The Parisian Professor

The Parisian Professor

Joseph Sciuto

IGUANA

Published by Iguana Books
720 Bathurst Street, Suite 303
Toronto, ON M5S 2R4

Publisher: Meghan Behse
Editor: Lee Parpart
Front cover design: Meghan Behse

ISBN 978-1-77180-407-3 (paperback)
ISBN 978-1-77180-408-0 (epub)
ISBN 978-1-77180-409-7 (Kindle)

This is an original print edition of *The Parisian Professor*.

Dedicated to Lee Parpart, editor and friend,
who makes everything I write so much better.

Chapter One

The rarest creature in the world is an honest person. I don't remember which philosopher said this, but for some reason it has always stayed with me … even through the most difficult times in my life, like at this very moment.

***

I sat across from Abdul Haqq and silently watched as the young man said a short prayer before touching his meal. I understood enough Arabic to silently translate his words: "All praise is due to Allah who gave us food and drink and who made us Muslims."

Abdul was a young graduate student at the local technical university, École des ponts ParisTech. I knew more about him than he realized. I knew, for example, that he had emigrated from Algeria with his parents when he was very young, and the circumstances of his adoption, and the fact that he had an adoptive sister.

But these were just the facts in his file. As I got to know Abdul, it was all the intangibles that began to matter most: his essential sweetness, combined with his rakish charm and brilliant mind. A pleasant-looking man with a round face and eyes that crinkled with kindness when he spoke, he was fluent in English and French as well as in Arabic, and seemed to get along well with almost everybody. It was difficult to dislike this young man, as I quickly found out while pretending to be a student at the same university.

Unlike other students from his background who stuck to socializing within their communities, Abdul Haqq was quite outgoing and made friends with just about everybody. He could often be seen flirting with the pretty young women on campus, and he was quick to help any struggling student who was having difficulty with a project.

It wasn't long after we met that Abdul introduced me to his adoptive parents. A few days later, I would have the distinct pleasure of meeting his sister, Gabrielle. At first it was uncomfortable having to pretend that I didn't know about the horrifying circumstances of Abdul's adoption. I was relieved when he finally told me the whole story, so I wouldn't have to worry about slipping up and referring to it. I could have told him I saw an old news story, but that would have been stretching things. It had been over a decade since *Le Monde* and *Le Figaro* were full of stories about his biological family being blown up by a suicide bomber while strolling across the Champs-Élysées. All five of his sisters and brothers and his two parents were killed when the terrorist accidently detonated the bomb strapped around his waist. By some amazing good fortune, Abdul, who was just a kid, had become separated from his family and was wandering around lost when the bomb went off. It wasn't until hours after the explosion, after all the debris and body parts were removed from the scene, that the Paris police picked him up, identified him, and placed him in an orphanage.

Luckily for him, a Lebanese Christian family that had recently immigrated to Paris read about the tragedy in the newspapers and decided to adopt him. Little Abdul was already well-schooled in the Muslin faith and deeply religious for a small child, and his adoptive parents decided it was not in his best interest to force him to become a Christian. From the time he came into their home, they never failed to encourage him to continue to practice his religion. They considered themselves progressive, and after fleeing Lebanon due to all the sectarian violence, they weren't big on religion, anyway.

We were sitting at a small table in the back room of Chez Marcel, a hundred-year-old bistro tucked away on a small street off Boulevard

Raspail near Montparnasse on the left bank. We were the only people dining, and at a small bar about thirty feet away, Elijah and David, two crazed Mossad agents, were laughing and drinking while pretending to chat with the bartender and actually keeping an eye on me. They were here to make sure I did the job correctly, and if not, they would clean up my mess. Somehow, even after four years as an operations officer working for the CIA, I still had plenty of people looking over my shoulder, not quite convinced that I was the best man for the job. This, despite the fact that, by all of the usual measures, my recent three-year stint in Kabul had been a success. I was assigned to our embassy there, and I made a lot of contacts for the agency. I also participated in a number of successful operations that saved lives and provided us with invaluable information. I may not have been James Bond, but I sure as hell didn't need to be babysat by these two Israeli soldiers while doing my own job.

Elijah was the less subtle of the two. He kept banging his beer stein on the bar and side-eyeing me as I ate my steak and frites. It was annoying, but I had to keep my cool. I was already hoping that this would be my last job with the agency. It was becoming increasingly clear to me that I was destined for a different line of work. The stresses of the job were really meant for someone with steelier nerves and a better poker face. I stuffed a French fry in my mouth and resolved to get through this job with as little drama as possible. And on the face of it, the task was simple enough. I'd been transferred to Paris a few months earlier, was set up with my own little apartment, and was registered as a graduate student at the university. My only real job was to befriend Abdul and find out if the agency was right about his ... extracurriculars. My bosses believed he was involved in manufacturing sophisticated bombs to be used by suicide bombers for an Islamic terrorist group with ties to Hezbollah in Lebanon, and I was there to prove the case and turn him over to the CIA.

I knew for a fact that I wasn't the agency's first pick for this job, but I had a few important things going for me. At twenty-nine, I still looked young enough to be a graduate student studying abroad, and it didn't hurt that I had an undergraduate degree in engineering and spoke fairly fluent French. But after everything I'd accomplished in Afghanistan, I still felt a little silly playing the part of a spoiled American kid, carrying around a backpack stuffed full of engineering and chemistry textbooks.

Usually one of the most difficult jobs working as a covert agent is to gain the trust of the source, which in this case was Abdul. In this case, it was dead easy. In fact, it was Abdul who introduced himself to me on the first day we had a class together. I sat right across from him and he leaned over and asked me, in French, what I thought of the two girls in the front row. He used the word "bonne" to describe them, and I knew from brushing up on current Parisian slang that this was not quite as innocent as it sounded. It was short for *bonne à baiser* — "good to fuck."

I smiled knowingly and said, "The blonde and the brunette?"

"Yes, Americans, no doubt. Facile! We'll ask them out after class."

"Okay, that sounds like fun," I said as we shook hands and exchanged names. During class, Abdul was all business, raising his hand and participating and offering all the right answers. But as soon as class was over, he was equally focused on our planned conquest. He grabbed me by the elbow and steered me over to where the girls were standing, packing up their books. We introduced ourselves, and Abdul took the lead, saying a bunch of smooth stuff and asking the girls out for a meal. After giggling like a couple of teenagers, they agreed to meet us at a little bistro not far from the campus. As Abdul had predicted, they were American, and ready for a little ... cultural exchange.

During my four years as an undergraduate back in the states, I never once got so much as a smile out of the one or two good-looking girls in my science classes. Now here I was in Paris, and after just a few hours of amiable chatting and four bottles of wine, these two beauties were ready and willing.

Abdul disappeared with one of the girls through the back door and that was the last I saw of him that night. The other one, Jennifer from Nebraska, was literally climbing all over me like I was a mountain. Fending her off might have been the most difficult and frustrating assignment I'd had since leaving Afghanistan. Quite simply, she was hot, and it didn't help that I had not been with a woman in years. But there was no way I was going to compromise my assignment, or Jennifer, by establishing any sort of relationship with her, especially not a sexual one. She could easily become collateral damage and I could never, in good conscience, allow that. Thankfully, the poor girl got sick and vomited all over me, and whatever desire I might have had vanished. After cleaning up, I put her in a cab, and told her I would see her in class. From that night on, she could barely look at me without apologizing a thousand times.

For the next couple of weeks, Abdul and I hung out day and night. After being away from school for so long, I was rusty when it came to physics and mathematics, but that was no problem; before leaving the university grounds, we would go to the library and Abdul would sit there tutoring me until every problem was solved and the answer double-checked. It was all so easy for him. He could solve a highly technical math problem in a fraction of the time it took me to get a less elegant solution, and he did it all with a smile.

We would then go out and eat at the finest restaurants, drink and party until the wee hours of the morning, and never once did he let me pick up a check. He always carried around wads of cash, and never paid with a credit card. If he was a terrorist, he certainly didn't belong to any ascetic organization.

As a cover story in case I needed to get away for a while, I told him my mom back in the States had been ill for a while, and that I was worried about her. Never once after I told him that did he fail to ask about my mother. He would inquire after her health at least twice a day and ask if there was anything he could do to help her, such as pay medical expenses or send her gifts to cheer her up. The guy was as charitable and as empathetic as anybody I had ever met. I showed more signs of being a terrorist than he did.

Even so, a bomb was about to go off in my life, and it was named Gabrielle. The day I met her was the same day I first noticed

Elijah and David watching me in a bistro during my lunch with Abdul. I'd endured their antics all during our meal and finally left the bistro with Abdul. I was on my way home to my little apartment when we came across Gabrielle on the steps of the American University, where she was studying to be an artist. Little did I know that all the self-restraint I'd been able to exhibit with Jennifer a few days earlier would vanish in an instant at the sight of this incredible creature.

I've never been a big believer in love at first sight, but with Gabrielle, there was no other explanation. It had to exist, or I was going crazy. How do I put this? She was the most stunning creature I had ever seen — a tiny thing, slim to the point of waifishness, with gorgeous, long, dark brown hair, parted in the middle, and the most beautiful, olive complexion. When I met her, she wore a simple white dress with a narrow, red leather belt around her waist, a light wool coat, and stylish black boots. She looked like she'd just stepped out of a Chanel ad. She was so perfect that I was immediately afraid that she wasn't real, or that at any moment she might vanish. Her delicate features reminded me of both Ingrid Bergman and Audrey Hepburn, and her smile was instantly bewitching. At certain angles and in certain light she could look almost like a child, with her sweet dimples and her precious little teeth, so white and so straight. All of these characteristics combined, but especially her smile, made her extremely dangerous.

I hung back while Abdul and Gabrielle talked, unable to take my eyes off of her. Abdul gave her some money that she had asked for, and she quickly thanked him and turned away, saying she was late for class. Abdul and I went our separate ways, after making plans to meet later that evening. I was starting to walk back toward my apartment when I heard a voice from behind me. I turned and saw Gabrielle walking toward me, smiling. I knew from that moment that I was doomed.

"So, tell me Nicky, do you always fall in love with a girl after only twenty seconds?" she asked.

All of my CIA training lay in a puddle on the ground. I couldn't remember my own name, let alone the recommended strategies for not falling in love in the field. After a long pause, I finally forced out a reply.

"I didn't know I had fallen in love," I said, almost choking. No one would believe me. I didn't believe myself.

She smiled at me appraisingly, and said "Uh-huh." Then she pushed one thin forefinger into my chest and said, "Okay, Nicky. Have it your way." But she didn't turn and leave. She stood there, arms folded in front of her, gently mocking me with her coy smile.

I was trying to shake off the feeling of having been bewitched. I called to mind the wizened, friendly face of my first mentor at the agency, Donna Low, the senior officer in charge of recruits. I remembered her advice to me that first summer after I joined the agency: "Never let your heart, or *any other bodily organ*, do work best performed by your head." She had stared at me pointedly, smiling just a little, when she said it. That was seven years ago, and the penny had just dropped. Some agent I was, taking seven years to get a dick joke.

I almost laughed at the memory and exerted all my will to force my heart rate down, imagining Donna Low's face in front of me instead of Gabrielle's, and said, "I thought you had a class to get to?"

"I do, I do, but missing one class won't make me any *less* likely to become the next Rembrandt or Monet — or, for that matter, the next Suzanne Valadon."

I couldn't tell what she meant by that — whether she was praising herself or denigrating her own abilities, so I just kept quiet. Then, suddenly, we were on the move, as she looped her arm in mine and we began walking along rue Saint-Dominic, in the direction of the Esplanade des Invalides.

She looked up at me, her face now three inches away from mine, and like a beautiful sorcerer casting a spell over her helpless prey, asked, "Isn't Paris lovely, even in late winter?"

"Beautiful…" I stammered, not knowing to what or to whom I was referring — just trying to stay in the conversation and keep floating along beside her. At that moment, I didn't know where I was, who I was, what my assignment was, or what was in the best interests of my country ... I was doing my best to ignore the goosebumps that were running up and down my body as this earthbound goddess squeezed my forearm and touched her shoulder to mine.

Suddenly, she stopped us in mid-stride and turned around to face me. Her expression was soft, knowing, and grave all at the same time. She placed both hands on my arms and said, "Wake up, Nicky. You're not dreaming ... the girl you are going to marry is right here in front of you. Hopefully, you won't mess it up."

Now I really was awake, and defensive, but on her terms instead of my own. It took me a moment to speak, but when I did, I made a small effort to defend myself. "What makes you think I might mess it up?" I asked, staring into her eyes, battling for position.

"Because," she said, softly, "you are an American, a very handsome American, living in Paris, where there are many temptations."

"And you suspect that the temptations might be too great for me to resist?" This was getting a little easier.

"You are a man, after all, and if Adam could be gullible enough to eat the forbidden apple offered by Eve, I don't see why you might not be just as gullible and foolish."

"Maybe if Adam was looking at you, instead of Eve, he might never have taken a bite," I said.

I knew this was a half-baked analogy as soon as the words came out of my mouth, but she spared me by laughing softly and leaning in closer.

"I think you need to go back and read your Bible," she said, teasingly. "You seem to have misinterpreted the meaning behind the story."

"Well, maybe we can read it together and you can explain it to me."

"I don't think so, my little Nicky. I don't waste my time on such nonsense anymore. Hopefully, you don't lose sight of your dream and taste the milk of any of these French *putins* who so pollute our lovely city." She looked at me hard and said, "If I catch you cheating on me one time, your dream will evaporate as quickly as it materialized. I don't forgive such transgressions."

She smiled as she touched my wrist and asked, "Do you understand?"

"Quite clearly," I replied. Then I asked, "And does the same hold true for you?"

"Of course. If you like, I will even wear a chastity belt."

"That won't be necessary. I would hate to have you wear anything that might inhibit you in any way."

"So thoughtful," she said, smiling. "Why don't we take a walk through the gardens at Tuileries … such a lovely day to walk beneath the spare winter trees and to learn a little something about my little Nicky."

I was starting to recover my equilibrium, and now I was gripping her arm as tightly as she had been gripping mine. We stayed that way, glued at the hip, alternating between French and English like a couple of Montrealers, without even noticing when we were speaking in one or the other language.

"What do you want to know?" I asked her, as we exited the Esplanade des Invalides and continued east toward the Tuileries.

"So many things. So many," she said. "I'm sure behind that handsome face and pleasant demeanor you have some amazing stories you would like to share with your future wife."

I knew I should be trying to keep things interesting by resisting her utter confidence in our future as a couple. I tried to get myself to say something like, "You're awfully sure of yourself, aren't you?" But it was futile pretending that we weren't made for each other — that we weren't two figures trapped in a painting together for centuries, becoming conscious of each other for the first time.

"To be honest, when I look at you, every story flies out of my head. I can't remember anything from before we met less than an hour ago. How is that possible?"

"It's possible," she said. "Just ask the poet Rilke and the painter who he, and he alone, called Merline. They knew all about love that transcends reason."

"The things you pick up in art school…" I said, impressed.

"A lot of art school is just art gossip," she said, waving her hand. "Which reminds me, Nicky … there is no need to pretend that you are a graduate student. You might be able to fool my stupid brother, but one look at you and I could easily tell that you have no interest in your studies."

"Why would you say that?"

"Because I just know."

"Know what, Gabrielle?"

"That no one who carries himself like you do has any interest in attending a university. You're a man of the world, not a man to be tied down in a classroom. Am I wrong?"

I suddenly felt my mission kick in. Why would she say this? Had my cover been blown before I even had a chance to investigate Abdul? I tried to sound casual, as though her misunderstanding was a source of amusement for me, but the truth was, she had me rattled. I went on the defensive.

"I'm a graduate student, and if you have any doubt you are more than welcome to go to the university's registry's office and check for yourself." I smiled at her calculatedly, and watched for her reaction. It was, at most, inscrutable. A lightness played around her emerald green eyes as she waved aside my offer.

"How generous of you. No, thank you. I have no doubt that you are registered … but a serious student? No, not my handsome fiancé." She ignored my puzzled look and took me by the arm and we entered the Tuileries.

As we walked through the gardens, Gabrielle skipped and danced around me, held my hand and then dropped it, and delighted in pointing out a Pin de Corse tree — a Corsican Pine — that she said was the pride of the Tuileries in late February, and her personal favorite. She seemed to have forgotten all about my seriousness, or lack of seriousness, as a student, and I began to forget, too. We were just two lovers walking through Paris.

After a little while, we sat down on a bench across from the Louvre. She leaned against me in silence. I asked, "Maybe one day you can take me on a tour of the Louvre?"

"I would love that, Nicky," she said as she suddenly laid her head on my lap and stretched out along the bench, with her coat pulled across her body, looking up at my face. "I could look at the *Mona Lisa* for hours. So many tourists complain that they don't see what's so great about it — especially Americans, like you. The type that prefer looking at the Kardashians. But me, I see the mischief behind the smile and a million little plots going around inside her head."

"Is that so?" I asked, as I tried not to confuse my real identity with my cover identity.

"And what do you see?" she asked.

"I haven't looked at the painting in years, and never up close, so I really couldn't tell you."

"Well, then we definitely have to take a tour of the Louvre. Certainly, before we leave Paris," Gabrielle said.

"And when are we planning on leaving Paris?"

"As soon as possible," she said. "Once you formally propose and we get married."

I smiled at her absolute confidence in our future together. "And where do you propose we live?"

"Anywhere you like. After all, you're the man of the world. I'm just a struggling art student, still living with her parents."

"Oh, you're so much more than that, Gabrielle."

"And what makes you say that, my handsome boy?" she asked as she reached her hand up and touched my lips.

"Just a very strong hunch."

I looked down into her eyes and suddenly my fingers were caressing her lips and a second later she was sitting up and we were kissing. For an agent to lose track of time is rare and totally against training and protocol, but I couldn't tell you how much time passed before we finally came up for air. Even then, we just hung there, our faces inches apart, smiling at each other with dewy eyes.

"Did you enjoy?" she asked, in French.

"Very much so," I replied, in one of the two languages, though which one I couldn't say, any more than I could tell you whether it was raining or snowing or sunny at that moment. We were on our own planet, with its own time, its own hybrid tongue, and its own weather. She threw her arms around my neck and we kissed, again.

"A little taste of what you will be missing out on if you're ever tempted."

My phone rang and it was a text message from Abdul asking me where we wanted to meet tonight.

"From your brother," I said to Gabrielle. She grabbed the phone, looked at the message, and started typing. "He has a date tonight," she wrote, "so you're on your own ... good luck chasing your whores. Gabby."

"That was kind of rude," I remarked.

"You think so? I mean, if you want to go out with Abdul tonight, please go right ahead. I just didn't think you wanted your dream to explode so quickly in your face."

"Don't be like that, Gabrielle."

"Don't be like, what? If you want to go out with Abdul, please do. I laid down my conditions. Just don't think in a few months when you go back to your America that I will be just another story among your many conquests. I'm not for sale!"

She got up from the bench and started to walk away. I reached out and grabbed her wrist and pulled her back and said, "I don't behave like that, and for the record, you might be my dream, but it's not like I'm mincemeat."

"Mincemeat, is that like hamburger?"

"I guess so; I never thought about it."

"Well, just for the record, I don't think of you as just hamburger. Where do you plan on taking me to dinner, Nicky? I'm starving." We walked toward Le Fumoir, which was close to the Louvre. The sun was starting to set and for a moment we had to shield our eyes, and when I looked back at Gabrielle, it was almost a relief to notice that she didn't look quite as stunning as she had up to that point. I thought I might be saved, but a few seconds later, after my eyes cleared, the dream was back, and I followed her like a little puppy.

We sat at a nice table in the corner and before looking at the wine list and menu she asked, "You do have money, Nicky?"

"Not much," I said, looking at her casually. "I figured we could go Dutch."

"Dutch?" she asked. "What does that mean?"

"It means, whatever you order you pay for, and whatever I order I pay for. Abdul did give you a stack of money."

"Enough for cab fare home and to pick something up at the grocery store. You are American, aren't you Nicky?"

"Yes, but when in Paris one behaves like a Parisian."

"I think we should go," she said as she started to get up out of her chair and I took her hand and sat her back down.

"I'm joking with you, Gabrielle. I have money for both of us. Please order whatever you like."

She looked at me suspiciously and blushed. "Joke, like Jerry Lewis?"

"Yes, but not as funny. My God, you are adorable."

We each ordered an aperitif while deciding on appetizers. Gabrielle drank her entire aperitif before I had time to taste mine. She ordered another one and nearly drank that one as quickly. "You might want to slow down; otherwise I might have to carry you home."

"I don't think so, Nicky. I've already told you don't expect any favors until we are married."

"I didn't mean it that way."

"I know," she said. "I was only joking, like your Jerry Lewis."

I laughed but nevertheless quickly ordered a number of appetizers: salmon trout tartare with pressed caviar and tomatoes, porcini mushroom tartlets, and herb-and-lemon-poached baby artichokes.

Gabrielle looked at all the food and remarked, "So you *are* a rich American."

"No, just trying to impress the girl of my dreams."

"Merci, c'est très gentil," she said.

"Tout le plaisir est pour moi," I said.

"You speak well," she said.

"Your English is great, too."

"Well, it's mandatory in French schools."

"You must be very popular with the men in your university classes."

"Why would you say that?"

"Because you are undeniably the most beautiful girl in the university."

"If you say so."

"I doubt I am the only one who does."

"The men are all pigs, like my brother, and the girls are whores."

"All the men you meet are pigs?"

"Every one of them. But not you, my little Nicky, right?"

"No, ma'am — I mean, non, mademoiselle," I replied with a tinge of fear if I contradicted her. Gabrielle was only about five-foot-four, but already I could sense that I didn't want to get on the wrong side of this complex, beautiful, and sphinx-like creature.

"Do you speak any other languages besides French and English?" she asked as she took a small bite of a cracker covered with caviar and salmon.

"A smattering of Spanish," I replied.

"No Arabic?" she asked.

"No! Why would you think I speak Arabic?"

"Because there are many Arabs living in France and in your America. Abdul is a Muslim and my parents and I are from Lebanon. Christian, not Muslim."

"And you speak Arabic?" I asked.

"Yes," she replied as she took another bite from her cracker and pronounced it "délicieux!"

"Well, maybe you can teach me Arabic?"

"Maybe," she replied, pensively. "Maybe sometime, Nicky."

I picked up the wine list as I watched her eat tiny portions as though she was suspicious that it might be poison ... not at all like she was savoring every taste.

"Do you have a favorite wine?"

"Whatever you like. After all, you are a man of the world, whereas I still live with my parents."

I ordered a bottle of the Bouchard Aine & Fils Bourgogne pinot noir, a good, reasonably priced wine. Gabrielle liked it so much that we had two bottles during our main course. For after-dinner drinks we each had a kir royale, and for dessert, we split a crème brûlée.

We walked out of the restaurant at about ten o'clock and got into a cab. It wasn't particularly late, especially not for Paris. Actually, this was the time Abdul preferred to hit the nightclubs. I was drunk, a couple of drinks away from being plastered, and with any other girl I would have asked her if she wanted to go to a club and listen to some music, but this wasn't any other girl ... it was Gabrielle.

I played it safe and had Gabrielle give the driver the address to her parents' apartment. Throughout our long dining experience, Gabrielle and I had talked freely and laughed frequently. Suddenly, in the back seat of the cab it felt like we were strangers, with only a few words passing between us.

The driver stopped in front of her parents' apartment and I walked her up the few front steps of the building. I asked, "Can I call you tomorrow?"

"Of course," she replied as she looked up at me with her glistening, emerald eyes seemingly studying every aspect of my face.

"And do you think you might be free to go out tomorrow?"

"Yes, Nicky."

"Great," I said. "I had a wonderful time tonight."

"Me too."

"I'll see you tomorrow," I said as I started to turn back toward the cab, and she grabbed me by the arm.

"No goodnight kiss?" she asked as I turned back around and lowered my head and kissed her.

"Nice?"

"Yes, very nice."

"Maybe tomorrow we can practice some more?"

"Maybe," I replied as I gently ran one hand through her hair and kissed her on the forehead. Then I turned and walked back to the cab and got inside. I looked out the window as she stood there, an ethereal beauty that even the greatest romantic poet would have difficulty describing. She waved goodbye as the cab drove away.

"Mademoiselle is very beautiful," the driver remarked.

"Yes, she is," I replied.

Chapter Two

I climbed the creaky stairs to my apartment, opened the door, and stumbled inside. I put on a pot of coffee, and stood there watching it drip. I was tired and still quite drunk, but my mind was working overtime. I did not believe in consequences. In the world I was currently employed in, it was stressed that there was no such thing as a consequence. I started my day as an operations specialist pretending to be a student, and ended it engaged to a woman who seemed to materialize like an angel from heaven. She was the type of girl I fantasized about my whole life, except for the fact that she spoke with a French accent and lived in Paris, which only enhanced the fantasy.

I poured myself a cup of coffee and took out my file on Abdul. I had been over it hundreds of times. The information on his adopted family was limited and the only part of it that was highlighted said, *not under suspicion*. I had not given it any thought before, but since when was a suspected terrorist's family *not under suspicion* ... unless they were the informants.

Gabrielle seemed to know things about me that only my handler knew, such as the fact that I was pretending to be a student, and that I was a man of the world who had witnessed many things. She had also asked me if I spoke Arabic, which would be highly unusual for an American, unless he lived or worked in a predominantly Muslim country like Afghanistan.

If she was an informer, she was using a highly unusual tactic to keep an eye on me, a tactic that limited my ability to gather information on her brother. I closed the file and put it away. I lay down on the bed and fell asleep as quickly and suddenly as Gabrielle had materialized before my eyes.

The following morning I woke to my phone ringing. It was Gabrielle, and whereas many of my ideas and deductions from the previous night when I got back to my apartment and looked over the file were a bit hazy and confused, I couldn't help but feel a little suspicious.

"Good morning, Nicky," she said brightly.

"Good morning, Gabrielle."

"Did you sleep well?"

"Yes, the minute I hit the bed I was out cold. And how about you?"

"I slept wonderfully. I had much to be happy about. I had a wonderful time last night. I only hope you have not changed your mind about the things we discussed?"

"No, Gabrielle; why would I want to throw away the dream I have harbored my entire life?"

"Because I imagine you have had many girls in your life and at first sight you fell in love with them, too, non?"

"Non, I mean no," I said. "I have not had many girls in my life and you are the first one I fell in love with at first sight."

"That's very sweet, Nicky, but I find it hard to believe."

"Unless you know something I don't know, I am telling you the truth."

"How could I know for sure something like that? We just met."

"You like to surmise, like that whole thing about me pretending to be a student."

She laughed and asked, "Did I surmise wrongly?"

"Yes."

"Well, then I apologize."

"No need to apologize, or to feel sorry. I like the way your imagination works."

"My imagination? How do you mean?"

"I love the way your mind works — the way you put things together. It's just one of the many reasons why I find you completely irresistible."

"So … I guess this means we are still engaged and will soon be husband and wife?"

"Oui."

"And where shall we live … in America?"

"Yes, if that's okay with you … but would your parents be upset with you living so far away?"

"Yes, of course, but they understand. They like you very much."

"But they only met me once."

"They are also very good at surmising."

"So it runs in the family?"

"Except for Abdul — but then, he is adopted."

"Are you free for dinner tonight?"

"I thought you wanted to spend the whole day with me? After all, we have much to discuss."

"I forgot that I had classes today."

"Oh, yes, you are a student," she remarked dryly.

"And so are you?"

"Yes, but not a very obedient one," she replied.

Chapter Three

I made it to the classroom with only a few minutes to spare and sat at the desk next to Abdul. He had a big, silly smile on his face, and before I had even finished pulling my notebooks out of my knapsack, he asked, "So … are you in love with her?"

"Yes," I replied without hesitation and he bowed his head despairingly.

"Barely a month in Paris … barely enough time to sample the wonderful and willing ladies of the city … and you fall in love with the one 'chienne' who I wouldn't wish on Shaitan."

"Do you always talk about your sister in such glowing terms?"

He simply nodded and a moment later replied, "Compared to what she probably said about me…" He suddenly stopped as he continued to nod his head and then he leaned over and asked, "Did you at least shag her?"

"No, we didn't have sex," I replied.

"A goodnight kiss on the cheeks?"

"No, on the lips," I replied proudly, then immediately felt like a silly teenager.

"Oh là là! Maybe a year or two after you're married she'll let you shag her."

"Is there something I should know about your sister that you're not telling me?"

"Oh, you mean, apart from the fact that she's nuts?" he asked. I just stared at him until he continued. "Yes, she's beautiful … even a blind man could see that. And if she wasn't my sister, and I saw her sitting by her lonesome self at a bar, I would be quick to introduce myself and try to bang her."

I was sitting beside a man who was talking about his sister — okay, adopted sister — like she was a common whore. He had flat-out told me that he wouldn't wish her on the devil. Was this just a severe case of family dysfunction, or was I the target of some sort of insidious disinformation campaign? Bits and pieces of this scenario were starting to feel eerily familiar to the tribal insanity I had just witnessed in Afghanistan.

If it was just a family drama, I knew I could deal with that. My own family is borderline crazy, so I'm fully trained in the subtle arts of mental and emotional manipulation — which, come to think of it, is probably the main reason why I make a half-decent field agent. Yeah, there was never a dull moment in our household, and the dysfunction continues to this day. My mother doesn't speak to me, for reasons neither of us can fully remember. My father was a bigwig general in the US Army, but he was forced to resign after they found out he was having an affair with a female subordinate half his age. Since then, he has been working as a military contractor in Iraq. He has made enough money to buy two homes in the Hamptons on Long Island, a block or two from Steven Spielberg. Naturally, my mother forgave his transgression, because it's not like she saw much of him anyway, and now that the money is pouring in she can afford to go to the best plastic surgeon and get herself a boy toy on the side. My older sister is a narcissist. She has never passed a mirror without stopping to admire her own perfection. Of all of them, the only person I truly trust and relate to is my younger sister. She's an angel. Before I joined the CIA she was my closest confidante, and the one family member I could say I love unconditionally. She was born with a disability that limits her mobility, but that has not limited her from doing anything she puts her mind to. On top of all that, she is as quick as a whip and looks like a Greek goddess.

My father, once he was rolling in cash, set up trust funds for all three of his children. But since his new job and my current job could easily be perceived as being in conflict with each other, I have kept my distance. I haven't spoken to him in four years — even though he's the one who urged me to join the CIA and championed my decision. I put my younger sister in charge of my portion of the money. It wasn't like I had a choice. My mother and older sister would think nothing of stealing — or, should I say, borrowing — the money from me and never telling me about it.

So I knew I wasn't in a great position to disparage another family, considering how many conflicts I had with my own. But I had to admit, Abdul's words had really thrown me. Never in my life did I think I would hear a brother call his sister a whore or admit to another human being that if he wasn't related to her, he would have no problem picking her up at a bar and having sex with her. I didn't care if they were siblings by adoption instead of birth. This kind of talk went so far beyond the bounds of good taste that I didn't even know how to react to Abdul's words, or how or whether to defend Gabrielle against his insults. But Abdul was right about one thing: Gabrielle was as quick to insult him as he was to insult her. She had had no problem confiding in me her disgust with her brother, describing him as a pig among pigs. If they really were just a dysfunctional family, they were out of my league. I thought I knew all about domestic conflict, but this was taking family feuding to a whole new level. I was at sea with it all, unsure what to say or how to make peace.

So far, my mission was seemingly stalled. I had very little, if any, proof that Abdul might be involved with terrorists or be building sophisticated bombs. He never talked politics, except for the micro-politics of picking up girls and shagging them. He completed his class assignments with astonishing ease, and he gladly helped me with my assignments whenever I was stuck. He drank like a fish and, to my surprise, he even did quite a bit of cocaine. I was having trouble reconciling any of this with the stories I heard about him while I was being briefed for this assignment. For one thing, he didn't seem at all devout. The only time I saw him pray was before he had dinner in the evening, and if he happened to be in the company of females, he had no problem skipping that little ritual. His hands looked like he had them manicured, and displayed none of the grit and scars often associated with the hands of people working with explosives.

The one thing I could not explain was where he got all the money. He threw cash around like a gangster in a Mafia movie. He never used a credit card and refused to let me pay for anything, and it's not like we were hanging out in dives. We ate and drank in upscale, fashionable restaurants where the ultimate prize was usually a barstool away ... Americans and other foreign tourists visiting Paris and behaving like Parisians.

Terrorist organizations didn't usually reward devout followers with huge sums of money, especially not the type of money that Abdul was throwing around. He could be making money doing other students' projects; many foreign students had money to throw around, and paying Abdul a thousand dollars to do a project could be well worth it to them, especially if it left them free to spend their time enjoying Paris. That was one possibility as I continued to search for more.

***

I opened the door to my apartment and decided to grab a nap before going to pick up Gabrielle. Before I had a chance to lie down on my bed, my phone rang, and it was Gabrielle. She wanted me to pick her up an hour early. After all, I was supposed to spend the whole day with her, and coming an hour early shouldn't be much of an inconvenience, since all my classes were done for the day. I guess she didn't think that I might have any homework to do. She wanted me to meet her parents. I reminded her that I already met her parents.

"That was before we were engaged," she replied. "My mother is so excited that she's already planning our wedding."

I was silent for a long moment as I realized that all this talk about getting married was very real for Gabrielle, even though we had only met yesterday.

"Is something wrong, Nicky?"

"No!" I replied, as I desperately tried to think of something to help me get a grip on a situation that seemed to be taking on a life of its own.

"You still want to get married?" she asked in a voice riddled with concern and anxiety, which was not like my Gabrielle.

"Of course, I still want to get married. You're all I think about, my lovely Gabrielle."

"That's sweet, Nicky."

"I'll be leaving in a few minutes."

"I'll meet you outside the building and then we'll go up and see my parents."

I said a sweet goodbye and hung up the phone, then put on a clean shirt and a sport coat. After all, I wanted to make a good impression meeting her parents for the first time as their daughter's fiancé.

Chapter Four

I got into a cab and we drove to Gabrielle's apartment. She was waiting for me in front of the building dressed in a simple red dress, similar to the white one she'd worn the day before, but this time with a white belt around the waist and a comfortable pair of loafers. She was stunning, and though I knew nothing about women's fashion, even I knew that a dress like the one she was wearing cost nothing, and that one could probably pick one up in a thrift store for under twenty dollars. Abdul was certainly not sharing his money with his sister, the "chienne."

Gabrielle and Abdul's parents lived in an apartment on the eastern outskirts of the city, in a lower-middle-class suburb populated by a mixture of native-born Parisians and immigrants. Abdul had his own apartment, closer to the city center, which I had not yet visited. The center of Paris was expanding outward, like Manhattan, and literally pushing the citizens living in the outer suburbs further and further away from the tourist-dominated, wealthy core.

I paid the cab driver and as I turned around, I was greeted with a kiss from my beautiful fiancée. She took me by the hand and led me up the stairs of the building and into her parents' apartment, where I was greeted with kisses on the cheeks by both parents. Her father opened a bottle of champagne and passed around glasses to everyone. He raised his glass and welcomed me into the family with a brief toast, during which he quoted Molière: "Vivre sans aimer n'est pas proprement vivre." To live without loving is to not really live.

Gabrielle clapped her hands like a little girl, kissed her parents, and then kissed me. I don't know if what I felt toward Gabrielle was true love, at least not yet, but I could say with a certain amount of clarity that I was totally infatuated with her. She was like a lovely white rose in a garden of thorns. The only question — and it was one that was only beginning to take shape in the furthest recesses of my mind — was whether she would turn out to be not a rose at all, but the most poisonous plant, or the sharpest and most dangerous thorn, in the garden.

She gave me a tour of the apartment that culminated with her bedroom. It was amazingly organized and uncluttered, with only a few pictures on the wall: one of the Statue of Liberty and another of the Lincoln Memorial. She walked over to an easel and flipped forward a page with a canvas portrait of me in front of an American flag. It was quite stunning and I hate looking at pictures of myself. It was difficult enough looking into the bathroom mirror each morning.

"I thought you said you had no talent?"

"It is easy to paint when the subject is someone I am madly in love with, and what I said was that I would never be a Rembrandt or a Monet or a Suzanne Valadon."

"How about a da Vinci?"

Gabrielle sighed knowingly and said, "There will never be another da Vinci, my handsome Nicky." Then she reached up, wrapping her delicate hands loosely around my neck, and asked a question of the sort that, I was beginning to realize, only Gabrielle could ask. "Please tell me you love me as much as I love you, and promise to marry me and never leave me?"

I was taken aback, I won't lie, but I heard myself replying without hesitation. "I promise a million times over," I said, as she threw her arms around me and we kissed. This beautiful creature, my dream girl, was begging me to love her forever. That, in itself, was blowing my mind, but there was also something in her tone — a hint of need, combined with a bald insistence — that was putting me slightly on edge, even as I couldn't quite believe my luck. It was as if she was preparing me in advance, knowing I was to find out something about her that could challenge that love.

After we reconvened in the living room and Gabrielle's father gave one more toast, Gabrielle and I left the apartment. Her parents were going away for a couple of weeks to visit family in Spain and they asked me to please take care of their daughter while they were gone. Where exactly Abdul fit into this family I could not figure out. When he introduced me to his adoptive parents there was warmth and love between them, but I could see now that it was nothing close to the level of warmth displayed by Gabrielle and her biological parents.

We got into a cab and I told the driver to take us to Les Papilles bistro in the Latin Quarter. Gabrielle said that she didn't think we should go there because it was expensive and there was no reason to impress her, since she was already as impressed as any girl could be with her fiancé. This stopped me in my tracks. I looked at her and asked a question that had been on my mind since she first mentioned marriage. "How could you be so certain about me? We have only known each other for a very short amount of time."

She replied, "Because when I first looked into your eyes I did not see lust, but love and compassion."

The cab stopped at Les Papilles and we got out and walked in through its sunflower-yellow facade. I had made reservations and we were seated right away at a small, simply dressed table next to a wall lined with wine bottles. The place was famous for two things: the food was fabulous and the chef did the ordering for you.

As we waited for our aperitifs to arrive, I took Gabrielle's hands in mine. Unlike her brother's hands, they were scarred and gritty, just as one expects a painter's hands to be. Deep in the creases of her palms I could see bits of paint that seemed to have settled in permanently. "I know, I desperately need a manicure … maybe on our wedding day."

"Your hands are perfect, like the rest of you," I said as a playful smile crossed her lips. Gabrielle was behaving differently than yesterday. She was hesitant and mindful, whereas yesterday she spilled over with confidence and was carefree … dancing to her own tune.

The dinner was fabulous, as advertised, and after leaving the bistro we took a cab back to the Tuileries Garden. It was a crisp, clear night and musicians were playing to throngs of tourists and Parisians. We sat on a bench, away from the crowd but in clear view of the Louvre. Gabrielle cuddled up close to me and I asked her to tell me something about her past.

"What do you want to know?" she asked.

"Well … do you remember much about living in Lebanon?"

"Not much," she replied.

"Do you have any desire to visit there?"

"No," she replied, as I felt her body tense up.

"Any relatives still living there?"

"A few, I think."

I looked at her and asked, "What's wrong, Gabrielle? Do you not like talking about Lebanon? At one time it was referred to as the French Riviera of the Middle East."

"Not for me, Nicky. Not for any of us in the Christian minority there."

"What do you mean?"

Gabrielle went silent and pulled a light cardigan she'd brought with her around her body, crossing her arm over her chest. She looked at me and then looked down at the ground more than once before she finally spoke.

"I don't know if I should tell you," she said.

"If we're going to be married, I think you need to feel that you can tell me anything."

"I know," she said, biting her lip.

"You don't have to tell me tonight. I'm sorry—"

"No, it's okay," she said. "It's a terrible story."

"Okay," I said, getting worried.

"When I was ten years old there was a tragedy in our family. I was walking home from school and I was pulled into an alley and then taken into a building that was controlled by Hezbollah."

"My God—" I said.

"Nicky, it was really bad. I was raped. I was raped and beaten by four members of the terrorist group. They called me a filthy whore and spit on me when they were finished."

I listened, unable to speak or even fully process what she was telling me. I looked at her as the memory of what had happened brought tears to her eyes, and I felt tears welling up in my own. When I was finally able to speak, I said, "That is the most terrible thing I've ever heard. I'm so, so sorry that happened to you."

"Thank you," she said quietly.

New questions began occurring to me as I regained my composure. "Did you report them to the authorities?"

"That would have been useless. The police were afraid of them and would have done nothing. I told my girlfriend who was Jewish and she told her parents. She then took me to her parents' house and I stayed there until two Mossad agents, Elijah and David, came and talked to me. After that, I got into a very big truck with them and we drove around the Muslim section of the city and I pointed out the men to them. We followed them in the truck and when we came to an isolated area, they jumped out of the truck and took down the four men in what seemed like half a minute. It was like watching a movie. They chained the unconscious men to each other and threw them in the back of the truck where Elijah watched over them.

"We then drove far into the desert and stopped at a cave where an older lady met us. The men were brought into the cave, which was well-lit with many candles, and they were tied tightly to the back wall of the cave. They threw water into their faces and they woke up."

"What happened then?"

"They were shouting at the men in Arabic, 'Did you touch her?' The men didn't say anything, but they were refusing to look at me, and finally they all started shouting in Arabic, something that basically means 'Satan's whore! Long live Allah.'"

"David spoke to them calmly in Hebrew, saying 'You are the whores and Allah will not save you.'

"Then David took out a pistol and placed it in my hand. Then he placed his hands over mine to steady the gun. The woman was protesting loudly, saying, 'No! No! She is just a little girl.' But David told her to be quiet, and said I needed to learn.

"He pointed my hands with the gun at the first man's groin. I had no idea if we were just going to scare him or pull the trigger, but David guided my hand and we both pulled the trigger and suddenly there was blood everywhere and the man was screaming in agony. With David guiding my hand again, we did the same to the other three men, shooting them all in the groin. The screaming was terrifying and the prayers and pleading to Allah bounced off the walls, unanswered."

I was listening to her with my mouth open, amazed that she had lived through any of this.

"I'm guessing that wasn't the end," I said.

"No, it wasn't," she said. "David handed me to the lady as Elijah walked back into the cave with a canister of gasoline, which he poured over the four crying men. The lady took me outside and from the shadows across the ground I could see the flames anoint these four beasts and I could smell the dirty stench of their disgusting bodies as they burned."

When Gabrielle had finished speaking, she moved away from me and sat, staring ahead. She looked smaller and more uncertain than at any time since I had met her.

Finally she spoke in a whisper and said, "And now do you still love me after the way I have been soiled, degraded and dishonored?"

I had heard some terrible stories and witnessed some horrific things since joining the agency, but what Gabrielle just told me was one of the worse I had ever heard, and was made worse than anything by the fact that it happened to her.

The fact that I couldn't speak seemed to agitate her, and she asked again, "Are we still getting married, or would you like more time to think it over?"

I looked at her and saw that she was trying desperately not to add to the tears she had already shed. I said, "I thought you said you knew the type of man I was?" I reached over and pulled her close to me. Her beautiful face rested lightly against my chest as she stood there next to me, still tense. I ran my hand through her hair and said, "I doubt I could love another human being any more than I love you right now." I lifted her face up off my chest, and said, "Yes, I am still marrying you. Since the moment I saw you, I knew that if I was ever going to get married it had to be to you. You're the one dream I refuse to ever let go of."

I reached down and kissed her as tears rolled down her cheeks and pooled at our lips. I knew, right then and there, that my sole purpose in life was to protect and love Gabrielle.

Once my mission was over and all the loose ends were tied up, I would quit the agency. I had known for a while now that I was not made for this type of work ... my own father, a thirty-five-year veteran, a general, for God's sake, had sold out. Our president sells out our country on a daily basis, enriching himself, and putting the very people who safeguard our country at risk. Yes, I love my country, but I could no longer serve it in this fashion.

I took Gabrielle home, and left the cab waiting outside as I walked my fiancée to her door. Neither of us had fully recovered from the emotional story she'd shared, but in her case the effect was physical; she kept her head bowed the whole time we were climbing the narrow staircase to her parents' apartment. At the top of the stairs, I lifted her chin up and looked into her eyes and said, "Please, don't get into the habit of casting your face and eyes downward. That prevents me from seeing the most beautiful face and eyes in the world."

She hugged me for a long time as I whispered, "I love you so much and can't wait to call you my wife." When she was safely inside, I returned to the cab and had the driver take me back to my apartment. In the lobby of the building, I noticed the headline on an English-language newspaper: "CONVICTED UKRAINIAN GUN RUNNER AND DRUG SMUGGLER, DMITRY KOLOMOISKY, MOVED FROM PRISON TO HOSPITAL."

I took the paper up to my apartment and read the story. Dmitry had a very short time to live. The story said he was dying from complications from cancer, but I knew better. The Russians had got to him. He had become a real obstacle in their attempt to take as much territory away from Ukraine as possible. He had been opposing them every step of the way since they took over the Crimean Peninsula and most of the Donbas region of eastern Ukraine in 2014. At the moment the Russians controlled about ten percent of Ukraine and were looking to take control over much more than that. The Ukrainian army had fought gallantly against the much-better-equipped Russians, and had lost fourteen thousand soldiers and civilians and tens of thousands wounded.

With US aid to Russia on and off, and our president siding with the Russian president, a former KBG agent, over our own intelligence agencies, we had reached the unbelievable position where a sitting US president had become Russia's greatest asset. Not even the great science fiction writer, Ray Bradbury, could have predicted the scenario that was still unfolding in our nation's capital, with our sworn enemy, Russia and its president, now calling the shots.

Dmitry hated the Russians and their imperial design on his native country. He had a long memory of the reign of terror inflicted on his people by Stalin, whose policies had led to the deaths of eleven million Ukrainians. Dmitry and his pals loved to tell the story of how the Russians were so bad that the Ukrainians actually sided with the Nazis when they invaded and pushed into Russia.

Dmitry was actually providing life-saving military equipment to the Ukrainians, out of his own pocket, while the US Congress and our president were arguing over debunked theories that Ukraine, not Russia, were the ones who interfered with our 2016 elections.

I finished reading the story and looked one last time at its picture of an emaciated Dmitry lying in a hospital bed. It stung to see this man, who was well-known as an anti-Russian patriot, looking so weak and near death. It even felt personal to me. Dmitry and I had met a bunch of times while I was stationed in Afghanistan, and for some reason he took a liking to me. I felt like he viewed me almost as a son, or as someone who he could mentor. One time when we were sitting at a café in Kabul, he turned to me and said, "Nick, you're in the wrong profession. Get out while you still can. Go back and be an engineer." That had seemed peculiar at the time, but now I felt he was right. I was in the wrong field altogether.

Dmitry had even saved me once. I'd been working with an informant who I thought was reliable, but they passed me some bad information, and I handed it to my station chief, who relayed it to our military. It was Dmitry who somehow found out about it and rushed to let me know it was a trap. Without this information, I would have been responsible for numerous US and civilian Afghan causalities. Dmitry saved many lives, and spared me a lifetime of insufferable agony. Had the plot succeeded, no amount of penance would have helped lift my guilt. I would have been lost.

It was easy to cast Dmitry as a bad guy, and in a strange way he took pride in his reputation as a high-flying rebel and a thorn in the Russians' side. As he would jokingly say in Ukrainian, "At least I earned it." And while that was true, he had also done the right thing when lives were at stake, and I would always be thankful.

My phone rang and it was Gabrielle. The girl who, just a day ago, seemed to be bubbling over with confidence and conviction had disappeared like a shooting star across a darkened sky. Suddenly there, and then gone. I picked up the phone and immediately could tell that she had been crying. No amount of assurances from me that I loved her and had every intention of marrying her could erase the lingering doubts she felt, and how could one blame her after what she had been through … four disgusting beasts raping a child, kicking and spitting on her after they were finished. Thankfully, they were punished accordingly. They had earned it! But their agony ended quickly, whereas Gabrielle's agony and shame continued indefinitely.

She was talking quickly now, telling me how much she loved me, and promising to make the best wife in the world.

"I have no doubt," I said, "and I am going to make you the best husband in the world, and I love you so much."

"Are we going to live in America?"

"Yes, I think that would be the best thing to do until we get settled, and then we can go anywhere you like."

"I have always wanted to live in America. We can visit the Statue of Liberty and the Lincoln Memorial."

"Yes, and many more wonderful places. After all, I want to show you off to as many people as possible. You are so beautiful, charming, and intelligent."

"Thank you, Nicky," she said. "I'm the lucky one."

We talked for a long time and she asked if it was all right if she called in the morning. She wanted her voice to be the first one I heard when I woke up. I told her I couldn't think of a more lovely sound to wake up to … tomorrow and forever.

It was love at first sight when I met Gabrielle on the steps of the university, but love at first sight could be quite deceiving once you start peeling back a layer or two. Watching her dance across the stairs of the university was like a mirage released from a prison in my mind … my perfect vision of a woman that I was fairly certain existed only in my unconscious. Yet, there she was. I could feel her hand running across my face, and hear her laugh, and she spoke English with a distinctly French accent. And then a layer was peeled back and another, and suddenly an emotional scar so large and an assault so devastating that just thinking about it made me cringe, and yet it was these dastardly acts and her fragile emotional state that bonded me so closely to her. It was love at first sight, no doubt, but it was not until she revealed these horrific acts and her fragile emotional state that I truly fell in love with the whole Gabrielle.

Only Gabrielle's mother had known about the rape, and Gabrielle had begged her mom to promise never to tell her father. She needn't have begged; Gabrielle's mother knew that it would be dangerous for Gabrielle if the rape became known, even by her husband. There was no telling how the men in their family and in the wider community would treat Gabrielle if they knew. Most likely, she would be considered tainted, and unworthy of marriage. The fact that Gabrielle's father never learned her secret helped to explain why her parents adopted Abdul and allowed him to practice his religion without interference. Gabrielle's experiences also helped to explain her disgust at Abdul's womanizing while pretending to be religious. I still had not seen any evidence that he practiced the Muslim faith or any other, apart from a simple prayer before supper, which he had no problem discarding if something better came along. I had no proof that he was a devoted and practicing Muslim. Unless this was his cover, and if so, he was a better actor than Olivier and Pacino put together. The man was a dog when it came to women ... going so far as to admit that he viewed his sister as hot, and that, if not for the fact that she was his sister, he would have no problem picking her up at a bar and shagging her.

I had decided to wait this assignment out, collecting and verifying the information as I discovered it, but after meeting Gabrielle, that approach went out the window. I still had not been to Abdul's apartment, and if he were actually building bombs, pieces of evidence would very likely be there. It was now time to get an invite, and if I found no evidence there or anywhere else very soon, I would ask to be taken off the case because I felt I might be compromised. I wouldn't even wait for re-assignment orders, or go to the embassy and hide out until they felt it was safe for me to leave. I would head straight back to the States with Gabrielle, and then quit.

I was hoping and praying that Abdul was innocent of all charges. Just because he was a wizard at chemistry, physics, and engineering, and was also Muslim, did not make him a terrorist. The evidence that was shared with me when I was given the assignment had always seemed thin, if not outright circumstantial. I was very fond of Abdul, very fond, and if being a pig was all he was guilty of, I could live with that.

It took me hours to fall asleep as images and scenarios involving Gabrielle, Abdul, and Dmitry passed before my eyes. Russians, Ukrainians, Mossad, Muslims, Kiev, my father, mercenaries, Kabul, my father, Dmitry ... "I earned it! I earned it!"

Chapter Five

I woke up to the sound of my phone ringing and naturally it was Gabrielle. It was like she was keeping tabs on me, but after a few moments the sound of her voice was like music to my ears. "Good morning, my handsome Nicky."

"Good morning, Gabrielle. How did you sleep?"

"Wonderfully. I dreamed about you all night. I felt like I was in paradise. Did you dream of me?"

"I did," I said, then quickly followed that with, "have you ever been to Kiev?" There was a long pause on her end.

"Kiev, where is that?" she finally replied.

"Surely, Gabrielle, you know where Kiev is? It's the capital of Ukraine."

"And why would you think I have been there? I don't understand. Is that where you want us to live instead of America?"

"No Gabrielle, I just had a dream that you were there. I don't want to live there."

"Good! I don't want to live there either. I want to live in America."

"And that's where we are going to live. It was just a dream, Gabrielle."

"I love that you dream of me, Nicky, but not in this place Kiev."

"I'll do my best, but you know how dreams are … you don't have much control over them."

"If you think about us living in America more, you won't have these stupid dreams."

"I didn't mean to upset you. All day long I will think about us living in America."

"Good! Are we going to spend all day together? You promised!"

"No, I did not promise. You know I have classes all day."

"No! You pretend to have classes," she replied angrily.

"How can you be so sure I'm not a serious student?" I asked.

"Because I know, that's how. What do you think I am, stupid?"

"I never said you were stupid. I just want to know how you can be so sure I am not a student. Why would I lie to you about that?"

There was another long pause on her end and I asked, "Are you still there?"

"Yes, Nicky, I'm here," she said. "If you would rather hang out with Abdul, then hang out with him. I don't care anymore. Do you understand? I don't care!"

"You know that's not true."

"I don't know anything. I'm stupid!"

"Stop it, Gabrielle! Stop it! You're acting like a child."

"Screw you!" she said. "You ask me about this Kiev, and then you tell me I'm acting like a child."

"You know what, I don't think we should see each other at all today."

"You don't want to see me at all?" she asked, as her voice dropped to a near whisper. "Fine!" She hung up, and I couldn't help but think that she was already acting like an American. A minute later, my phone rang and it was Gabrielle.

"I'm so sorry, Nicky. A thousand apologies. I don't know what came over me. Please forgive me. Tell me you still love me. Please! I love you so much. I will even learn everything there is to know about this place Kiev. Please!"

It was shocking to hear her beg so openly. A girl so beautiful that when we walked into a restaurant every guy turned to look at her. She was like a beautiful flower, but without any thorns attached to the stem. She was so fragile that a gentle wind could knock her over.

"Of course, I still love you, Gabrielle. Did you forget that you are the girl of my dreams? Nothing is going to stop me from loving and marrying you. Nothing!"

"Merci, Nicky. And are you going to come over and see me after your classes?"

"Yes, and I am going to take you out to a beautiful bistro, and we are going to have a wonderful time."

"No, Nicky! I don't want you spending so much money on me. I can cook, and we can stay at home. My parents left this morning, and we can have a romantic dinner all by ourselves."

"We can do that after we are married and living in America. We only have a short time left here in Paris and I want to take advantage of all the great food. We might not be coming back to Paris for a very long time. Do your parents understand that?"

"Yes, but they can come and visit us in America, right?"

"Of course, sweetheart. I need you to promise me something. In a very short time I will be able to explain everything to you, but in the meantime, you need to stop worrying about me cheating on you or not wanting to be with you. There is nothing I would like more than to be with you all the time, and soon that will be the case. Trust me, my beautiful, Gabrielle. Please, just trust me, and promise me, no more fighting."

"Yes, my handsome, Nicky. I promise. I'm a jealous fool! I know, but it's because I love you so much."

"And I love you so much and I feel like the most blessed person in the world to have you. It's not very often that one's dream comes true, and every time I look at you it is like a miracle."

"Thank you, Nicky. Thank you."

"And I promise to always protect you, Gabrielle. No one is ever going to hurt you."

"Merci, Nicky."

I could hear her crying ... crying like a child, and in a sense she was still a child ... forever frozen in a time and place by events so horrifying that they defined her. The monstrous attack she had suffered, and the bloody vengeance that she had been coached to exact from those men, had left her permanently scarred. The evil done to her as a child was still suffocating her, repressing a beauty, a laughter, a smile, and a grace that could otherwise have enchanted and mesmerized a world in disarray. I resolved in that moment to do whatever I could to help her heal. It would be my life's work, and if it took me the rest of my life, so be it.

Chapter Six

I strapped my backpack on and walked out of my tiny apartment. It was a sunny morning in late February and as I walked to the university I could not help but wonder what Paris was really like when Hemingway, Fitzgerald, and James Joyce roamed these very same streets. World War I had just ended a few years earlier, and whereas the city was populated with many aspiring artists and writers, there were many more crippled and mutilated soldiers on every corner and alleyway of this famous city.

It was Oscar Wilde who said, "When good Americans die they go to Paris." I had always considered myself a good American, but at this moment, if I was to die and found out that Paris was Heaven ... well, then I might consider Hell a better alternative. I was sure that this had more to do with hating my job than with the city itself. Paris was beautiful, as always. But my reasons for being here were becoming more odious to me by the day. I entered the university and went straight to my class and sat next to Abdul. As he smiled his hello and as the professor ambled in and began arranging handouts on a table, I reflected on the fact that for the last four years, I had been living a lie ... *pretending*, as my lovely Gabrielle likes to say. As I listened to the soft scrape of chalk on a board that began filling up with equations, I was filled with new hope that this, now, might finally be the beginning of the end of that lie.

Abdul was in the same bubbly and joking mood that he seemed to be in most days. He immediately started in on his sister, asking if I had at least "got to first base with the stuck-up bitch," since I had been spending so much time with her. I doubt he knew that first base was a baseball term, but he had probably heard it used numerous times by the Americans who dominated the tourist clubs where he was a regular.

"No," I said, "and I'm getting really tired of putting up with her bullshit."

"Good, so you see, I was right. She is just one pretty face in a city of beautiful women that are willing and ready. Why limit yourself to a stuck-up virgin who doesn't possess anything different than all these other women … except her inability to have fun and let go?"

"You're right. How about after classes we go have a few drinks in your neck of the woods?"

"Great, and I can show you my apartment where all the action takes place."

At times, it was like he was reading my mind. It all seemed too easy. He introduces himself to me, we become instant friends, and he helps with my assignments, and pays for everything. I ask to visit his part of the city, hoping he will ask me up to see his beautiful apartment that he is always bragging about, and naturally, the next thing out of his mouth is an invitation to show me his apartment. It was like he had a copy of my playbook … as if he got an advanced copy of a test and had already filled in the answers.

Right after our classes ended, we jumped into a cab and drove to the 8th arrondissement, also known as the Golden Triangle, located between three of Paris's most famous boulevards: Avenue des Champs-Élysées, Avenue Montaigne, and Avenue George V. In short, this was the Park Avenue of Paris, a place where bankers, CEOs, investors, and movie stars live, not graduate students.

We sat at a table at a fashionable bistro, and the waiter, Antoine, greeted Abdul like they were old pals. Apparently, Abdul frequented this establishment quite often … so often that Antoine asked if he wanted "the usual."

"Oui, mon ami," Abdul replied. "The usual, and a few appetizers."
A few moments later, Antoine brought over a bottle of Poujeaux

Bordeaux and poured a tiny amount into Abdul's wine glass. He swirled the wine around, took a whiff, and then a taste … hesitated a moment … and declared, "Magnifique!" Antoine smiled, poured wine into my glass and then the same amount into Abdul's glass. He then left to check on the appetizers as I took a sip of the wine and Abdul asked, "And what do you think?"

"Magnifique," I replied. The bottle went for $225.00, fairly cheap for this type of establishment and in this part of town … about the same amount it would have cost to buy his sister ten new dresses.

He tapped my glass with his glass and made a toast: "To no more Gabrielle."

We drank up and I remarked, "I haven't broken up with her yet."

"But you will?" he asked, sounding quite anxious.

"Yes, but I thought I would take it a little slow, like over a couple of days. Like today, I am supposed to meet her at five, but I'll show up about an hour late. She hates that. Tomorrow it will be something else. Hopefully by day three it will be all over."

"Are you crazy? Why would you waste an extra minute with that bitch? You want to get it over quick. Tell her tonight to get naked. That you're tired of her nonsense, and if she's serious about you that making love now or two years after you're married should not make a difference. That will have her threatening to cut off your balls as she kicks you to the street."

"Have you always thought so highly of your sister?" I asked.

"I have tried everything with her, but from the moment she looked at me after her parents adopted me she has been nothing but nasty. I love our parents as much as she does. You don't think I know how fortunate I was to be adopted, after having lived in that foster home? I know. And I'm always trying to give our parents money, trying to get them to move out of that neighborhood, but they are too proud to take it. Finally, after years of attempting to give them something back, I was able to convince them to let me pay for their vacation to Spain to visit relatives. I love our parents more than anything in this world. It's her, and it's always been her. Our parents tell me to help my sister, that she needs new clothes and supplies for school. I give her money and she barely acknowledges the kind gesture. She makes it sound like it's the life that I lead, chasing women and drinking, but it has nothing to do with that. Before I knew anything about women, she was horrible to me … from the time I was adopted as a ten-year-old she's been nothing but a bitch."

"Have you ever tried to talk to her about it? Really sat her down and tried to find out why she behaves the way she does toward you?"

"A million times, but she always just brushes me off like a piece of dirt." He refilled our glasses and continued. "You know what I think her problem is? I think she … how do you say it in America … plays for the other team."

"You think Gabrielle likes women?"

"What else could it be? Wherever she goes she has guys looking at her and she looks back like she would like to kill them. The only affection she has ever displayed toward a man is our dad, and I don't think that counts."

"How about me? I've kissed her a number of times and she seemed to like it."

"She's real good at make-believe. Honestly, I think the only reason she has shown interest in you is because she wants to get back at me. She's knows you're my best friend, and she just wants to get between us. She's evil."

We ate our appetizers, had another bottle of wine, said our goodbyes to Antoine and other members of the staff and left. We got into another cab and drove a mile away from the Golden Triangle and into another district, which was like a step down from the Triangle … more like the residences on First or Second Avenues in Manhattan.

We entered Abdul's building, where we were greeted by the concierge, and took the elevator up to the tenth floor. Abdul opened the door to his apartment and we walked into a space that was tastefully furnished, modern, with all the latest digital devices on display. From his living room window we could clearly see the Arc de

Triomphe de l'Étoile. Yes, this was the type of apartment that you could bring women to in the hope of seducing them.

He poured us each a hundred-year-old cognac, in a warm sniffer, and started showing me around the apartment. It was a one-bedroom with a separate, enclosed alcove that was filled with neatly stacked and labeled boxes. On a nearby worktable sat a stack of leather wallets, maybe thirty of them, and several stacks of microchips. I asked, "What's with all the wallets?"

He picked up a wallet and opened it and smiled at me as though he wanted to tell me but wasn't sure if he should.

"What?" I asked, laughing. "Is this how you're paying for your swank apartment? With a roaring trade in leather goods?"

"They're just not wallets, they're … explosive devices."

"You're joking."

He opened the wallet that had a place for credit cards, identification, family pictures, and cash. He held the wallet closer to my face and lifted a flap to reveal a panel behind the place for pictures. Woven into the panel was a tiny button and a little piece of white plastic, smaller than a Chiclet.

"What is that?" I asked.

"That's the bomb," he said. "Right there."

"Very funny."

"I'm telling the truth, man. You press the button and boom! Everyone within thirty feet of you is either dead or severely wounded."

"That's crazy."

"What's so crazy about it?"

"Well, let's just assume for a moment that you're telling the truth, which you're fucking obviously not. Why would anyone want to carry around a wallet that might explode and kill them? I don't understand."

"There's a safety feature, like a catch on a gun. And there's a timer that you can set for fifteen, thirty, or forty-five seconds before it goes off … plenty of time to get at least a hundred feet away."

"You're serious."

"I'm dead serious."

"And who buys these wallets from you?"

"Americans like yourself … businessmen and women, CEOs of big companies, people with money."

"But why?"

"For the same reason you Americans love your guns. For safety, and they're undetectable."

"Only Americans buy them?"

"No … Russian oligarchs, Arab sheiks and kings — people with money who want an extra layer of protection."

"Terrorists?" I asked.

He swung his head around and glared at me. "I would never sell to terrorists. I can't believe you could even suggest such a thing. Horrible! My family was killed by terrorists."

Could he be playing me for the stupidest human being ever, the most gullible … or was he actually naive enough to believe that these wallets weren't getting into the hands of terrorists? My phone buzzed and I looked down at the screen. It was Gabrielle, asking where I was and what time I was going to pick her up.

"The bitch!"

"Of course, who else."

"Stop being a gentleman and end it tonight. She either gets naked and fucks, which is one in a million chance, or she kicks you out and the nightmare is over."

I shook my head as I looked at the shipping boxes full with explosive wallets. I asked, "How many in a box?"

"Usually twenty-four."

"And how much do you get for a shipment that size?"

"Thirty thousand American dollars. First, a courier delivers the money and then I arrange for them to be shipped to the buyer."

The apartment buzzer went off and Abdul excused himself and went over to talk into his intercom. I used that time to quickly scan the shipping labels attached to the boxes. It looked like many of the boxes were being shipped by boat. From what I could tell, it looked like they were departing from the Port of Marseille, traveling all the way around Italy and up through the Port of Istanbul and into the Black Sea, then docking in the ports surrounding Crimea — the part of Ukraine occupied by the Russians. It was a roundabout route, but probably the safest when it came to shipping illegal contraband. Turkey, a member of NATO, and Russia, NATO's main adversary, had recently become buddies, and had joined forces with the Syrians to slaughter the Kurds after our president, the leader of the free world, deserted the Kurds at the behest of Turkey's leader. The president of the United States was Russia's greatest asset, and here was Abdul, casually confiding in me about profiting off this ungodly mess.

From the labels, it was clear that some of Abdul's cargo headed for the United States. Those boxes left from a port at Brittany, stopped in the US Virgin Islands, and then in Puerto Rico, and eventually docked and unloaded at the Port of Miami.

The cargo headed to the sheiks and kings was naturally headed to our friends in Saudi Arabia.

Abdul explained to me the intricate design woven into each wallet. The wires were so thin and had been covered so carefully with beautiful leather art work that there was no chance that a normal person would suspect anything was strange about the wallet. The bomb itself looked tiny and when I asked, "How do you manage to get such a deadly explosion out of such a small bomb?"

"Physics, Nick. Physics!" He handed me two wallets and told me to keep them as souvenirs or, "if you want to do the world a favor, detonate one in front of Gabrielle and quickly take cover."

"That's not funny," I angrily replied.

"No, it's not funny but it would be the humane thing to do … unless of course you're still in love with her?"

"I just don't want to harm her in any way. It might not have worked out, but that doesn't mean that I want to see anything bad happen to her."

"Wow! A few more kisses and you might actually be licking her ass clean after she uses the toilet."

"That's truly disgusting. How about one more cognac before I have to leave?"

"Of course, my friend. You're going to need all the liquid courage you can get just to face the rage of Gabrielle for being so late." He took my sniffer and walked into the living room. I quickly took out my phone and took as many pictures of the wallets, boxes, and shipping labels as I could. I put my phone away as he walked back into the room with the sniffers of cognac.

"She called, again?" he asked.

"Of course," I replied, shaking my head and shoving my phone in my back pocket. Then I asked, "So how much money do you usually make every month from your business?"

"Between sixty and ninety thousand US. I've been looking for a partner to help with the shipments and the admin. I could see you being good at this, and I trust you … so if you want in, just let me know. No more living in a small, decrepit apartment. You'll have a place with a view, beautiful women, fine restaurants, and no Gabrielle."

"I'll seriously think about it," I said. "The money would certainly make my life a lot easier. Just give me a little time. I really appreciate the offer."

"For my best friend, anything."

Chapter Seven

I got into the back of a cab and laid my head back against the cushion. I literally had everything I needed. Abdul had given me a tour and the blueprint to the whole operation. I should be passing this information onto my handler at this very moment, but I couldn't. I wasn't thinking straight and it had nothing to do with the alcohol in my system. Abdul trusted me … he called me his best friend … and I liked the guy, despite his beef with Gabrielle. That I could write off as a misunderstanding. He didn't know about the trauma that had shaped her opinions of Muslim men. These were the things that a veteran agent — someone who was actually made to do this type of work — would immediately put out of his mind. A real professional would already have handed over the information to his handler and disappeared. But, I wasn't a professional, and I wasn't made for this type of work. I knew that now.

The cab stopped in front of Gabrielle's building. I paid the driver and got out of the cab. Gabrielle was not waiting by the stairs like she had been the previous times I had visited. She must have been pissed off and gone back into the apartment to pout. I rang the outside doorbell to her apartment a number of times, waited about five minutes, and then called her phone.

She answered, "Hello!"

"Gabrielle, I have been ringing the outside bell for quite a while. Are you home?"

"Where do you think I would be … while you were spending precious time with my brother. Do you know how late you are?"

"Enough, Gabrielle. I'm going back to my place. Apparently, you weren't listening to anything I said this morning. Good night." I hung up the phone and walked down the stairs and started walking in the direction of my apartment, hoping a cab would come by. I had had it with Gabrielle and her childish behavior. Tonight, I would go to a bar and hopefully pick up some lovely American girl and actually have sex. It had only been five years that I had been intimate with a woman, and since I might never have sex with Gabrielle, why bother with her childish games? I would find another girl of my dreams without all the baggage attached.

Suddenly, I heard someone calling my name and of course it was Gabrielle. I turned around and she was running toward me wearing the same white dress she had on the day we first met. She literally jumped into my arms and kissed me so passionately that if I didn't know better I would have thought she was an imposter.

"S'il-te-plaît, Nicky, dis-moi que tu m'aimes. S'il-te-plaît! S'il-te-plaît! Please, tell me you love me ten times. Please Nicky, please!"

I told her … maybe nine, ten, or thirteen times … who could keep count at this stage of the game? She was so beautiful … so damaged, so fragile, so helpless … and I was a conflicted, hopeless CIA operative who couldn't make a decision about something as black and white and as simple as whether to turn in an individual who was building wallet-size bombs that could only be used by terrorists and anarchists whose main objective was to use violence to overturn democratic governments.

Dmitry was right; I wasn't made for this type of work, and no amount of training could change that simple fact.

I took Gabrielle's hand and we hailed a cab and drove to a restaurant. We ate at a small bistro, and the entire time I could not help but feel that we were being followed. I was not being paranoid. After three years in Afghanistan I had developed a sixth sense for when there were eyes on me. The only thing I wasn't sure of was if the eyes were on Gabrielle or me … or both of us.

After dinner, we got into another cab and drove to Gabrielle's building. I had the cab wait as I walked Gabrielle upstairs to her parents' apartment. The street was unusually quiet for this time of the night. I could see a couple sitting in a car a little ways up from the building. I couldn't tell if they were making out or just sitting close together and talking. I took Gabrielle's hand and walked back down to the cab. I told the driver that we were going to take a walk because it was such a beautiful night. I paid him and he drove off.

Gabrielle asked, "What's going on, Nicky?"

"I've decided to stay in your apartment tonight. I don't want you staying by yourself. I'll sleep on the couch."

She cuddled up really close to me and all I could think of was that we were sitting ducks for anyone who might want to target us. We quickly walked up the stairs to the building and entered her apartment. Gabrielle locked the front door as I walked through the rooms and closed all the windows and drew the curtains.

"What's going on?" Gabrielle suspiciously asked.

"Nothing! I'm just being overprotective when it comes to you. Get used to it, Gabrielle, because it won't be any different once we are married and living in America."

She smiled and walked into the kitchen to make us some tea. The apartment was in the back of the building, so I had no view of the front street. If we were targets of a hit, it would have happened outside, but I was more than certain that we were being watched.

I walked into the kitchen and came up behind Gabrielle and asked, "Did you wear your white dress tonight because you know how much I love it on you?"

"I don't have much money to buy clothes, and so I only have a few dresses to pick from, but now that I know how much you like me in it I will wash it more often and wear it."

"You won't have to worry about money when we are in America, and I will see to it that you have all the dresses and clothes that you like. That's a promise."

She turned around and looked at the stove and poured the boiling water into the teapot. She said, "I don't need new clothes as long as I know I have you."

I turned her back toward me and remarked, "You will always have me, but I still want to spoil you and give you things you could not afford."

She sat down at the kitchen table and she poured two cups of tea and put a baguette between us. She moved her chair closer to mine as she slid over her laptop computer that was on the table. She opened the computer and images of Kiev came up. "I spent most of my day learning about Kiev. I know how important it is to you, and so it's important to me. It looks pretty and if that is where you really want to live I will go with you."

I touched her hand and said, "That is so sweet of you. You really are a doll, but I don't want to live there. I want to go back to America with you. I'm sorry I gave you the wrong impression."

"No, Nicky, it was my mistake. I'm so stupid…"

"No, you're not. You're considerate and kind and the love of my life. You're perfect!"

She blushed like a little girl and replied, "Merci, and you are the love of my life."

I reached over and kissed her on the lips. Then we sat there in silence, each of us taking tiny bites of the bread. Finally I looked at her and said, "Tomorrow, I want you to pack a suitcase with everything that you need and everything that is important to you. Do you have a passport?" She nodded yes.

"Can I see it, please?" I asked, and she walked into her room and came back with her passport. She gave it to me, and everything seemed in order, and not even a passport photo could distort the beauty of her face. "I am going to be taking this with me tomorrow because I will need it to purchase the airplane tickets."

"We really are going to be leaving for America very soon?"

"Yes, my angel. Very soon."

She clapped her hands and said, "I am so happy, but when are we going to get married?"

"In America, very soon after we arrive. I promise."

"Thank you, Nicky."

"Thank you, Gabrielle, and thank you for loving me and wanting to be my wife. It makes me very happy."

I reached over and kissed her passionately, and for a short, blissful moment the fate of her adoptive brother did not intrude upon my thoughts. She opened a closet, and took out blankets and a pillow and fixed up the couch for me to sleep on. She then went into her bedroom to change into her pajamas.

A few moments later, she emerged wearing a pair of Mickey and Minnie Mouse pajamas. They were a little small for her, faded, and probably had been washed a thousand times. "And don't you look adorable."

She spun around like a dancer and behaved like she did on the stairs of the university when I first met her. Hopefully, America and a new life and beginning would make the joy she was exhibiting at this moment an everyday occasion.

Gabrielle had me lie down on the couch, and gave me the unique pleasure of being tucked in by the most beautiful girl in the world. She kissed me demurely and said good night, and then walked into her bedroom, closed the door, and *locked* the door. The click of the lock was quite loud.

I should have fallen asleep immediately. I had enough alcohol in me to tranquilize a horse, between the two bottles of wine and the cognacs I'd had with Abdul and the couple of glasses of wine I drank at dinner with Gabrielle. But I tossed and turned. I still had concerns that Gabrielle and I were being watched, though by whom was anybody's guess. But what really kept me up was the situation with Abdul. There should not have been any situation at all. I should have contacted my handler, met with him, and handed over all the evidence I had collected, no questions asked. That more or less would have been the end of my time in Paris. Abdul would be whisked away to an interrogation room where he would be pumped for names of contacts higher up the chain, and I would have disappeared.

But it wasn't that simple anymore. I had gotten close to Abdul, and despite the line of work he chose, I really liked him. Even so, I couldn't help being baffled by his complete lack of common sense. How could anybody be so stupid as to believe that the wallets he manufactured with such skill were being used by his buyers for self-defense? Or that they would somehow, magically, never find their way into the hands of terrorists like the ones who killed his family? It seemed impossible that anyone as smart and charming as Abdul could be so deluded. But he really seemed to believe that what he was doing was no big deal. Maybe somebody told him that to make him feel better, and it was convenient to believe it. Maybe he was a trusting simpleton when it came to politics. Whatever the reasons for this massive blind spot in Abdul's understanding of what he was doing, that willful or genuine naivete made him especially dangerous to civilians and democracies around the world.

I was thinking way outside the box to try to save him ... so far outside the box that I could be accused of treason. I thought of alerting him to the situation, and to my real job as a CIA operative, and hoping he would take that information and quickly skip town with his money and go live in a friendly country like Russia. But then, every time I read about a suicide bomber detonating a device and killing hundreds, I would be hammered over the head with the real possibility that Abdul had something to do with manufacturing that bomb. Could I live with that uncertainty? Probably not, or not very well. My training had taught me to be level-headed, to suppress my emotions, but I always had more nerves than the other recruits, and I was more prone to guilt. Donna Low had identified these traits in me back at the training academy. She had said that they would make me a good agent, one with "ethics and compassion" to go along with my "nerves of steel." But I wasn't sure my nerves had ever been as steady as they needed to be. And this whole situation with Abdul was starting to feel like the toughest challenge I would ever face. It was all just more proof that I was wrong for this job and needed to get out. But how to get out without implicating myself, or Abdul?

I rolled the problem around in my mind, considering one solution after another. I could go to the French authorities and alert them to the situation. It would be subverting my supervisors at the agency, but the French were much less likely to torture and kill him. He would end up in jail, but he would probably be kept alive. And I wouldn't have to hammer myself over the head each time I read about a suicide bomber. This felt like a win–win scenario, except for the fact that I would be dishonorably discharged, or worse, from the CIA for directly contravening orders and scuttling an intelligence operation by handing the target over to a foreign power. The French police could never be trusted to keep my secret for me. They weren't spies. They didn't have the discipline to lie well.

I could go to another country's spy agency, like Mossad, and let them take the lead on the case. They might be willing to take the credit for the arrest and work with me to construct a believable alibi that would prove to my bosses at the CIA that I had nothing to do with botching the case. Then I realized what a crazy plan this was. Imagine, thinking Mossad was a better and more humane agency than the CIA. That's how screwed up and desperate I was at the moment. No, that would be handing Abdul to the wolves. And while Mossad wasn't necessarily the only option, I couldn't immediately think of another country's spy agency that had strong enough motives to want to intervene, and that would work with me on a story to save my hide.

It was hours before I fell asleep, and then suddenly I was awoken by screaming coming from Gabrielle's room. I quickly got up off the couch and ran to her room. I banged loudly on the door and just about the time I was going to simply knock it down, the door opened and Gabrielle ran under my arm and straight to the bathroom. I quickly looked into the room to be sure there was no one there, and found it empty.

I then ran to the bathroom and watched in horror as Gabrielle slumped on the floor by the toilet and violently vomited for a long time. I could not believe that there was that much contents in her little stomach. There was vomit everywhere, especially all over her. When she finally stopped, I moved closer to her as she fell backwards, limp, and passed out on the floor. I could not wake her.

I grabbed a washcloth, wet it, and tried as much as possible to clean her face and to make sure the vomit was out of her mouth so she could not drown in it.

I took a blanket off the couch and laid it across the bathroom floor. I slid Gabrielle onto the blanket. She was as pale as a corpse, as if all the blood had been drained from her body. The top parts of her pajamas were soaked in vomit and there was no way I could leave her like that. I walked into her bedroom, and grabbed one of her clean shirts. I walked back into the bathroom and started to unfasten the buttons of her pajama top. I could not worry about what she might think when she finally woke up and I didn't give a damn at this point. The buttons all unfastened, I separated the two sides and looked down at her naked stomach and breasts. Apparently, she did not tell me the whole story about the rape. She had scars across nearly her entire body and chest and what looked like burned cigarette marks tattooed on her breasts. She had not only been raped and spit on, but also mutilated by those four bastards. She wasn't some stuck-up bitch like Abdul was fond of calling her. She was ashamed of her body, humiliated, and that's why she refused to take her clothes off and have sex, or allow herself to get intimate with anyone.

I slid off her dirty pajama top, used the wet cloth to wipe away as much of the vomit as I could, then gently helped her into the clean shirt that I'd found in her closet. She was still out, though her eyes fluttered slightly and she once tried to say something before fading out again. I then picked her up carefully and carried her to the couch and laid her down, then rolled her onto her side in case she were to vomit again.

She was breathing normally and a little color was finally coming back into her face. I took the time to go back into bathroom and clean up all the vomit. I did not want her waking up to that mess.

I poured myself a large glass of water and sat in a chair across from the couch. There were parts on the bottom half of her pajamas that were still soiled. I didn't dare take them off, not so much because I didn't want to hear her protests, but more because I was scared of what else I might find. She was ten years old when this rape, assault, and mutilation took place. Ten years old! A child! I had never been able to comprehend the terrible atrocities that human beings were constantly showing themselves capable of committing against one another. I watched Gabrielle sleeping and was filled with sadness at the legacy of this horrific abuse. What could possibly have prompted the attack? Were these men simply monsters who took a random opportunity to satisfy their sick need for power? Or was it a religiously motivated hate crime? Was Gabrielle targeted because she was part of the Christian minority in her home country? I knew about many such attacks, and I knew these events to be every bit as horrifying as the attacks that happened elsewhere in the world against other religious groups, including Jews and Muslims. Every one of these groups had been attacked for their religion and had since perpetrated attacks on others. Every religion had its extremists who believed that their god and their faith were the only correct ones, and every church had monsters who were willing to use violence against non-believers. But a child of ten! The mind couldn't contain it, couldn't make room for the idea that there might be any common humanity in those four men who perpetrated this assault on a child. As I watched Gabrielle's breathing catch and return to normal, I knew in my heart that if these four bastards were alive and in front of me, they would suffer the same fate that they suffered all those years ago. They deserved to have their balls shot off and be scorched alive repeatedly until the end of time. And yet, and yet — they were human. One had to admit that. They were as human as Gabrielle and I were, and they had no doubt suffered for their own beliefs, for their own histories. They had suffered on their way to becoming the men they became. Their actions, and the fate they suffered in that cave, proved that much of humanity was simply lost.

Gabrielle, meanwhile, was also lost, and had been left to bear all of the pain — her own, and theirs, for what had been done to them in her name. The enigma that was Gabrielle was becoming clearer by the day. The present situation I found myself in was still fuzzy and indistinct, fraught with problems of life and death, good against evil. My Catholic upbringing did not make the situation, the answers I was seeking, any easier to obtain. In a family where my mother, father and older sister could at best be called very lax Catholics, and at worst be called amoral, the burden of conscious action and belief frequently fell on my baby sister and me.

The acrid smell of vomit permeated the apartment. The lovely lady on the couch needed the type of help I wasn't sure I could deliver, but I would give it everything I had. The scars, mutilations, burned marks, and her fragile and deeply troubled state of mind made me even more attracted to her than when I first saw her on the steps of the university. Back then, it was her face and her eyes and easy demeanor that so drew me to her, but now it was the whole person that I was in love with.

The hours ticked away, and I could see that it was starting to get light outside. Gabrielle stirred and then opened her eyes and looked across at me. She tried to get up, but I gently held her down on the couch and told her not to move. I opened the refrigerator and filled a glass with ice cubes. I sat down beside her, and put an ice cube in her mouth. "You got sick during the night and you need to rehydrate yourself." She sucked on the cube and then I put another into her mouth. She was still confused, as I patiently placed one cube after another into her mouth.

I grabbed the leftover baguette from the night before and fed her tiny pieces. I asked, "Are you feeling any better, my beautiful angel?" She nodded as she looked down at the clean shirt I had put on her. "And now you know everything, my handsome Nicky. Please don't feel sorry for me. You should just leave and try never to think about me again. I understand, believe me."

She turned on her side and buried her face into the back cushion of the couch. I turned her back around, "Do I look like the type of guy who would leave his bride stranded at the altar? We have a whole life before us, a life that is going to be wonderful and fun and filled with love. Please, don't destroy that dream, please."

She gently ran her fingers across my face and said, "I love you so much."

"And I love you so much," I replied as I went to kiss her on the lips but she stopped me and continued, "We can kiss all you want, but please let me clean up and brush my teeth first. It will be a lot more fun then."

I laughed and remarked, "But first you need to eat a little more and drink a lot of water."

"Oui, Nicky."

"Good girl," I said as I held another tiny piece of bread to her mouth and she parted her lips.

Chapter Eight

Gabrielle took a shower and cleaned up. I could hear her brushing her teeth and gargling for a longer than usual time, and after that I could hear her softly singing a little tune I didn't recognize, in French. She walked out of the bathroom wearing a simple blue dress, like all the others, with a white belt tied around her waist. She was sparkling as she threw her arms around me and we kissed passionately for a long and amazing time.

She twirled around, like a ballerina … like an angel who had a wing clipped, only to see it finally grow back, stronger and more beautiful than ever. I took her by the waist and looked into her emerald green eyes and said, "Tell me I'm not dreaming?"

"You're not dreaming," she reassured me as she twirled around and then flung her arms around my neck and we kissed over and over again.

I promised Gabrielle that I would stay with her all day long, but I reminded her that she needed to pack because we really were leaving for America in a couple of days. While she packed, I decided to walk to the market and pick up some food. I walked out of the building and before I walked a hundred feet I could feel someone walking close behind me. The back door of a parked car suddenly opened in front of me, as the person behind me put a gun to my head and said, "Get in."

I bent down and slid into the back seat of the car. It was foolish to even try to escape. The gentleman in the front turned and looked at me as the other gentleman shut the back door.

The gentleman up front remarked, "So you're the American that our lovely Gabrielle is so madly in love with."

I asked, "Are you David or Elijah?"

"I'm David and the gentleman with gun pointed at you is Elijah. And Gabrielle is like a daughter to us and her love for you is a little disconcerting."

"And why is that?"

They both laughed as David remarked, "You might be a terrible operative, but please don't play dumb with us. It's insulting! Don't you think, Elijah?"

"Very insulting," Elijah agreed as he shoved the barrel of his gun into my side.

"Surely, the CIA hasn't changed its playbook so much that it preaches that it's okay for its operatives to fall in love with a source's sister and take her back to America and marry her?" David asked.

"No, they haven't, but in two days my assignment here will be finished and my career with the CIA will be over. And when I leave Paris and go back to America it will be with Gabrielle, and the quicker we get married the happier we will both be."

"Wow! Our lovely Gabrielle is very good at pretending. I often thought she would make a wonderful actress."

"What is that supposed to mean?"

"Some women who experience what she did as a child grow up to be warriors. Gabrielle has grown up shattered and tormented, as fragile as a newborn, and Elijah and I have always felt a sense of responsibility and guilt over how we handled the situation. We were young and crazy and carried the revenge too far. The bastards deserved everything they got, but we should never have forced that child to pull the trigger." He looked at me closely and continued, "If this turns out to be some type of farce you are playing with Gabrielle, what we did to the four terrorist bastards will look like child's play after we get through with you. If you so much as disappoint her, let alone hurt her…" He stopped short, as the pain on his face said it all. "Have you been in touch with your handler about the information you found out yesterday about that simpleton Abdul?"

"No, not yet," I replied.

"For what it's worth, he's dead. Send whatever code or message you were going to send to him, anyway. The person responsible for his death is expecting it."

"And who might that be?"

"The CIA chief, right here, in charge of your embassy: a short, weaselly gnome known as the professor. He'll get back in touch with you quickly and ask to meet. Agree to whatever plan he proposes. We'll be there with him. We're the ones who notified the CIA about suspicious activities surrounding Abdul. What we didn't know at the time was that the professor was the buyer behind the whole operation, paying Abdul thirty thousand dollars at a clip and getting a half a million dollars in return from Ukrainian nationalists working for the Russians. We get first crack at Abdul, pretending that he's a threat to Israel, which is what we originally thought, but that information turned out to be false."

"What's going to happen to Abdul?" I asked.

"We'll interrogate him, and then ship him off to Israel. The idiot can actually be of some use to us. His design for those wallet-size bombs was quite ingenious. The good news for him is that we allow him to live. There's nothing more dangerous than a simpleton with one deadly skill. Especially one gullible enough to believe that the wallets were being sold to law-abiding citizens for their own protection. What a dope!"

Elijah laughed at that and they traded looks before David turned back to me. He reached into the glove department of the car and pulled out two plane tickets.

"Tonight you sleep in your own apartment," he said. "Pack only what is essential to you and leave the apartment as though you were coming back. Tomorrow, take the tickets with you to the meeting with the professor and us. Make sure you put them in that stupid-looking backpack, and wear it to the meeting. Give the professor the pictures you took and the wallets that Abdul gave to you as souvenirs. He'll look surprised, but don't fall for it. He'll then tell you to carry on as usual, as a student, and to continue to get information on Abdul.

When you leave, go to your classes as usual. Tell Abdul that you have a family emergency and have to fly back to America immediately, but that tonight you would like to have dinner with him because you don't know how long you might be gone. Make the reservation at Chez Marcel Bistro for seven o'clock. Have dinner, have a few drinks, and get out of there by eight. There will be two cabs waiting outside the restaurant. You take the first one. If Abdul wants to come along just tell him you have a few friends you want to see before leaving and you need to pack because you will be leaving early.

"He'll take the second cab. Elijah will be driving it. He'll take Abdul to a secret location where we will interrogate him before shipping him back to Israel."

Elijah picked up the narrative and said, "The cab will drop you off at your building. Go into the building like you would usually do, but instead of going up to your apartment, take the stairs down to the basement. The door on the far end of the basement will lead you to an underground tunnel. Take a flashlight and walk the entire length of the tunnel. That will leave you about a half a mile from the building. You will most likely hear a loud explosion shortly after entering the tunnel … that will be your apartment blowing up, courtesy of the professor.

"Stay out of sight for at least two hours, and then take a cab to Hôtel R de Paris. Gabrielle will be waiting for you in room 405."

David handed me the plane tickets. "The following morning you leave very early for the airport. You go to the El Al terminal. At the receiving desk you hand the attendant the two tickets for you and Gabrielle. The tickets are marked in an invisible code, that the attendant will notice when she scans the tickets. She will notify a supervisor who will come and take you to a back room where the two of you will wait until it is time to board. The plane will take you to Tel Aviv where a car with Israeli government plates will pick you up and take you to a hotel. You can stay in Tel Aviv as long as you want. You are safe there, and if it weren't such a nightmare I would say get married there and enjoy the pleasures the city has to offer. When the two of you are ready to go to America, I suggest you also take El Al."

"How am I going to explain all this to Gabrielle?" I asked.

"Not to worry, we will be doing all the explaining. We're going back to her apartment with you."

The three of us got out of the car and walked to the building. I knocked on the apartment door, waited as Gabrielle looked through the peephole, and then she opened the door and screamed, "Oh my God," as she threw her arms around David and Elijah and kissed them over and over again.

We entered the apartment as I locked the door behind us. She threw her arms around me and asked, "So you have met my Nicky?"

"Yes, we have met your Nicky and we have had a long talk, and Elijah and I have made it perfectly clear to him that if he doesn't treat you like the princess you are, there will be a severe price to pay."

"Not to worry. He loves me so much. He would never hurt me. Isn't that so, my sweet Nicky?"

"Yes, that is definitely true," I replied as I reached down and kissed her on the cheek. The steely look the two men maintained during our whole conversation in the car disappeared as they looked at Gabrielle. Their faces had relaxed, and they looked at her with love and caring in their eyes. It was as though they had gone back in time and were looking at the innocent ten-year-old child who had been savagely assaulted.

Elijah took her by the hand and led her to the kitchen table. "We have a lot to talk about, Angel, and there is no need to worry because it is all good."

"How about I make us something to eat first?" she anxiously asked.

"No sweetheart, we just ate a short time ago."

"Something to drink?"

"No! Come and sit down." She sat down next to Elijah, with me on the other side of her, and David sitting directly across from her. David remarked, "Now I want you to listen and any questions you have you can ask later."

"Okay," she replied as she nodded.

"Good! First, your fiancé works for the CIA, the US Central Intelligence Agency."

She looked up at me with her eyes wide open and full of suspicion. David reached over and grabbed her hand and she looked at him. "If he didn't work for them you guys never would have met and fallen in love. He's one of the good guys."

I reached over and took her hand. She immediately withdrew her hand and David remarked, "That is not the way you treat a person you love, and who loves you just as much and has risked his life to protect you. Do you understand?"

"Yes," she replied as she took my hand back, and looked down at the table. David reached over and lifted her chin up. "He's resigning in two days from the CIA and everything he has promised you he definitely intends to follow through on." He looked at me pointedly and said, "Right?"

"Yes, every last promise I intend to keep," I replied as I affectionately squeezed her hand.

"I gave Nick two plane tickets to Tel Aviv, and from there you can go onto America as soon as you want. You will be leaving in two days. In the meantime, and this is very important, Gabrielle, you are going to do exactly what I tell you. Nick is going back to his apartment tonight to sleep, and do not, under any circumstances, try to persuade him to stay here. Any important files you have on your computer, put on a flash drive, and any important telephone numbers on your phone, write down on a piece of paper. Tomorrow morning, around eleven, I am going to come over here and take your computer, phone, and any other digital devices you have and destroy them."

"Why?" she asked as she looked across at me, Elijah, and back to David.

"You know why, Gabrielle. Don't worry, your future husband has plenty of money and I'm sure he will gladly buy you the latest state-of-the-art computer and phone."

I stopped being surprised by how much these two gentlemen knew about me. Yes, I had plenty of money, but at the moment it was in my little sister's name. I could get it at any time, but up to that moment I thought I was the only one who knew about it.

"Tonight you pack all the belongings you want to take with you to America. After I confiscate your devices, I will drive you to the Hôtel R de Paris. You will stay there until the following morning when you and Nick will leave early in the morning to go to the airport. Nick will meet you at the hotel tomorrow night at about eleven."

He took both her hands and looked straight at her and continued. "Under no circumstances are you to allow anyone into your room. You are not to order room service or pick up the phone in your room if it rings. I will bring plenty of food with me when I pick you up in the morning. I will give you a phone to use in case of an emergency. The only visitor you will let in is Nick when he calls the phone I give you between ten and eleven. Do you understand?"

"Yes," she said quietly. "Can I call Nick in the morning like I usually do to wake him up around seven o'clock?"

"Yes, but do not talk about any travel plans, or the CIA, or anything related to what we just talked about. Speak in very general terms. Like two love birds … that should be pretty easy."

We all laughed and then Gabrielle asked, "How worried should I be?"

"There is no reason to be worried. Elijah and I will always have eyes on the two of you. And after tomorrow you get to live the life of a princess … a life you richly deserve."

Chapter Nine

I watched from the kitchen table as Gabrielle kissed and hugged David and Elijah goodbye. She then locked the door and walked into the kitchen and sat down at the table across from me. She looked at me for quite a while before she spoke.

"The CIA … like James Bond?"

"No Gabrielle, nothing like James Bond. I thought you might know."

"And how would I know?"

"Because you have always told me, from the first day we met, that I could stop pretending to be a student when I was with you. That I was a man of the world."

"Yes, Nicky, a man of the world. A person who travels a lot … who travels to different countries to climb mountains and navigate rapids … not a person who kills people."

"I have never killed anyone, so please don't let your imagination run wild."

"But there are people who want to kill you? Why else would David and Elijah come up with this plan to sneak us out of the country?"

"They're simply helping to protect us … to safeguard me against any potential danger."

"Absurd! It is their job to kill bad people."

"Are you going to follow the instructions they gave you?"

"Yes! Are you going to make it back to the hotel?"

"Yes!"

"Promise?"

"Yes, I promise," I said. I took her hand and continued, "No one is going to take my dream away from me."

"It's my dream too, Nicky."

I reached over as tears started flowing down her cheeks. "I love you so much, Gabrielle." We kissed as her tears mingled with our lips and we started to laugh.

"And Abdul, how does he fit into all this?"

"He'll be okay," I replied, hoping against hope that she wouldn't pursue the issue of Abdul.

"And what does okay mean?"

"Just that, Gabrielle; he's going to be fine."

"So he has nothing to do with this business that you, the CIA man, and David and Elijah, two Mossad agents, are so concerned about? You just happened to become his best friend while pretending to be a student?"

"Yes, we just hit it off. Your brother is a very likeable guy once you get to know him."

"You are a very poor liar, Nicky. If anything happens to you and I find out he was involved, I will kill him. You understand?"

"You will not be killing anybody, and nothing is going to happen to me."

She looked at me really hard with her emerald green eyes that seemed to stab at my heart and read my mind.

"And how did David and Elijah know so much about our relationship?"

"I have stayed in touch with them ever since that awful experience, and I thought they would like to hear the good news about the two of us. They care for me very much."

I lowered my eyes and looked at her paint-stained hands. I asked, "And how is your portrait of me coming along?"

"I have not worked on it since you've seen it. Tonight, when I can't sleep because I will be so worried about you, I will work on it."

"So tomorrow night I might get to see the finished project?"

"Yes!"

"Do you want me to write down all the instructions that David told you to follow so you won't forget anything?"

"No, I am not as stupid as you might think."

I laughed, "That thought has never crossed my mind, I can assure you."

I sat in Gabrielle's bedroom and watched her pack as we talked about America and the Statue of Liberty. Her wardrobe was very clean and quite outdated. But Gabrielle was so beautiful that she could wear rags and make them sparkle like a new line of clothing from Valentino. She didn't have the type of body that one sees on models walking down the runways in New York or Paris. She was petite, with an angelic face, and when she didn't seem to carry the weight of the world on her shoulders, she moved with a grace and ease of someone walking on air. As I sat there looking at her, I realized that for the first time in my life, I loved everything about another person. I also remembered that we hadn't known each other very long, and knew I would have the pleasure of finding out more about her, and getting to love those parts of her, too. I couldn't imagine learning anything that did not inspire a deepening of the love I already felt. It was a wild and completely new sensation. I didn't try to explain it or share it with her. I just sat there and enjoyed it, but of course she noticed something was up and smiled at me quizzically.

I reached into my pocket and took out a piece of paper. On it were written a phone number and several verification codes that would give her access to enough money to allow her to live comfortably for the next twenty years. I motioned her over, and she came and sat on my lap. I handed her the paper and said, "In case something happens to me…" She already started to object and I put a finger over her lips. "Please, just listen. In case something happens to me, you call the number on this paper and enter the codes. That will give you access to enough money to live very nicely for a very long time. Don't argue with me, and whatever you do, don't lose the piece of paper."

I picked her up and laid her on the bed and we kissed for a long and wonderful time and then I simply held her as I kissed the back of her neck as I watched tears fall from her eyes and onto the sheets of the bed.

Chapter Ten

I took a cab to my building and entered the lobby. I took the stairs down to the basement to check on the door that opened to the tunnel. It was just as David had told me. I then walked up to my apartment and took out a secure phone and typed a cryptic message to my now-deceased handler. In less than five minutes I received a message back telling me to meet at eight o'clock in the morning at a café in a poorer district of Paris. I used a code to confirm the meeting.

I then called up Abdul who was naturally at a club. Right away, he asked me to come over. I told him I had a family emergency … that my mother was very sick, which when I thought about it wasn't that far from the truth … she was seriously out of her mind … and that I would be leaving for America the day after tomorrow. He agreed that we should have a farewell dinner and when I told him that I would like to eat at Chez Marcel, he warned me that there weren't many girls that hung out there. I told him I wasn't really in the mood, with my mother being so sick, and I was on a tight schedule.

He then asked if I had made any headway breaking up with his sister.

I told him that everything was going as planned until I dropped her off at her apartment, and she got horribly sick. "She was vomiting all over the place," I explained. "I felt guilty and stayed overnight to take care of her."

"You are such a fool. She probably got wind of you wanting to break up with her and forced herself to get sick. Like I have told you, she's very good at pretending."

"Well, maybe I will get lucky and by the time I come back to Paris she will have forgotten me."

"She's a conniving bitch and will be sending you text messages all day asking about your mother … making you feel even more indebted to her."

The music got so loud in the club that I couldn't hear him anymore. We decided to talk about it the next day. I put the phone down and I sat very still, staring at the table and then across at a small mirror on the wall. Never in my life had I felt more like I was betraying a friend. David and Elijah were killers, and they probably thought I was really stupid to fall for their story that they were going to ship Abdul back to Israel. The Israelis were really smart and inventive and anything Abdul came up with they came up with a few years earlier. I had one option left and that was to inform the French authorities about Abdul's activities, merchandise, and place of residence. They would arrest him, confiscate the explosives, and have it all over the news. Mossad and the CIA wouldn't be able to do shit. In fact, the French would be so outraged with both agencies for not informing them of their involvement and suspicions about Abdul, and allowing a lingering threat on their soil to fester to this point, that there would be accusations flying wildly between the intelligence agencies of all three countries. And in the end, Abdul would get a fair trial and be spared certain death.

The downside would be the threat that such a plan would have on my relationship with Gabrielle. According to David and Elijah, my station chief in the Paris embassy, the professor already had a kill order out on me. That wasn't at all surprising, especially if he was making the fortune they said he was making off of Abdul's explosives and was put in charge of the Paris embassy under direct orders from our treasonous president. And whereas David and Elijah would never hurt Gabrielle, they might not be so kind to me. I was sure Gabrielle and I were being watched right now and so it would be nearly impossible to get away.

I did not have time on my side, and I was only certain of two things: Abdul's enterprise had to be shut down, and our embassy station chief had to be eliminated. Abdul's explosives weren't just being shipped to the US or Saudi Arabia; they were ending up in Russian-occupied Crimea and were being smuggled into the democratic country of Ukraine for the sole purpose of slowly and methodically destabilizing the country so that the Russians would once again be in total control. Ukraine's desire to be part of NATO and the European Union was a threat to the Russians. Once the Soviet empire collapsed, Stalin's buffer zone against the west was eliminated. Ukraine, Poland, Belarus, Romania, the former East Germany, and Kazakhstan were for decades puppet satellites protecting Russia's border from imminent, unimpeded attacks such as the ones the Nazis launched against them during World War II. With the former satellite countries drawing closer to the west, practicing democratic principles, and wanting to join NATO, Russia's borders were no longer protected ... if anything these former occupied countries despised the Russians.

I knew that Russia and its former KGB operative president hungered for the days of the old Soviet Empire, and its invasion of Crimea, a part of Ukraine, was a stepping stone in its desire to rebuild barriers against the west and destabilize the region. Turkey, a member of NATO, was drawing closer to Russia every day. Syria, and its diabolic leader, had become allies with Russia, whose military and firepower had assured that the regime and Bashar al-Assad were going to survive ... giving Russia a firm footing in the Middle East, which is what it had always desired. And of course the president of the US and the leader of the free world is Russia's greatest asset. Whatever the Russian president has on our fearless leader must be so incriminating that our president is actually doing Russia's bidding in trying to undermine the greatest alliance ever formed ... NATO. Presidents Roosevelt, Truman, Eisenhower, Reagan, and George H.W. Bush must be turning over in their graves ... not to mention Churchill, General George C. Marshall, every soldier who ever fought, died, and was wounded in their efforts to secure peace and freedom for our country and the world, every CIA operative, spy, intelligent officer, and all of the embassy officials who have sacrificed so much for our country and the world. As far as I was concerned, the entire Whig Party, which collectively refused to stand up against our rogue president, all deserved a special place in Dante's Hell, right next to Lucifer.

I started to pack everything I needed into my backpack, leaving behind enough stuff to make it seem like I was definitely coming back to the apartment. I looked once again at my files on Abdul and his family and at my most trusted contacts in the agency. Suddenly, I came across the name of Michael Levine, a CIA pilot who was grounded for his overly aggressive actions in Afghanistan. He was a renegade and a superb pilot who was re-assigned to fly some big shot general around in a US-owned plane to every country in NATO. I was the only one who stood by him when disciplinary actions were taken to remove him from the agency. The Afghan government accused him of killing civilians, but I knew that claim to be totally false; I was in charge of supervising and overseeing his actions at the time, and he was nowhere near the area where the civilians in question were killed. The agency needed a scapegoat and it was Mike. He was removed from the combat area, but my testimony in the case saved him from being fired. He always told me that if I needed anything he would be there for me, even if it meant losing his job, because as he said, he had "no use for the motherfuckers," and his only interest was in receiving a paycheck and "flying the dickhead around."

It was a one-in-a-thousand chance that he would be in France with the dickhead. I took out a burner phone, a disposable cell, entered a code that identified that it was me, and dialed his number. After it rang twice, Mike answered and recognized my voice immediately.

"Dude, how are you?" he asked.

"I'm okay. Sort of. What are the chances you might be around Paris for a few days?"

"As good as they ever will be. I flew into Vatry Air Base yesterday with General DH. We're scheduled to be here for another five days. I was actually thinking about driving up to Paris. It's only about 100 miles."

"How would you like to fly me to New York late tomorrow night?"

"Well, I do like New York a million times better than Paris. We'll be staying in the city?"

"As long as you like. All expenses on me."

"And does that include enough coke to keep me up for the whole flight?"

"Yes!"

"They've turned on you?"

"Yes!"

"It's that motherfucker in the White House. He's put pressure on the agency to put his men into certain embassies that benefit his own political survival. Is it just you, or are there other passengers?"

"One young woman."

"Good looking?"

"Yes, she's beautiful and I think I am engaged to her."

He laughed. "You think? Does she have a sister, or a really good-looking friend who would love to see the Big Apple?"

"Not that I know of. Sorry."

"Well, then you want to bring a lot of extra coke to make up for it."

"I'll see what I can do. One tomorrow night sound okay?"

"Perfect."

Mike gave me directions on how to get to the base, and where to park the car. The former Vatry Air Base, now Châlons Vatry Airport, was about a hundred miles east of Paris. It was a NATO base back in the 1960s and now it was being used as a cargo and transport base. The French government, with an eye on public sentiment, was very sensitive about letting military aircraft from other countries fly over French air space; in the mid-1980s, they refused to allow the US to fly over France on the way to bombing Libya after that country was tied to a number of terrorist acts against civilian planes. The Reagan Administration understood the politics and the sentiment of the French people, and never made a big issue over the episode. Today, with little or no understanding of international issues, the administration would use such an episode as proof that NATO was useless and that we were paying too much to keep it afloat. All of this was total bullshit.

After I hung up with Mike, I finished packing. Tomorrow, after classes, I would destroy my laptop and the cell phone I had been using to communicate with Abdul and Gabrielle. From then on, I would be using burner phones that I would dump after one call. I lay down on my bed and knew I needed to get some sleep, but it wouldn't be easy. Just then, my regular phone rang and it was Gabrielle. Regardless of how many times I told her not to call me except for the one time in the morning, she just couldn't help herself. She was worried because she hadn't heard from me since I left her apartment hours earlier. I apologized and told her I was really tired and would talk to her in the morning, but she just kept on talking, telling me how much she loved me and having me repeat how much I love her. I had to stop her from divulging information about our plans about half a dozen times. Finally I said one last time that I loved her, "more than anything," and simply hung up.

Abdul and the Mossad twins had told me how good she was at *pretending*, and let me just say, if she was pretending to be crazy, she was doing a hell of a job.

Chapter Eleven

After a few hours of sleep I was woken up at six in the morning by my phone ringing. Naturally it was Gabrielle. It was like a repeat performance from the night before, except this time she cried throughout. Maybe it was just that I was new to this whole love thing. I had never had a steady girlfriend in my life, and certainly never had a girl even come close to saying she loved me and wanted to be with me for all eternity. Working for the CIA, despite what you might see in the movies, does not present one with many opportunities to truly fall in love. Yes, sex and money were two of the most powerful weapons in recruiting foreign agents, but you were never supposed to feel anything, and most of the time you didn't.

Falling head over heels with Gabrielle, the source's sister, was definitely forbidden ... but then I was through with this insane life after tonight, or so I hoped. I was quite sure many other agents as stupid as I was, who had made similar mistakes, thought they were done with the agency too ... only to be found months or even years later, floating in a pool of blood in their own deluxe bathtubs.

Anyone who became a CIA operative for the adventure that such a life presented could be quite sure that they would not last long. Adventure-seekers had a way of ending up dead in remote villages in Siberia and other far-flung places. One had to be smart, a true patriot, and be willing to do certain things that any conscientious human being would not do ... or, like myself, have a father who was a general in the army who championed my decision to join the agency and serve his country.

After talking to my highly anxious fiancée, I retrieved my handgun from under the bed. It was a standard-issue military P320, 9mm semi-automatic, manufactured by the German company SIG Sauer. It was the first time I would be carrying a weapon since being assigned to Paris. Contrary to what one sees in the movies and reads in spy novels, most CIA operatives carry only one weapon, the above-mentioned handgun, and many don't carry any weapons at all. And unlike the impression created by James Bond movies, being an agent doesn't translate into frequent firefights. If you're doing your job well, there should be few opportunities to use a weapon at all. In fact, after four years in the agency I still had not fired my handgun or any other weapon in a defensive, combat situation, and I was hoping to keep that streak alive … unless of course my lovely Gabrielle continued to behave insanely, and then I might have to use the gun to kill myself.

I put the gun in my backpack, along with the wallets from Abdul, and the pictures I'd taken of the boxes and their address labels in his apartment. It was all I planned on handing over to the traitorous professor. I took one last look around the tiny apartment and then closed my eyes and visualized everything I had to do today and tonight. The burden of guilt was so heavy that I was quite certain that I would be flying back to the States tonight with Mike … if I managed to stay alive that long.

Chapter Twelve

I walked into the café and immediately spotted David sitting at a table in the back. He was sitting next to Elijah, who had his back to the door, and another man who I assumed was the professor. I couldn't just walk over to the table because none of us were supposed to have met, so I stood there by the hostess stand, looking like a jackass. The place was very crowded and loud, which was more or less what I expected. When meeting your handler, or in this case the murderous station chief, you either had to choose a crowded place where it would be difficult for anyone to overhear your conversation or someplace completely deserted. I was happy that we were meeting in a bustling restaurant because that made it highly unlikely that I would be blown away.

A young female hostess approached me and asked, in French, if I was waiting for someone. I told her I was, but that I didn't know what they looked like. She smiled and took me over to the table where the professor and the Mossad twins were sitting. The professor thanked her and looked up at me.

"Nick?"

"Yes," I said, extending my hand and settling into the only other empty chair at the table. The professor introduced me to David and Elijah, and we all pretended to be meeting each other for the first time. Then I sat quietly and looked across at the professor, taking in his strange appearance. He looked like a character out of a Joseph Conrad novel. Small and studious looking, his body was twisted like a pretzel.

He wore rimless glasses and his eyes were two little brown dots, like the eyes of a mouse. His face was pale and wizened, and he wore a fedora and a long overcoat, despite being inside the café on a warm day. I suspected the coat was there to conceal his deformed body. A walking cane hung from the back of his chair. The three of them were drinking what looked like triple espressos.

"I'm sorry James couldn't make it," the professor lied. "He had a family emergency."

"Oh, that's unfortunate," I said, feigning ignorance. "Hopefully, everything will turn out all right." I thought of my deceased handler and marveled at the nerve of this vicious little gnome, who was so convinced that he could commit murder and get away with it.

"Oh, I'm sure it will," the professor said with a slight laugh. His voice was squeaky and irritating and his lips were slanted as though he had suffered a stroke. He kept stirring his espresso as he dropped one lump of sugar after another into the cup. I ordered a single espresso and it arrived while the professor made small talk.

"How are you liking Paris?" he asked.

"It's quite beautiful." I replied.

"Yes, especially during this time of the year. And the women?"

"Also quite beautiful."

"Yes, quite gorgeous. I especially like the petite ones, with dark, straight hair, and that olive skin that is like fine silk. And you, Nick, what type do you prefer?"

"I guess all types. I really haven't been able to give much attention to the women. I have been so busy with school."

"Of course, school can be all-consuming, especially when studying subjects like engineering and chemistry. I don't know if you've heard about this, but I was a professor once. I taught chemistry and math. I have always enjoyed working with formulas and devising experiments."

I smiled and nodded and took a sip of my espresso. Then I reached into my backpack and took out the folder that contained the photos and notes from my trip to Abdul's apartment. I slid the folder over to the professor and he took a quick glance inside, then closed it. I then gave him a small gift box that contained one of the wallets. "And this is a gift from one of your former students."

"How thoughtful," he remarked as he opened the box and took out the wallet and pretended to admire the gift. "What an ingenious design, and such soft leather." He opened the wallet and took a quick glance at the instructions I had taped to the inside of the wallet. "Please tell the student how grateful I am."

"I definitely will," I replied as David slipped me a piece of paper with a phone number and instructions.

"Please give him a call as soon as you have a chance," the professor said, before asking if I had time to stay and enjoy a meal.

"I really can't, but thank you. I don't want to be late for my first class." I gulped down the rest of my espresso and stood up and grabbed my backpack.

I shook each of their hands as the professor remarked, "Don't forget to take plenty of notes." They all laughed as I walked out of the café and got into a cab.

The professor had made it crystal clear that he knew about Gabrielle, which did not surprise me. It was a veiled threat that if I didn't follow orders, she would be collateral damage.

Chapter Thirteen

The cab dropped me off at the university. As I walked up the stairs, I could not help but feel the burden of my predicament. I thought about the difference between my carefree days as an undergraduate in the States — where life consisted of partying and chasing girls that I never seemed to catch — and my pretend graduate school days in Paris. It was starting to feel like I was in too deep — playing the part of Judas while at the same time protecting a girl who was tormented by her past and who was now a potential target of a twisted, deceitful, traitorous gnome.

I walked into class and was immediately greeted with a big hug from Abdul.

"Your mommy is going to be okay," he said as he pulled out of the hug and held onto my shoulders.

"I hope so," I replied. Then I whispered into his ear, "Do you think you can pick me up an ounce of cocaine?"

"Of course," he said, surprised but eager to help. "Right after this class."

"Thanks."

"That's quite a bit for you."

"You haven't met my family."

"And they haven't met Gabrielle."

"And they never will," I replied.

"Praise be to Allah," he said as he folded his hands and looked up to the heavens.

Immediately after class, Abdul ran off to purchase the cocaine. I called David and told him that everything was set for seven o'clock at Chez Marcel. I also added that I didn't appreciate the veiled threat against Gabrielle and that if so much as a hair on her head was touched I would kill everyone involved.

He replied with a laugh, "Calm down, cowboy. Nothing is going to happen to your precious Gabrielle."

"Nothing better!" I angrily replied and hung up the phone.

Abdul met me in the men's bathroom and handed me the coke. I tried to pay him but he refused.

"A gift to my best friend," he said. "Return quickly and safely. That is all I ask."

If he wanted to make it harder on me, he couldn't. I knew he was a good man, caught up in a deadly game that he just didn't seem to understand. He left the bathroom and I walked into a stall and opened my backpack and nestled the coke into the very bottom. I was suddenly carrying around a bunch of burner phones, a handgun, and an ounce of cocaine. If a cop stopped me and checked my backpack I wouldn't have to worry about betraying anyone — I would be the one behind bars.

Chapter Fourteen

Classes that usually seemed to go on forever flew by during my last day in Paris. In the end, I was left with no choice when it came to handling the Abdul situation. In the hands of the professor, the gnome, he was dead. The Mossad twins would probably also dispose of him. They were killers. They had tried to play on my sympathies, and their confession that they went a little too far with Gabrielle's rapists by having her pull the trigger played well at first, but as I looked into their eyes while they talked to Gabrielle and the professor, I had no doubt that if they had to do it all over again, they would not only have her pull the trigger but would also get her to light the match. The Davids and the Elijahs of the world saw everything in black and white. It was probably that mindset that had allowed Israel to survive, surrounded for the longest time by countries that wanted to annihilate the Jewish state.

I had no doubt that they cared for Gabrielle, but I didn't know how much they would care if she was Muslim, or even considered Arab. Of course, there were plenty of Lebanese nationals who would like to claim Gabrielle and her family as belonging to the Arab world. But as members of Lebanon's Maronite Christian community, Gabrielle and her parents likely viewed themselves as Phoenicians, not Arabs — descendants of an ancient civilization that predates the Arabization of the Middle East. I couldn't help wondering how much of David and Elijah's sympathies for Gabrielle could be traced to their distrust of Arabs. Anti-Arab sentiment ran high among every Mossad agent I had ever met, and the causes of Islamophobia, as it was now referred to by many left wing pundits, were not hard to understand. It all went back to a simmering distrust of how the Allies had approached World War II. While the Nazis went about exterminating over six million Jews, Roosevelt and Churchill turned a blind eye to the situation. The Allies could have bombed the railroad tracks that were carrying the Jews, like cattle, to places like Auschwitz, but they didn't. Many Allied planes loaded with bombs flew right over the tracks. The Jews have never forgotten that. When Arabs talk about annihilating the Jewish state, and peace groups talk about Jewish atrocities against their neighbors, Jews are understandably concerned. They well remember how the world ignored their plight during the Holocaust, and as a result, Israel remains on high alert, ready to defend itself vigorously against all threats. The entire Middle East remains locked in perpetual conflict. Mossad agents are taught that when Arabs talk about peace, it's time to prepare for war. It would be hard to imagine a reality in which David and Elijah's response to Gabrielle's trauma was completely free of this historical baggage.

At a little before 6 p.m. I walked into a bathroom in an isolated part of the university. I checked carefully to make sure that no one was in there. I walked into a stall and locked the door. I reached into my backpack and took out a burner phone. I dialed the Paris police and asked to speak to the captain. It took some convincing, but they finally put him on the line. I told him in no uncertain terms that at 7 p.m. and no sooner a cache of terrorist explosives, designed as wallets, could be found In Abdul's apartment. I gave them the address and the building number and stressed that they must not move until 7 p.m. I then told them that at 8 p.m. I would be walking out the front door of Chez Marcel, and that I would be getting into the first cab, and the terrorist suspect, Abdul, would be getting into the second cab, which would be driven by Mossad agents acting illegally on French soil without the authority of the French government. They should follow the second cab because it would lead them to a Mossad-owned building where they planned on torturing the suspect and then killing him. I stressed over and over again not to come in with sirens blaring … to stake out the place quietly and follow the second car, and I made sure they knew that the Mossad agents were deadly and would use force against them. I hung up, smashed the phone against the toilet, and dumped it into a trash can.

I walked out of the bathroom and took out another burner phone and called Mike and told him we were on for tonight, and that I had all that he asked for neatly packed in a large bag. I then smashed that phone and dropped it into another trash can.

I then walked outside and took out another burner phone and made arrangements with a car rental place to have a small luxury car parked behind the hotel where Gabrielle was staying. This was to happen at exactly ten o'clock, and they were to leave the keys under the front seat. I gave them an unidentified credit card that I used for such transactions and waited on the phone while they processed the hefty down payment. Everything went through. I then smashed that phone and dumped it into another trash can.

Earlier in the day, I had destroyed the hard drive on my laptop and dumped the whole computer in a trash can off campus, along with the phone I had used to call Gabrielle and Abdul.

After completing these steps, I noticed that my heart was racing. I composed myself by slowing down my pace and walking around the campus for a few minutes. I looked at the buildings and watched the students coming and going all around me, and briefly envied their normal lives. Then I exited the campus and met Abdul and we took a cab to the bistro.

Chapter Fifteen

It was ten minutes to eight as I looked across at the bar at Chez Marcel. The Mossad twins had left a short time before and the only one at the bar was the bartender, who I was pretty sure was a Mossad agent too. I had seen him talking to David and Elijah, and he had that same look about him: all three of them were beefy, quick-witted, and hyper-alert to their surroundings. Abdul and I were finishing off our after-dinner cognacs. He paid the check and we got up and left the restaurant through the front door.

There were the two taxis parked outside the bistro and I told Abdul that it would be better if we took separate taxis because I needed to make a few stops and say goodbye to a few friends before going back to my apartment to pack. We hugged and Abdul whispered into my ear, "I love you like a brother. God be with you."

I replied, "And I love you like a brother, and God be with you." We kissed on the cheeks and then I got into the back seat of the first cab. It took only a few seconds before the first hot tears rolled down my cheeks. I waved goodbye as the driver pulled away and I watched Abdul get into the second cab. The driver turned the corner as I said a prayer for my friend. I didn't even have to tell the driver where to go. Ten minutes later, he dropped me off at my building. He said, "Good luck and a happy life." I stepped out of the cab and paid the driver as though I was paying a regular cab driver. I watched the cab pull away as I stepped into the lobby of the building. Instead of going up to my apartment, I walked down to the basement. I took out a small flashlight from my backpack, turned it on, then opened the door to the tunnel and closed it behind me. The tunnel was dark, and it had a rancid smell like a city sewer, which I figured was right below the tunnel. I hurried through the tunnel, knowing damn well that if everything didn't go as planned, and the time frame wasn't followed correctly, that I would be met at the other side of the tunnel and that would very likely be the end of me. Suddenly, I was knocked off balance and went flying off the walls of the tunnel. My apartment had apparently blown up and by the sound and force of the explosion they didn't leave anything to chance. I prayed that the few other residents of the building were okay.

I quickly got back on my feet, took my handgun out of my backpack, and started to run toward the end of the tunnel where I was met only by darkness, dilapidated buildings, and in the distance, the glitter of city lights.

I shut the flashlight off. If there was someone out there looking for me, why make it easier for them to find me? I climbed up an embankment, slipping occasionally, digging my hands into the soiled earth, which was littered with animal feces, as I passed decrepit structures that must have at one time made up a small community. I followed the glittering lights in the distance. For the first time in my life, I felt like a man without a country. A boy raised in a military family where the only thing I ever remember my father teaching me were the words to the Pledge of Allegiance and the lyrics to the National Anthem. I didn't grow up idolizing sports heroes like other children in school, but men like George Washington, Alexander Hamilton, Nathanael Greene, General Ulysses S. Grant, President Theodore Roosevelt, and General George C. Marshall.

And now, under a canopy of stars, in the city of love and lights, I felt like a man who had auctioned off his soul and conscience ... still searching for the elusive truth.

Chapter Sixteen

I jumped into the first available cab and told the driver to take me to Pitié-Salpêtrière Hospital. I put my handgun and my flashlight back into my backpack as I tried hopelessly to clean the slime and dirt off my hands. The driver must have thought he picked up a homeless man. I smelled like human garbage.

He stopped in front of the hospital. I paid the gentleman, got out of the cab, and started walking up the front steps of the hospital. It had an infamous history dating back to the seventeenth century when it was used as a factory to produce gunpowder, and then as a prison for prostitutes and a hospice for the mentally ill. At its lowest point, the hospital housed a rat population ten times the human population of the city.

By the time of the French Revolution it had become the largest hospital in the world, with a capacity of ten thousand patients. Later it became famous for its humane treatment of the mentally ill, and as the place where some of the earliest, pioneering psychiatrists took up residence and published famous studies on the treatment and causes of mental illness. Sigmund Freud passed through the doors of the hospital as a young man, and his theory of psychoanalysis can be traced to lectures he attended at the hospital in 1885.

By the mid-twentieth century it had become one of the most esteemed hospitals in all of Europe. Many famous celebrities were treated there, including Princess Diana, Josephine Baker, Prince Rainer of Monaco, and the famous philosopher Michel Foucault.

The first thing I did when I walked through the doors of the hospital was go into a bathroom and clean up. I then took out my American passport and papers saying I was an employee of the US Embassy. I walked up to the front desk and asked to see Dmitry Kolomoisky. The attendant, an older lady, looked at me suspiciously and said, in French, "No visitors allowed."

"I'm here from the US Embassy," I said, taking out my passport and embassy papers and handing them to her.

"No!" she replied forcibly.

"Please, let me see your supervisor," I said as she continued to shake her head. I pressed on, begging and demanding to speak to her boss immediately.

She held onto my papers as she picked up a phone and called her supervisor. I waited about half an hour before an attractive, middle-aged woman arrived and talked to the attendant. The woman, who was indeed a supervisor, took my papers and asked me to follow her. She took me to a small waiting room and we sat down. "I am under strict orders not to allow anyone to see Mr. Kolomoisky," she said.

"I understand," I replied. "And I am under strict orders to see him before he dies. Many lives depend upon it. Many lives."

She looked at me and then down at my papers as I begged, "Only ten minutes, please."

"All right," she finally said. "Exactly ten minutes."

"Thank you so much," I said as I followed her through a maze of corridors and wards, suddenly understanding why it took her half an hour to walk to the front desk. We finally arrived in a gray, depressing ward that looked like it was from the Middle Ages. One old, male custodian mopped the floors. We stopped in front of a door. The supervisor held onto my papers and passport as I entered a large, dimly lit room. The space was empty apart from one bed and one patient: my old friend, Dmitry, who lay there, hooked up to an IV drip and a heart and lung machine. I walked over to the bed and looked down at him for a few moments until he opened his eyes. A slight smile crossed his wrinkled and sunken face.

"Saint Nick," he said in a voice that was quiet and raspy but still full of confidence and humor. "Are you here to take me to Heaven?"

I took his hand in both of mine and said, "I am here to visit my friend and to ask you if there is anything I can do?"

"Then you shouldn't be here, my friend. It is very dangerous for you." Dmitry was no older than his mid-fifties and yet when I looked at him he looked like a man in his nineties, pale and emaciated. The only resemblance to the man I knew in Afghanistan was in his locks of thick, blond hair.

"The Russians?" I asked.

"Always those sons-of-a-bitches. You Americans and Brits should have let the Nazis destroy them. You could have then destroyed the Nazis."

"The bastard out-maneuvered us at Yalta."

"The bastard played you guys, and your Roosevelt, from the beginning of the war." He coughed violently and then continued. "Stalin killed my parents and my little sisters and brothers and now his offspring has finished me off. You Americans make war very profitable for men like me, especially when you don't know the good guys from the bad guys."

"You got some measure of revenge," I remarked as he shook his head.

"They have no respect for human life ... not for their own kind, never mind for non-Russians. Unless you kill every last rat, they will forever feast at the banquet of humanity." He had another violent coughing fit and rested for a moment before continuing. "You need to be very careful, my friend. The bastard in your embassy is no good. He is like me, but with no conscience. He is evil like the devil and dangerous and malicious like Stalin." He closed his eyes as I held his hand. His grip tightened one last time around my hand as he whispered, "I have earned this, my friend. I have earned it!"

The machines sounded alerts as the supervisor rushed into the room with a doctor and a nurse. She ushered me out of the room and a few minutes later I watched from outside the room as they covered the face and body of my friend.

The supervisor handed me my passport and papers and said, "He was a bad man, an evil man, oui?"

"No, he was a good man who they made into a bad man."

I walked out of the hospital and called Gabrielle on another burner phone and told her I would be at the hotel in less than half an hour. I couldn't tell her any further details because I was certain her burner phone, given to her by the Mossad twins, was tapped.

Chapter Seventeen

I got into a cab outside the hospital and asked the driver to drop me off a block away from Hôtel R de Paris. I entered the hotel through a back entrance and walked up the stairs to the fourth floor. I knocked on room 405 and Gabrielle let me in and immediately started kissing me and telling me how worried she was and how happy she now was that I came back to her. The girl was crying and talking at the same time. I put my hand over her mouth as I quickly looked around the room and at her open suitcase on the bed and what looked like a new spring coat beside the suitcase. I whispered into her ear, "Please be quiet." I took my hand away from her mouth as she looked up at me with anxious eyes. I grabbed the coat off the bed and took her by the hand and led her into the bathroom. I turned on the shower and motioned for her to sit on the toilet seat.

"Please, just listen and answer my questions."

She nodded and fixed her eyes on mine. I could see that she was scared, but there was no time to waste, and I didn't have it in me to start playing Sigmund Freud and try to calm her down.

"How many burner phones did David and Elijah give you?"

"Three. Two are in my suitcase and the other one is on the table by the bed."

"Who brought you here?"

"David."

"Was he in the room by himself at any point?"

She thought about it for a long moment and then replied, "I had to use the bathroom once but I was only gone for a couple of minutes."

"Do you have anything in that suitcase besides clothes and the burner phones, anything that you definitely need to take with you?"

"The portrait I am painting of you. I have it in a picture tube so it won't wrinkle."

"We need to leave the suitcase and everything in it right here in the hotel."

"No! What is going on?"

"Don't argue with me, Gabrielle. You need to trust me … otherwise there is no reason for us to be together." I picked up the new jacket and asked, "A present from David and Elijah?"

"Yes."

I pulled a set of keys out of my pocket and pressed my thumb into the middle of the small black keychain that I had been using since I first joined the agency. Out popped a thin steel blade, a little shorter than a match. Gabrielle stared in horror as I used it to slice through the jacket's lining, from nape to hem.

"What are you doing?" she protested, but I held my finger to my lips and glared at her and she quieted down.

I felt inside the lining but found nothing. Then I ran my fingers along the collar until I found what I was looking for. I ripped into the collar with the blade and pulled out a small lump of plastic and metal and showed it to Gabrielle. "A tracking device. Apparently, they really want to keep an eye on you. I need to run my hands through your hair and check around your ears."

"Do whatever you want," she replied. Tears of betrayal were running down her cheeks. It suddenly occurred to me what a blow this would be to her already fragile sense of trust. Gabrielle had known these two men since she was ten years old. She'd met them on what must unquestionably have been the worst day of her life, and she really believed that they loved her like a pair of protective brothers. I took pity on her and cupped her cheek in my hand for a moment before forcing myself to get back to work. Holding her head with both hands, I ran my fingers through her hair and checked her ears, but found nothing. I then had her stand up and said, "I'm sorry, but I need to be sure they didn't sneak anything else onto you. It's easier than you think, especially when you trust and love the people."

I slowly ran my hands across the top half of her red dress and then took her white belt off and examined the underside. Somehow, they had managed to sneak another tracking device inside the buckle. I detached it and showed it to her and threw it on top of the discarded jacket. I checked to make sure the belt had no other devices inside it before I tied it back around her slender waist. Then I checked the lower half of her wardrobe, including her shoes, and found nothing else. I then told her to go back into the room and grab her purse. I looked through her purse and found still another tracking device. I took out her slender wallet, which included photos of her parents, identification, and very little money. I found no devices in the wallet and put it into my backpack, along with her passport.

I took her by the hand and assured her that everything was going to be okay, and that in a very short time we were going to be husband and wife and living in America. I don't know if she heard a word I said. She was in shock. With me holding her hand and guiding her, we left the room and walked down the stairs. We walked out the back entrance and quickly crossed the parking lot to get to the car that I had rented.

Chapter Eighteen

I opened the passenger's side door of the car and Gabrielle sat down. She was staring hopelessly out in front of her as I put her seat belt on and said what was in my heart — that she was the most precious piece of cargo I would ever carry, and that I never wanted anything bad to happen to her. I kissed her on the head and she forced a little smile.

I took the key from under the front seat as I put my backpack in the back seat. I started the car up and headed east to meet Mike. I had literally taken everything away from Gabrielle, from every stitch of clothing she owned to her two most trusted friends in the world. To a certain extent I had also taken away her adopted brother, who she swore she hated, but who I was convinced she loved deep down. She'd had her innocence ripped away at the tender age of ten, and unlike some women, who would have used such a violation to become warriors later in life, my beautiful Gabrielle would forever be a victim. She asked for her wallet and I reached into my backpack and took it out and gave it to her. She looked down at the pictures of her parents and asked, "Will I ever get to see them again?"

"Yes, I will make certain of that … I promise."

"What did I do to make and David and Elijah mistrust me so much?"

"You didn't do anything. If I am sure of anything in this world, it is that those two love you more than any person in this world. It is me they distrust."

"But I told them how very happy you make me. I told them so many times."

"I understand, Gabrielle, but it is the nature of the business that they are in, and the business that I was in, to be suspicious of everyone … especially people in the same line of work. They suspected that I was just using you, and would discard you once I was finished with my assignment."

"And are you just going to discard me and leave me in America to fend for myself?"

"I have risked everything, Gabrielle, to protect you and to have a long and happy life with you. Please, don't ever think I would discard you for anything."

She looked out the passenger's side window and asked, "Where are we going?"

"We are going to meet my friend who is going to fly us to America in a US government plane."

"But the airport is the other way," she remarked.

"We are going to meet him at an old NATO airport that the French government still allows some high officials from other countries to use when they come and visit. My friend flies around a big shot general in the US Army and it just so happens that he is staying in France for a week, which gives my friend the opportunity to fly us to America."

"And won't he get into trouble if the big shot general finds out that he is flying us to America in a US government plane?

"I can't talk about that," I replied.

"Of course not…"

"Please, don't start, Gabrielle. Please, don't."

"Whatever you say, Nicky. My life is in your hands. For all I know, you can stop the car at any time, kill me, and dump my body on the side of the road. It is in the nature of your job, isn't it?"

"Shut your mouth! I don't kill people, and that's one of the reasons we are in this situation right now. I refused to simply turn over an unarmed suspect to be butchered and killed by your friends.

If you suddenly feel so threatened by me, why don't you just take this car back to Paris once we get to the airport. You'll live a very comfortable life. I gave you the phone number and the codes you need to access all the money you want. Don't even wait to get back to Paris; you can start withdrawing the money once we arrive at the airport."

She looked at me and started to cry. "I'm sorry, Nicky. I am just so scared and confused. I love you so much."

"And I love you so much, girl of my dreams."

Gabrielle looked at me and smiled, and for the first time since she'd greeted me at the hotel I could see a glimmer of happiness in her eyes.

As we headed toward the airport, I kept a close eye on the rearview mirror to make sure we weren't being followed. After traveling nearly halfway there, not only did I not see any evidence of us being followed but also the road going in both directions was mysteriously devoid of any traffic. It was as though Gabrielle and I were the only two people in the world … traveling through a sea of darkness and isolation. I kept to the speed limit because the last thing I needed was to be stopped by the French police, especially since I was carrying an ounce of cocaine, a handgun, and a bunch of burner phones in my backpack. The idea that I was carrying an ounce of cocaine to give to Mike, to use while he was piloting a plane with Gabrielle and I on board, did not seem as outrageous at the time of the request as it did now. Back in Afghanistan it was common knowledge, at least to me, that he flew helicopters and planes while he was high on stimulants like cocaine and amphetamines, not to mention caffeine, all the time. My only hope was that he was not also drinking alcohol. The coke he could keep out of view of Gabrielle, but the booze wasn't so easy to cover up, especially if you got close to him and could smell it on his breath.

I was used to Mike being a renegade. He enjoyed having a good time, and that was to be expected in a business like ours, where any moment might be your last. If Gabrielle didn't take to him, I would have to find a way to help her see his better qualities. I knew him to be an honest broker who understood right from wrong, and good from evil. The false charges that were brought against him by the Afghan government and then litigated by our military contradicted everything he stood for as a man and a professional. He would never hit a target if he had the least suspicion that innocent civilians could be killed or maimed.

Gabrielle had become very quiet and withdrawn. It was as if she had curled up inside a shell. In the short time I had known her, I had become used to her doing this whenever she felt threatened. She was small to begin with, but when she curled up in the fetal position she could pass for a ten-year-old child. As we drove in silence, the quiet time allowed me to return to my obsession about devices that could be used to track us down. Despite all of my precautions back at the hotel, using burner phones just once and dumping them, and leaving no digital footprint that the Mossad twins and the professor could use to track us down, I knew that there were two things I had overlooked: Gabrielle's laptop computer and cell phone. The Mossad twins had said they would destroy both devices, but that was about as likely as them making good on their promise to keep Abdul alive and ship him off to Israel to be used as an asset.

They would be going through her computer, if they hadn't already done so, and what they would find was her intense search and interest in Kiev and Ukraine. This might seem a little unusual to them, but to the professor it would send up warning signals that could make him even more dangerous and traitorous than he already was. Dmitry knew about this sick son of a bitch, and that alone told me the professor was a major player and quite deadly. After all, he blew up my apartment. Gabrielle and I also had that surreal discussion about Kiev on our phones, and if they were listening in that would send up even more warning signs. Exactly how close the Mossad twins and the professor were was pure speculation on my part, but in the business we were all in, speculation was taken seriously.

As the old saying goes, "Everyone has their price," and that includes Israeli loyalists like David and Elijah. If they were in with the professor that would not necessarily endanger the Jewish state, because as I found out, nothing was really being shipped to the Middle East or the US. The labels were pure camouflage ... everything was going to the Russian-controlled Crimea, and being smuggled into the democratic country of Ukraine that the Russians were trying to overthrow. The money being made was huge ... the difference between living in Tel Aviv or on the French Riviera. If they were working together, everything that had occurred — including the blowing up of my apartment — could have been staged to simply throw me off. Of course, it was all speculation.

I slowed down as the airport tower came into view. I parked the car close to the gate that Mike told me about. I texted him a code as I gently touched Gabrielle and said, "We're here, beautiful lady."

Chapter Nineteen

I helped Gabrielle out of the car as I grabbed my backpack. She was wobbly and she held onto to me like a frightened child holding onto a parent. Mike opened the gate and greeted the two of us.

As he came toward Gabrielle, she suddenly straightened up like a soldier accosted by a sergeant. Mike greeted her with a big smile and said, "So you're the beautiful girl who my friend has fallen madly in love with. It's very nice to meet you."

"Very nice to meet you," Gabrielle anxiously replied.

Mike was tall — about six foot, four inches — with broad shoulders. He was ruggedly handsome, and many of the more liberal women who attended the university in Kabul were in love with him. The same went for the girls working at the embassy. His swagger was magnified by a strong Bronx accent, and he came from a part of the Bronx called Parkchester, which he talked about with a fondness that bordered on obsession. As he liked to say, "I spent my teenage years getting high and playing basketball day and night, during rainstorms, blizzards, and heat waves. It was the happiest time of my life."

Unlike me, who grew up idolizing men like George Washington, Alexander Hamilton, and General George C. Marshall, Mike grew up idolizing basketball players like Walt Frazier, Dave DeBusschere, Willis Reed, Jerry West, and "Pistol" Pete Maravich. His love of flying came about when he took his first plane rides to California, at the age of eighteen, to attend UCLA on a basketball scholarship.

After graduating and with no professional teams showing any interest in him, he joined the Air Force to pursue his second love in life. He spent ten years in the Air Force and then resigned. After flying for a commercial airline for a year it bored him so much that on a whim he decided to join the CIA. They were more than happy to have him. His first and only assignment was to Afghanistan, and whereas he could have easily transferred out a number of times, he became addicted to the excitement, the drugs, and the culture, until he was forced out. He was a few years from forty at the time, and a little less than two years shy of the ten-year requirement for a substantial pension, when I persuaded him to stay on and take the bullshit job with the general.

I wasn't sure if my lovely Gabrielle was attracted to Mike or just overwhelmed by his presence, but she did seem to come to life when she met him. This was no longer the same withdrawn young woman who had spent the car ride to the airport curled up in the fetal position. Instead, Gabrielle met Mike's eyes and smiled back at him and stood up straight. Mike didn't seem to notice anything unusual in her behavior, and he wouldn't have anything to compare it with anyway, having just met her. Once we'd said our hellos, he waved to the man in the tower, and then turned back to us and asked, "Do you guys have luggage?"

"No, this is it," I replied.

"Forced to travel light?" he jokingly asked.

"Yeah, you could say that," I replied as Mike closed the gate and we started to walk toward the plane, a Gulfstream G280 private jet.

"So, Gabrielle, do you have any sisters?"

"No, but I have an adopted brother," she naively replied.

"That's great, but I don't really swing that way. How about any girlfriends who happen to look like you?"

Gabrielle shook her head like a confused little girl.

"Well, it was worth a try," Mike remarked.

"Sorry," Gabrielle replied as Mike looked at her, then at me, and then back at her.

"Tired, are you?" Mike jokingly asked Gabrielle.

We climbed the stairs of the jet and entered through the cockpit. Mike ushered us into the cabin area that looked more like a luxury yacht than an airplane. It featured six rows of leather-cushioned chairs, two on each side of the plane, a sleeping area with two beds, and a small conference room, equipped with laptops and a large screen. Near all of that was a kitchen area and a full bar. I doubted Gabrielle had ever seen so much luxury in such a confined space.

Mike caught sight of her amazed expression and I could see him trying to make her feel comfortable. "Yeah, it's a sweet way to travel, on the taxpayers' dime," he joked. "All you need is a government job with a big enough title and limited knowledge, or a general with at least three stars on his uniform."

"Quite a jump from the planes you were flying in Afghanistan," I remarked.

"First class all the way, but with a lot less excitement." We stopped in the sleeping area and Mike turned to Gabrielle and asked, "Why don't you get some sleep, sweetheart? You look exhausted. We won't be taking off for at least an hour."

Gabrielle looked at me and asked, "Is that okay, Nicky?"

"Of course it's okay; you got permission from the pilot." She crawled into the bed and curled on her side, looking out at us with a glazed, sleepy expression. I covered her with blankets and leaned over and kissed her, then whispered in her ear, "I love you." Mike closed the curtains, giving her more privacy, and we walked to the front of the plane. I took out the ounce of cocaine and handed it to him.

He said, "I knew I could rely on you," and leaned over and kissed me on the head.

He opened the bag and took out a good portion that he placed on what looked like an old, dark album cover. He cut it into eight lines and took out a straw and snorted two lines up each nose, and then handed me the straw. I hesitated and he said, "Don't even dare say no.

It's not like you know how to fly this machine if I drop dead." I snorted two lines up each nostril and laid the straw down.

"Good stuff," Mike remarked.

"Yeah, I got it from a great source."

"What's wrong with Gabrielle; is she okay? A little timid for a French girl."

"She's been through a lot."

"So have we all, Nick. What's her story?"

I glanced toward the sleeping quarters and then at Mike, uncertain how much Gabrielle would want me to share. I hoped she would understand my need to level with an old friend who was doing us the incredible favor of flying us to safety. I lowered my voice and gave him the *Reader's Digest* version of the unbelievable terror that had been inflicted on Gabrielle as a child in Lebanon. Mike, who had seen and heard so much during his brief career in the secret service, sat in silence after I finished. He held his head in his hands for a moment before looking up at me and speaking again.

"She was *ten years old*?"

I nodded gravely, and saw his eyes go a little frantic and moist.

"What a bunch of fucking animals. Was anything done about it?"

"Mossad took justice into their own hands. Captured the four rapists, chained them to the wall of a cave, and steadied Gabrielle's hand as she pulled the trigger of a gun and shot the balls and dicks off the four pigs. They then doused the four screaming animals with gasoline and torched them alive."

"My God. Wow. That's … an awful lot for a little girl to go through."

"She's definitely damaged and tormented. She'll wake up in the middle of the night from a nightmare and vomit so violently that it's like her whole body is possessed by demons."

"And you're going to save her?"

"I hope so. She deserves better."

"Yes, she does," Mike said. He sat still for a few moments, then seemed to will himself to shake off the horrifying images that had just been flooding his brain. He stashed the cocaine under the pilot seat and said, "Guess it wouldn't be a good idea to ask her if she wanted a little coke."

"No, but that hundred-pound girl can drink. The first night I met her she out-drank me."

"Yeah, it helps with the demons … if only for a short time." We walked down the stairs and sat at the bottom steps of the ramp. Mike was waiting for the guy in the tower to give him clearance to take off.

"I see our friend Dmitry is dying."

"He died a few hours ago. I went to visit him. We talked for about ten minutes before he passed away."

"Are you out of your mind going to visit him when you have a target on your back?"

"I had to go see him," I said. "I owed him that much and more. He saved me endless torment. If not for him, I would have spent the rest of my life haunted by the deaths of dozens of soldiers and innocent civilians. I would have been eaten alive by guilt."

"I understand that, but no one understood the game better than Dmitry. I'm surprised he didn't get up off his death bed and throw you the hell out of that hospital."

"He tried. Let me ask you, would it have stopped you from going to visit a dying friend if the circumstances were reversed?"

"No, but I have been at this game a lot longer than you." He shook his head and asked, "The Russians?"

"Yeah."

"Wow, he hated those fuckers more than anything. I swear, if he had ever got his hands on an atomic bomb he would have dropped it on the Kremlin without blinking an eye."

"They wiped out his entire family," I remarked.

"I know the story, and I hate to admit it but if he wanted me to pilot the plane that dropped the bomb on those suckers I would have been happy to comply."

He looked up at the tower and said, "It's time to take off." We sat up, pulled the ramp closed, and walked back into the cockpit and pulled out the bag of cocaine. "But before we do that, it's time for a few more hits. He spread out eight more lines and we snorted two lines each. "You better go stay with your girlfriend during takeoff."

I patted him on the shoulder and said, "Thank you, Mike."

He looked straight ahead, out the cockpit window, and asked, "What were Dmitry's last words?"

"I earned it! I earned it," I replied as he shook his head and simply smiled.

Chapter Twenty

I walked back to the sleeping area and found Gabrielle sleeping like a little baby. I couldn't remember the last time I saw her so relaxed. I prayed that she wouldn't wake up until we arrived in New York, but like most prayers I didn't expect that one to be answered. I walked over to the bar and service area and poured myself a large glass of white wine. Whatever appetite I might have had before arriving at the airport was extinguished once I started doing the coke. Coke wasn't good for you, but if you wanted to lose weight, it was hard to think of a more expensive yet effective drug. I sat down in a seat that looked directly across at Gabrielle. The plane started to taxi down the runway. I glanced out the window as the plane took off. In an hour or so, we would be out of French air space. It was a beautiful country, and one I hoped I would never see again. Gabrielle would be enough of a reminder of the nightmare I was hoping I was leaving behind.

Mike was not the type of guy who would ever try to steal a guy's girlfriend away, or have sex with a married woman whose husband he knew. There were far too many girls out there to ever put up with those headaches. He would have laughed at Gabrielle's antics on the steps of the university the first day I met her. He wasn't the type who would even imagine such a nonsense notion as a girl of his dreams. He would have taken Gabrielle out to dinner and drinks and after getting nowhere that would have been the end of that relationship.

He could flirt with the best of them like he did when first meeting Gabrielle ... that was his way of making a girl feel better about herself, but that was it. When I told him about Gabrielle's rape and subsequent problems he really seemed to care for a few moments, but that was the extent of any sympathy he would show. For my part, telling him about the terror she'd experienced as a child was a gentle way of encouraging him to go easy on her. He liked to kid and joke and he could be quite funny, but my lovely Gabrielle wouldn't see the humor in it and most likely would go hide in the bathroom if he persisted in joking with her.

In the world that Mike lived in for nearly twenty years, Gabrielle's horrifying experience was just part of the everyday nightmare of being alive. The only difference between what David and Elijah did to the terrorist bastards and what Mike would have done was that Mike would have left the little girl out of it. He would have blown off their balls and sat back and enjoyed a few ice cold beers as he listened to their tortured pleas and prayers to Allah. He would have occasionally yelled back at them, "No one is listening, assholes. No one is listening." And then after hearing enough he would have doused them with gasoline, lit a match, and walked out of the cave and continued on with his life. The little girl would just have to deal with it like everyone else.

Mike was a man of action and he didn't give a shit about speeches and words of encouragement and hope. He was a Theodore Roosevelt type guy. If you wanted to show you cared you didn't speak about it, you took action. When he was accused of the hideous act of killing civilians, I took action and prevented this injustice from going any further. I put my job and future on the line for him, going against my superiors, and for that I earned his trust and friendship.

Gabrielle slept right through takeoff, and about half an hour later I got up, grabbed a full bottle of white wine, and went up to the cockpit to be with Mike.

Chapter Twenty-One

I locked the cockpit door and sat down next to Mike and handed him the bottle of wine that he took a big gulp from and asked, "Don't want the little girl walking in on the party?"

"Exactly," I replied as he handed me the bag of coke and told me to cut up eight lines, which I naturally did. "How does the weather look going into New York?"

"Great!" he replied as he snorted four lines and then handed it back to me and I snorted my lines.

"I was thinking of handing in my resignation shortly after I get back."

"I wouldn't if I were you. They think you're dead, blown up in that explosion. I would let them keep on thinking that until our fearless leader is kicked out of office and all his cronies are removed. You have to go on the assumption that they're all compromised like the freak in the Paris embassy."

"You think it goes that high up?"

"Right to the top of the agency and to the inept asshole he put in charge. What I don't understand is why our intelligence agencies, which he puts down every day while he sides with the Russians, haven't attempted to take him out, like they did with Kennedy."

"You think Oswald was working for the company?"

"Fuck no! That psychotic bastard just got to the president before we did. It was a lucky shot, one in a million. If he didn't screw up his original plan and had killed that celebrity-minded US general, he never would have killed Kennedy. The agency never got over Kennedy's betrayal at the Bay of Pigs. They spent months, if not years, training those Cuban refugees who they had befriended, building bonds of trust with them, only to have Kennedy pull back and leave them out there to be slaughtered and captured by Castro's army. It was the worst type of betrayal.

"The agency's plans for Kennedy were thwarted by Oswald's miracle shot. They had it all planned. They were simply looking for the right location and the right triggerman. How far up the chain of command it went is anyone's guess. But I have no doubt that current and former employees of the agency, after the Bay of Pigs fiasco, had a workable plan to assassinate the president."

"And the Mafia's involvement?" I asked.

"Hollywood make-believe," he said as he took another large gulp from the bottle.

"How's the general you're flying around?"

"Still a dickhead," he said, laughing. "Dude earned his three stars the old-fashioned way … sitting in a leather chair in a comfortable, air-conditioned control room in Florida, supervising operations on the ground in Iraq and Afghanistan. But I'll tell you, for a man almost seventy years old he can party … coke, booze, a coterie of high-class hookers in every city we fly into."

"Does he at least share?"

"He offers, but I don't bite because I know damn well that if the shit ever hits the fan about what's been going on he'll throw me to the wolves. But it hasn't stopped me from collecting evidence. I have tapes of him snorting coke, guzzling champagne and taking it up the ass from girls with dildos strapped to their crotches and him squealing like a pig. In a different line of work, I might have taken him up on his offers but if I have learned anything it is the higher up dickheads that pledge their loyalty to you, who supposedly have your back, who are the first to kick you to the curb when the pressure comes down on them."

He motioned for me to cut up more lines of coke and I obediently got to work and we snorted away. He remarked, "This is really good shit, nearly as good as the shit in Afghanistan. You need to give me the name of your connection in Paris because I'm quite sure the general has a few more visits planned for there."

"The connection was the *source*. Gabrielle's adopted brother."

He looked at me and shook his head and remarked, "Are you high on LSD or what?"

"No, at this moment I'm high on coke," I replied with a laugh.

"The *source* who very well might be dead right now, who you had a hand in taking down … you're engaged to his sister? The one sleeping in the bed back there with the scars across her body and the burned breasts?"

"Yeah, that's the one, and for all I know she might be the informer."

"She might be Mossad. Have you at least had her checked out?"

"No, it's not like they list their agents in a phone book. She hates her adopted brother and she's Christian."

"She's Christian? Like what the hell does that prove? How long have you known her? A week, ten days?"

"Something like that," I replied.

"And she just showed up in your life, poof, like in a fairy tale?"

"Yes, very much like that. She's not Mossad, or a terrorist, and she's certainly not working for that psychopath in the embassy."

"And yet you have no concrete evidence of any of that. Just a feeling, a love-stricken feeling?"

"And what would you have me do, Mike? You've seen her, you've spoken to her, what would you do?"

"I would roll that bed she is sleeping on right out the side door of this plane and into the ocean below. But that's not my call; that's your call, and as long as she is a passenger on this plane and the love of your life, I will respect her. I just don't trust her; at least not on the limited information you have told me."

"In the assignment notes it lists her brother as a probable source, but the sister and parents as not under suspicion."

"That's unusual. The family is usually always under suspicion."

"That's what I thought. After she and her family left Lebanon and moved to Paris, her parents — one not being aware of the rape — adopted Abdul who was just a child but had recently lost his entire family when they were killed by a suicide bomber who the authorities believe detonated his device by accident while crossing the Champs-Élysées on his way to the real target, a nearby bistro. The parents allowed Abdul to continue practicing Islam…"

"Which did not go over well with Gabrielle, who had been raped by four Islamic terrorists."

"They did not get along, or to put it more bluntly, Gabrielle refused to acknowledge all of Abdul's friendly overtures or his attempt to at least have some sort of a cordial relationship. She never told Abdul about the rape. She did not confide in him about anything and until this very day he is baffled by her contempt and outward disdain toward him."

"There's nothing so unusual about warring siblings, especially between a biological child and an adopted child. In fact, considering the circumstances, I would think it quite normal. The girl was raped by a bunch of pigs … every time she takes off her clothes, takes a shower, is having sex … the reminder of what happened to her is right there. I think it is all quite normal that she would behave that way toward her adopted bother, a member of the same brethren who debased and scarred her for life."

"Okay, so you agree that she's not a terrorist?"

"Probably not, but I'm not ruling out that she might be a Mossad agent."

"But at least they're on our side," I remarked.

"I don't know for sure who is on our side anymore. We have a renegade president living in the White House who has uprooted decades-old alliances and put out a welcome mat to dictators throughout the world. For the moment, at least, democratic countries and pro-democracy movements throughout the world are not looking to the old USA for guidance. We've betrayed the Kurds, we've given lukewarm support to the protestors in Hong Kong, we've allowed the Russians to run roughshod through the Middle East, and we've welcomed their interference in our elections. Every day is like the Bay of Pigs."

"That might be the case at the top, Mike, but that's not the case for the many, many patriotic Americans on the ground throughout the world, risking their lives, being away from their families, supporting pro-democracy movements like in the Ukraine."

"I agree, but if our leadership continues betraying and undermining the very values our men and women are fighting to protect throughout the world, the time will come when even these brave souls, or a lot of them, will throw up their hands and walk away. How many of our spies, working deep undercover, have been compromised and killed because of the clumsy way our leadership in Washington behaves and talks openly about sensitive, top-secret, matters?" He started to laugh as he took another big gulp from the bottle of wine and then continued, "For God's sake, you nearly joined that list."

I cut up another eight lines of coke and we snorted away; he was right, I nearly joined that list, and I wasn't sure I was out of the woods yet.

"We have become an unreliable ally, and when that happens we sow mistrust in all the other intelligence agencies we work with throughout the world, including Mossad."

"I still find it hard to believe that my lovely Gabrielle could be a Mossad agent. The informer, possibly, but not an agent."

"You're probably right. She probably found out about your daddy and the vast fortune he has been amassing, and simply decided to throw it all in and live the good life with the boy of her dreams."

"That son of a bitch was the reason I joined the agency."

"Yeah, and if not for him you wouldn't have met the girl of your dreams. Of course, she needs to be saved, but you're really good at that." He leaned over and kissed me fondly on the side of my head and continued, "And I'm living proof of that."

Chapter Twenty-Two

I walked back to the sleeping area and found Gabrielle still asleep. It was like some kind of miracle, and now after snorting coke for hours I really didn't think I could deal with her paranoia and neurotic behavior. I was just hoping that this miracle didn't end like a few other miracles of late … very badly.

As I pondered the two weeks leading up to our escape from Paris, I realized that Mike's suspicions about Gabrielle mirrored some thoughts I had vaguely entertained about her at various times. But, if she was a Mossad agent, a mole, her approach to seducing me and gaining my trust was not found in any CIA manual I had ever read, or in any of the other secret service handbooks that I'd been briefed on during my service. My training supervisor Donna Low had warned me about Russian agents posing as high-priced escorts and beauty queens, and about Taliban operatives pretending to be liberal university students in Kabul. Gabrielle didn't fit into any of those categories. Her behavior was at times erratic … her clinginess unsettling, and her need to be told she was loved bordered on the obsessive.

Gabrielle was so beautiful, she had me from the moment I laid eyes on her, and she knew it. Yet she also regularly did and said things that nearly turned me off, and I was her biggest admirer. I had serious doubts that any secret service could dream up a plan for anyone to entrap a man using such a chaotic strategy. Gabrielle's approach went beyond reverse psychology into total idiosyncrasy. Yet, if one were to do a psychological profile on me it would highlight the fact that I harbored rescue fantasies. I was definitely someone who liked to save others from suffering and injustice. Mike was one hundred percent right about me, and whereas in regular society those traits might be lauded, in the CIA they were traits that could easily be exploited by the enemy.

I opened another bottle of wine and headed back to the cockpit. I opened the door and locked it behind me, as I handed Mike the bottle and sat down.

"Still play ball?" I asked.

"I occasionally shoot around, but it's not so easy to find any half-decent ballplayers to play actual games with," Mike said. "The ones walking around wearing LeBron James jerseys are the worst of all."

"Are you still rooting for the New York Knicks?"

"Yeah, I'm a die-hard all right. The team hasn't had a winning season in nearly twenty years. What a crime, a New York team with all the money in the world and they still can't get quality free agents to sign with them … the front office and the owner are so terrible."

"Been home to Parkchester lately?" I asked as he laughed.

"Not in a number of years. The last time I was there it had changed so much I nearly vomited. Hemingway was right: you can never go back to the places you loved; you will only be disappointed. What are you doing, trying to get me down? Here I am on a wonderful high, piloting the latest Gulfstream jet, sitting next to my best friend, and here you are bringing up the hopeless Knicks."

"Sorry! Maybe I can help with that." I took out the bag of coke and cut eight lines and we snorted away.

"Where are we staying in New York?" he asked.

"Wherever you like. The Plaza?"

"No, I don't have much respect for the previous owner."

"Okay, how about the Maxwell Hotel between 49th and 50th streets, on Lexington Ave. It has everything, beautiful bar and dining area, gym, great rooms and accommodations."

"A steady stream of high-class hookers at the bar?"

"But of course," I replied as he passed the bottle back to me.

"And I get my own room, right?"

"You get a suite if you like."

"No, I don't need a suite, just my own room with a large bed. I don't want to infringe on your romantic adventures and I certainly don't want you intruding on mine."

I laughed to myself and said, "Ha, yes, our wild, romantic adventures…"

Mike looked at me and tried to read my meaning. "What, is the honeymoon over already?"

"More like it hasn't officially started."

"What?" He stared at me and said, "No. No way. Not again."

"'Fraid so."

"Who are you, Saint Frances? Nicky, I told you never to let this happen again. What is it with you and women who can't or won't put out?"

"I know," I said. "Believe me, I know. But it's different this time. I love her. I'm going to marry her."

"And you haven't slept with her."

"That's right," I said. I paused for a moment before sharing a concern that had been planted in my mind by Abdul. "There's also…" As my voice trailed off, I suddenly realized that I was a little too high to trust my own discretion.

"What?"

"There's a slight possibility that she might be frigid."

"Oh my God. Dude," Mike said, trying to process this news. Then he remembered the story I had told him about her attack in Lebanon and the damage that was done to her body. "Then how do you know about the scars on her body and burns on her breasts?"

"She vomited all over herself one night and then fainted. I had no choice but to change her clothes."

"Oh my God, you really are one fucked up dude."

"What do you expect? Look at who my father is."

"No, you're nothing like him. His problem is that he can't get enough pussy … whereas it doesn't seem to matter to you."

"Of course it matters to me, but it's not like I am going to force her. She's been through enough."

"I won't go through all the reasons why you never should have gotten involved with the *source's* sister. You could find that in every handbook ever given out at the CIA. What I don't understand is why you find it your responsibility to heal all her ailments when she's incapable of even getting intimate."

"I didn't say she couldn't get intimate. We just have not got there yet."

"You said she was frigid—"

"I said she *might* be."

"Might, is, whatever. If she has problems spreading her legs and enjoying it, she's frigid … at least in my book. I can't believe I am even talking about this shit with you … actually, I take that back. Of course, I can believe I am talking about this shit with you. Who else, in our profession, would find themselves in a position like this, other than you? Most operatives who find themselves compromised are seduced by beautiful, alluring women who reek of sex, but not you … you wind up with a woman who detests sex, and who probably hasn't had her legs spread since that awful experience. She probably doesn't even spread them when she plays with herself."

I quickly cut up four more lines — cutting our consumption in half — because this conversation was going off the rails, and he was flying a jet at forty thousand feet. I had lost sight of that fact a few times because the flight so far was as smooth as one could hope for, and he was a great pilot … even when high on coke. We snorted the lines and then Mike asked, "When was the last time you saw your father?"

"About four years ago, just before my first assignment. The optics of us being in touch just wouldn't look right."

"I can understand that, but in these four years you had to hear something about him."

"Yeah, from my baby sister. The only living person, besides the men under his command, that I'm certain he has ever loved."

"The sister who was born handicapped?"

"Yeah, the only one in my family that I'm certain I love."

"My God, it must have been a real trip growing up with that man."

"It was, but in all honesty he wasn't around that much. I give the son of a bitch credit though … he earned his stars. He was on the ground in Vietnam, Iraq, and Afghanistan. He went where his troops went. There is a part of him that has always remained a grunt. My mother would always remind my sisters and me to say a prayer for our father every night before bed. I doubt my older sister ever did, nor my mother. After that little reminder, she was usually out the door and into the warm bed and arms of a lover. But my baby sister and I always kept him in our prayers."

"And when he was home?" Mike asked.

"He was loud and obnoxious. He talked to all of us like he was talking to his troops. The flag hanging outside our house was like the most important thing in the whole house, besides my baby sister. God forbid, the light illuminating the flag at night ever went out and wasn't immediately changed. He would go bonkers."

I took a big swig of wine and handed the bottle to Mike. I continued, "I'll never forget the fight he had with my mother over my baby sister. My sister wanted to try out for the girls' freshman basketball team at her high school, but my mother was desperately trying to persuade her not to. I imagine she didn't want to see my sister get her feelings hurt. She had made great strides just being able to get out of her wheelchair and walk around the house on crutches. My father overheard the conversation, and he went nuts and started screaming at my mother in a way that I even felt sorry for her. He kept screaming, poking his finger into her chest, yelling, 'Don't you ever tell her she can't do something … you useless piece of shit. Don't you ever…' This went on for about fifteen minutes as my two sisters and I looked on. I thought at any moment he was going to whack my mother from one end of the kitchen to another, but he didn't. When he finally finished yelling at her, he turned around and softly asked

my baby sister when the tryouts were. She said, 'Tomorrow, Daddy.'
And he replied, 'You don't mind if I come and watch, do you?' And
she replied, 'Of course not, Daddy, I would love that.' He then kissed
and hugged her and said, 'I love you so much.'

"She was the only one in the family he repeatedly expressed his
love to. The very next day, he and I drove over to the high school to
watch the tryouts. On the way over, he said, 'I want you to promise
me that you will always watch over your baby sister. I can't count on
those two useless pieces of shit, but I can count on you.' I naturally
promised, and up to that point in my life that was the nicest thing he
had ever said to me. He stood on the sidelines of the basketball court,
and he made me stand right beside him, and watched as the girls ran
up and down the court, and my baby sister on crutches kept up with
them. I never saw him look so proud at another human being."

I paused as I took another big gulp from the bottle and Mike
asked, "And did she make the team?"

"Yes, she was undeniably the best shooter on the team and any
time the other team was hit with a technical foul she shot the foul shot
and never missed. She also played about five minutes of every game
and considering how difficult it was for her to move at times that was
quite amazing."

"She sounds amazing. Will I ever get to meet her?"

"Sure, but don't expect me to leave her alone with a pig like you.
I did promise to always protect her, and whereas she might be
disabled she is gorgeous and might actually give you a run for your
money on a basketball court."

"I wouldn't be a bit surprised," Mike replied with a smile.

"She's been in charge of my trust fund, slash, inheritance, which
keeps on growing as my father makes more and more money that he
simply sends her way. The man is pursuing the American dream with
a passion."

"How hurt was he when he was forced to resign?"

"According to my baby sister he was devastated. The military was
his whole life, and whereas he shouldn't have been screwing female

subordinates, it wasn't the subordinates that filed the complaints. The complaints came from male officers, just below him in the pecking order, who wanted him out of the way. He was very popular with the troops on the ground because he was right there with them. God only knows how many Purple Hearts that man received. He had become too big, a General Patton type, and he threatened the very type of general you fly around in this Gulfstream jet — the type who got his stars sitting in a command center in Florida. He felt betrayed."

"He did resign with his full pension in place?"

"Yes, but that was of little comfort to him. Never in my life could I have imagined my father working as an independent military contractor … literally working in concert with men like Dmitry, and getting super rich off the sacrifices of soldiers he so proudly commanded."

"It's a bizarre reversal, for sure," Mike said.

"And my baby sister and me benefiting the most," I shamefully remarked as a pang of guilt tore right through my body. I cut up eight more lines of the coke and we continued to snort away as we passed the bottle of wine between us.

Chapter Twenty-Three

There was a knock on the cockpit door, or at least that's what we thought we heard. It was hard to hear with the air pressure and the sound of the equipment in the room. The knock got louder, and then there was no doubt and we started to laugh. I got up and opened the door and Gabrielle looked up at me with puppy eyes.

"Is everything okay, Gabrielle?" I asked as she suppressed a yawn and nodded her head.

"Can I come in?" she asked.

"There's not enough room," I replied as I stepped outside and she looked around me and yelled to Mike, "Hello!"

Mike, without turning, waved to her as I closed the door to the cockpit, took her hand, and walked back to the sleeping area.

"Have I been asleep long?" she asked.

"Yes, you were out cold like a kitten. We'll be landing in about an hour."

"Do you think I can get something to eat? I haven't eaten in such a long time. I was so nervous."

I opened a cabinet in the kitchen area and found it loaded with what looked like a month's supply of potato chips, crackers, peanuts, and protein bars. I placed a few of each next to Gabrielle who sat back down on the bed and I asked, "Would you like a glass of white wine?"

"Please, Nicky," she replied as I poured her a large glass and handed it to her. I sat down next to her, as she opened a bag of potato chips and ate one chip at a time, slowly, like she was suspicious that they might be poisoned. "Are you coming down with a cold, Nicky? You sound so congested."

"No, it's just the air pressure at this height."

"I'm sorry," she remarked as she took a large sip from the glass of wine. She might eat slowly, but she drank quickly. I ran my hand through her hair and even though I was high as a kite, or to put it in proper context as high as the plane, I could not help but marvel at the unblemished loveliness of her face.

"We are going to be very happy in America, I promise."

"I know," she said confidently, in French. "We're going to be so happy, and I'm going to make you a great wife."

"And I am going to be a great husband. I love you so much, my beautiful Gabrielle."

She smiled and looked beautifully content — as calm as I'd ever seen her — as she reached out her hand and slipped it inside mine, letting her eyes return the compliment.

I got up and poured more wine into her glass and said, "And now I have to go back and sit with Mike."

"So soon?" she asked in such a pathetic fashion that if I wasn't dying for more coke I might have stayed.

"It's not fair, sweetheart. He has done us a huge favor, and I don't want him sitting alone."

"I understand," she said. "Please go sit with him." I kissed her on the forehead and walked back toward the cockpit. I locked the door, and sat down next to Mike.

"Is she okay?" he asked as I grabbed the bag of coke and cut up eight more line.

"She's like a battered boxer, but she'll be fine." We snorted the coke and drank the remainder of the wine in the bottle.

"I have a couple of tranquilizers that we can take when we land. They'll straighten us out some."

I looked at the bag of coke and for all we snorted, it really didn't seem like we made much of a dent. An ounce of coke is a lot, and for the first time in a few hours I thought about Abdul and the way we parted outside the bistro and him whispering into my ear, "I love you like a brother." I couldn't confide in Mike about my feelings of guilt over betraying him. He would just say, "You'll get over it," and then tell me that this was never the right profession for me, and to be glad I'm getting out. I wanted to steer clear of that whole conversation, so I asked him about himself.

"Do you still miss the action?"

Mike thought for a moment before launching in. "Not so much anymore," he said. "I mean, at first I was angry at what they did to me. I guess it was similar to what your father felt. I was pissed at being cut out of the action, as you put it. But then, after a little while, I found that I just didn't give a damn, and then I took pleasure in the fact that in a couple of years I would be done with the whole business, once and for all. The war in Afghanistan has never had a well-defined, clear, and realistic objective. You just don't go into a country that for a thousand years has had no conception of democracy, and think you can transform it into another America. It has always been a tribal country, ripe with corruption from top to bottom. Your friend during the day is your enemy at night."

It was all coming back to me now — the way a few lines of coke, or a dozen if we were being honest, could prompt Mike to answer a simple, yes-or-no question with a twenty-minute TED talk. I loved him for it, and I laughed a little inside, but I also listened, because he made a lot of sense.

"All right, Professor Snow," I teased him. "I asked you if you miss the action, but by all means, tell me the complete history of US–Afghan relations."

"Yeah, fuck you, buddy," he said, smiling.

"I'm kidding! Jesus. Talk, you silly m–f."

"All right, I will," he said with a laugh. "Yes, I miss the action. But like everything, it's complicated. I'm glad I'm out, but I don't regret being involved, and I sure as hell don't agree with people who toss around the idea that our soldiers and allies have lost their lives and been severely wounded and traumatized for nothing."

"Hell no," I said. "It's not for nothing."

"Right? Every time I saw an Afghan girl getting to attend university and studying to be a doctor, or an engineer, or just being free to write poetry and literature, and to live a life for herself, I felt proud because I knew we had something to do with that. It was because of our boys and girls in uniform that such a thing became possible. Yet, in the end it is up to the people of Afghanistan to decide their own future. We have shown them a taste of democracy, and if enough Afghan men and women want a free and open society they are the ones who are going to have to take up arms and fight to the death to achieve such a society.

"Revolutions such as the ones in America, or France, or even Russia don't succeed if the people of those countries are not willing to fight and die for change. Invading countries seldom succeed in changing the basic structure of another country without a majority of the locals being willing to fight and die for that change. True and lasting change comes about from within; autocratic rule comes about because of outside forces enabling dictators and tyrants."

"Amen," I said, taking another swig and passing the bottle his way. "Did you ever think when you were growing up and playing basketball all day, and getting stoned on park benches in the Bronx, that you would ever be talking about this stuff?"

"Back then, I couldn't even find Afghanistan, or Iraq, or for that matter France, on a map. I wasn't even sure I knew what was between a girl's legs, but once I found out I got addicted. I don't know if I ever got addicted to the action in Afghanistan, but I did realize early on that the Afghan culture went back a thousand years and, whether you agreed with its customs or not, to think that you could just walk into a country with that long a history and change its mindset was just plain stupid. Our mission from the beginning was simple — capture the bastards responsible for the 9/11 attacks, and rid the world of them. Use human intelligence on the ground to monitor the activities of terrorist organizations, and when the time is right, strike the leadership of these groups and send them into disarray and panic.

"If you suspect a country of developing nuclear weapons, like we do North Korea, destroy the facilities before they're able to produce a bomb. Let the world and the United Nations condemn you … like we really give a shit what Zimbabwe or Iran or Sweden say about us. Once we allow these rogue countries to produce such weapons, it's too late. Like the leadership in North Korea cares a fuck about its people? We can place sanctions on them all we want … the Russians and the Chinese will always be there and ready to bail them out.

"Enough talk about this shit; cut up double the amount. We've already started to descend." I cut up sixteen lines and over the next fifteen minutes we snorted it all. "The Big Apple, here we come." Mike gave me two tranquilizers and told me to take one once we landed, and if that didn't help bring me down enough, to take the other one. He was planning a big night, and he was expecting me to be in on the fun.

I walked back to the sleeping area and found Gabrielle passed out again. In my present condition, this was a godsend. I poured myself a large glass of white wine and took a seat directly across from her. I took the first tranquilizer and looked real closely at Gabrielle. She was undeniably broken, scattered at times into what seemed like a thousand different pieces. I had to close my eyes and think back to what seemed like an eternity ago, to the first time I met her on the stairs of the university. They all said she was really good at pretending, and her performance on the steps of the university was worthy of an academy award. I wondered, again, what parts of the Gabrielle I thought I knew would turn out to be real and substantial, and which parts would turn out to be chimeras.

I looked out the window, as the lights of the city became clearer and clearer. It was nighttime in New York, which was strange considering that it was nighttime when we left France. It was like time had stayed still, and only our place had changed.

We had just crossed the Atlantic and the pilot and I had snorted cocaine the whole way and drank three bottles of wine, and that seemed perfectly normal. My father was an arms dealer making a bloody fortune, and giving the lion's share of his profits to my baby sister and I, and that didn't seem to bother me at all. The girl of my dreams was, at the very least, mentally unstable, and I looked forward to helping her. Abdul, an idiot-savant who manufactured wallet-size bombs that he didn't even seem to realize would be used to kill innocent civilians, was the person I felt most sorry for ... who I felt I had betrayed. The guilt was overwhelming, and as we approached the runway I started to cry.

Chapter Twenty-Four

Mike landed the plane at a faraway runway at Kennedy Airport used by high-ranking military and US officials, and by foreign diplomats. It took me a good fifteen minutes to wake Gabrielle, and for a moment I thought I was going to have to carry her off the plane, and I was in no condition to do that, regardless of how little she weighed.

The airport officials working the area knew Mike, and we passed right through without any inspections. That was good because Mike was carrying at least a half-ounce of coke on him.

I called up the hotel and booked two suites. Mike deserved to be treated like a king. He did me a huge favor and I never knew when I might need him again. He was my most trusted friend, and that was becoming more and more important to me because I still wasn't totally certain about Gabrielle. Mike's initial comments about her, even though he sort of took them back, still rang loudly in my head. He didn't just say things for the sake of saying them. He was a straight shooter.

We took a taxi to the hotel and because it was quite late, the traffic into Manhattan wasn't too bad. We checked into our suites and met back down in the lobby after only fifteen minutes. The hotel restaurant was still open and the three of us sat at a booth. Gabrielle was finally coming to life, and after drinking a double espresso she actually was quite cheerful and entertaining, like on the first day we met at the university.

We ordered appetizers, and two bottles of white wine, and after taking the tranquilizers, both Mike and I exhibited something that resembled an appetite. Gabrielle, as usual, ate slowly, like she wondered if the food might be poisoned. Mike asked, "Is this how you stay so thin, Gabrielle?"

"I don't understand," she replied and then looked at me and asked, "What's he talking about?"

"He's asking if you manage to stay so thin because you eat so slowly that you wind up eating less."

She thought about it for a long moment and said, "It's the way I have always eaten, but maybe that is the reason I stay so thin." She smiled, and her dimples were in full bloom, and she looked like the most adorable doll I had ever seen, and her French accent only magnified the effect.

Gabrielle was the first one to empty her glass of wine. When I refilled it, she smiled and thanked me in French, teasing me by using the formal pronoun "vous," as though she were addressing a superior or someone she had just met.

"You're welcome," I replied as I reached over and kissed her on the head. Then I looked at Mike and said, "She might eat slow, but she drinks fast."

Mike laughed and asked, "Have you traveled much, Gabrielle?"

"No, this is the first time I have been out of France since my parents moved there over ten years ago. But, I am so happy to be in America. Nicky promised to take me to see the Statue of Liberty."

"Well, you're only a few miles away from it," Mike said as he downed the wine in his glass and refilled it to the top.

Gabrielle looked up at me and asked, "Maybe we can go tomorrow?"

"Maybe, but first we have to get you new clothes."

"Yes, I definitely need new clothes. Nicky wouldn't allow me to take the suitcase I packed with my old clothes."

"You can always walk around naked. I doubt anyone would complain," Mike remarked as Gabrielle suddenly lowered her head and I nodded at Mike to back off.

"I'm only joking. You would immediately be arrested, so I wouldn't recommend doing anything like that."

Gabrielle suddenly looked up and angrily said, "I would never do such a thing. In France, the whores might walk around naked, but never me."

Mike shook his head as he took another big gulp from his glass. I watched him make a conscious effort to ignore this strange moment and let this comment go, and I gave silent thanks for his restraint. Mike then asked Gabrielle, "Is there anywhere else you would like to go?"

"Yes," she replied. "I would like to see the Lincoln Memorial."

"And why that memorial?"

"Because I hear he was a very great man."

Mike lowered his eyes, and looked down at Gabrielle's hands and asked, "You paint Gabrielle?"

"Yes, or at least I try to paint."

"Don't let her fool you. She's an excellent painter," I remarked as I ran my hand through her hair.

"My Nicky says that because he loves me. Isn't that so?"

"I love you very much, but that's not the reason why I say that. I say that because I think you're an excellent painter."

"Thank you, Nicky."

"And who is your favorite artist?" Mike asked.

"Mr. da Vinci. His paintings are full of life and motion. They are like looking at a movie."

"You are a very perceptive young lady. I know very little about artists, but the few times I have had the pleasure to look at da Vinci's paintings I have noticed the same things, but for me they remind me of an airplane in motion, passing through the clouds, and touching Heaven."

Chapter Twenty-Five

After dinner, we all went back to our suites. Despite all the cocaine, the tranquilizers, traveling, and drinking finally caught up with Mike and me. I was exhausted, and after washing up in the bathroom, I walked into the bedroom and found Gabrielle passed out on the bed. I lay down beside her and simply looked at her lovely face. She was breathing softly and peacefully, like a newborn baby.

I closed my eyes and quickly fell asleep, and like in the movies, the lovely face of Gabrielle quickly dissolved into the jovial face of Abdul, and then into the scene outside the restaurant, beside the taxis, when we hugged and whispered to each other, "Love you like a brother." I then got into the first taxi and watched through the rearview mirror as Abdul got into the second taxi and disappeared as my driver turned the corner. The entire scene kept on repeating itself, until I finally found myself in the second taxi watching as Abdul slid into the back seat and looked into the smiling face of Elijah. He tried to escape as the latches on all the doors closed in unison, and Elijah pulled out a butcher's knife and said, "Your friend Nick says, hello, hello, hello … your friend Nick…" as he repeatedly thrusted the knife into Abdul's stomach, twisting and turning it, as he gleefully kept saying, "Your friend Nick says hello … hello, hello…"

I suddenly woke up and looked at Gabrielle, peacefully asleep, and quietly turned around and got up off the bed and walked into the living room. I sat on the couch and turned on the television and switched from the regular American channels to the international channels. I turned on France 24, a popular news channel, and watched as the French police knocked down the door of Abdul's apartment and seized the boxes full of wallet-sized bombs and other explosive devices and materials in that one side room. The cameras focused on the box labels and one could clearly see the destination countries — Crimea, the US, and Saudi Arabia. If one was to believe the Mossad twins, all of the bombs were to be used against Ukraine. They did not identify the terrorist suspect or suspects, but they said the police had numerous leads.

They interviewed the local authorities and the anti-terrorist units stationed around Paris, and then switched to the explosion at my apartment, which the authorities were saying was probably caused by a gas leak. They mentioned that the one body that was found was believed to be that of a US citizen, studying at one of the universities. I didn't even want to think who that body might belong to, but I was hoping that it was a corpse they had stolen from the morgue. The explosion was huge, but confined mainly to my apartment, and no one else in the building was killed or hurt.

I shut off the TV, and lay there until I fell asleep to the recurring nightmare of hugging Abdul outside the restaurant and watching him go off to be butchered in my name.

Chapter Twenty-Six

I woke up to the sound of Gabrielle's voice. She was standing over me with her hair still wet from just taking a shower. She was wearing a hotel bathrobe about five sizes too large, and she looked so adorable, like a photoshopped picture one sees in a women's magazine. She bent down to kiss me and her oversized robe accidently came loose … revealing her naked body: the scars, burns, and all the loveliness God could fit in her tiny frame. She immediately went to cover herself up and I put out my hand and said, "No!"

I stood up, and removed the rest of the robe as she looked up at me with the type of shame and fear in her eyes that one might see in the eyes of a child caught with her hands in the cookie jar she was told not to touch. I leaned down and kissed her, and said, "You are the most beautiful woman I have ever seen. The most beautiful." I picked her up, and carried her into the bedroom and laid her down on the bed. I took off my clothes, and gently kissed and caressed every part of her body, and she let me make love to her, and reader, she was not frigid.

Afterwards, we lay silently in bed for a few awkward moments and when she tried to get up I reached over and brought her back to me, "Oh, no, you don't."

She smiled and said, "I thought we were finished. Isn't that the way it works?"

"Not with me," I replied as we started to kiss again and after a few more minutes we were making love again. Her surprise and delight were so complete that she started giggling, and then crying, as I held her arms above her head and kissed her deeply.

How long we stayed that way I couldn't be sure. In the end we fell asleep with our bodies entwined. I woke to the feeling of her moving away, and I instinctively grabbed her by the hand and asked, "Where are you going?"

She looked at me and started to laugh and then replied, "I have to go pee, Nicky."

"Oh, okay, but hurry on back," I said as I watched her cute little butt wiggle off to the bathroom.

She came back and without hesitation curled up right beside me and said, "Tell me how much you love me, Nicky."

"I love you to the moon and back, and how much do you love me?"

"I love you to the moon and back and all the way to Heaven," she replied as I took her beautiful face into my hands and we kissed passionately. I was thankful that a barrier had been brought down, but also thankful that we had waited. Her readiness and willingness meant everything. I looked at her and knew, without either of us having to say another word, that this was love.

Chapter Twenty-Seven

I knocked on Mike's door and he let me into the suite. "Sleep okay?" I asked.

"Like a baby. Those tranquilizers are a godsend," he said as he looked at me rather oddly and continued, "You been a naughty little boy this morning, my little Nicky?"

I shook my head as though I had no idea what he was talking about … thinking the whole time that nothing got past him and what a wonderful CIA operative he made.

"Well, I hope you have plenty of money for me because I have lost time to make up for … in that naughty department. You understand, don't you?" he asked and laughed.

"Yes, I understand," I said, and handed him five thousand dollars. "Hopefully, that'll hold you over to this evening."

He flipped through the short stack of hundred-dollar bills I'd given him and said, "Wow! It's nice to be rich."

"I had my baby sister wire me the money. She was so excited to know I was back in the States."

"For her safety, you be sure to keep her away … at least until the election is over with and this whole nonsense blows over."

"I know," I said. "But she can handle herself quite well. She might have trouble walking, but that girl is a deadly shot, and she has a whole arsenal of weapons generously given to her by my father."

"She sounds like a hoot. Maybe, after I retire you can introduce her to me. She sounds like the type of girl I could settle down with."

"Surely, you're joking? I've already told you I wouldn't allow a pig like you within a hundred yards of my baby sister."

He laughed and then said seriously, "This is my last hurrah, Nick. In another year or so, once I'm through with this bullshit assignment, I'm done. I'll have two pensions to live off of. That should keep me comfortable for a long time. I have no intention of dying in the service of this country. I would rather be shooting hoops all day and drinking beer all night. Strange, but I feel my service would be better appreciated on a basketball court than it was in the field."

"You know what they say — don't quit your day job," I said with a laugh.

"Ha! I know. My shot at the NBA came and went. It just hurts to see so many brave and courageous people go completely undervalued by an establishment so corrupt and greedy that it bears almost no resemblance to the country that the rest of the world used to admire."

"I'm not sure how many countries actually admired us—" I said, but Mike cut me off.

"They did! They fucking did, whether they admitted it or not! They looked up to us and they wanted to be like us. We were cool and free and we gave people hope. This used to be a place where anyone who could get themselves here and hustle had a real shot at making a dream come true. Now it's a stinking cesspool of special interests and greed, intolerance, and stupidity at the highest levels."

"Preaching to the choir," I said, settling into a big armchair under the window. Mike was on a tear and he wasn't finished.

"It's sickening to watch the very principles that so many struggling countries have admired and tried to emulate be undermined every day by the very same scumbags that we, the people, elect. Your little girlfriend — excuse me, fiancée — is right. Lincoln was a great man, and so was Teddy Roosevelt, and Franklin, and Truman, and General Marshall, and Senator McCain, and the list goes on. Those were guys who knew how to work across the aisle to get things done. Now our politics are all about partisanship as a form of blindness. The day we crossed that Maginot Line and allowed a cult leader into the White house is the day we started losing respect around the world. That was also the day people like you and I became pawns, at times the very enemy of our own government, and our lives became meaningless, because the only thing these scumbags value is money and power."

He shook his head as he took a beer out of the mini-bar and downed it, then took two beers out and offered me one, which I declined. "Oh, I forgot, you're high on love."

"Still think she might be a terrorist or a Mossad agent?" I asked.

"Oh please, that child is lucky she has the courage to get out of bed in the morning. But it doesn't mean she wasn't the informer ... she could be clueless but dangerous."

"You do remember that you're talking about the girl of my dreams and the person I plan to marry?"

"You asked me what I thought, and I gave it to you straight. She's a charity case, but that's exactly the type of woman I would expect you to fall heads over heels for, because no one is more giving of himself than you. Saintly, is how our recently deceased friend Dmitry used to put it."

"I actually fell in love with her because of her looks," I remarked.

"Oh, I can definitely see that. She's undeniably beautiful. But love at first sight is like the setting sun ... lovely to witness until it fades to dark. Admit it, you really fell in love with her after you learned about her tragic past, right?"

It was hard for me to acknowledge it, but he was right.

"I knew it," he said.

"On second thought, I will have that beer."

He handed it to me and said, "You might as well; you're paying for it."

"I was looking at the French news and it showed the raid on Abdul's apartment and the explosion at my place. I have this funny feeling that Abdul is dead."

"Well, I hate to break it to you, but I can guarantee you that he's dead. Surely, two Mossad agents can outmaneuver the French authorities."

"I knew I couldn't trust them."

"Oh, I doubt they killed him, unless they're in on the business side of things. Mossad knows that a dead terrorist is a lot less valuable than a live one. I'll bet on it, that it's the station chief in the embassy ... the one they call the professor, that killed him, and at this very moment he is probably gleefully torturing the Mossad agents before killing them."

"Surely, they wouldn't be outsmarted by that weasel?"

"You underestimate the weasel. No one gets a reputation like his without earning it. The general mentioned him on numerous occasions, and after visiting the embassy in Paris he went so far as to say that the professor was a national security risk, and needed to be eliminated."

"A political appointment?"

"A hefty donation to the campaign and the inaugural balls and festivals. The same old story; qualified candidates need not apply ... only deep-pocket donors with little or no government experience." He finished off his beer and opened another as he looked very closely at me and continued. "If this is going down like I imagine, you need to be very careful because you will be the next one on his hit list."

"He already thinks he killed me. He's the one behind the bombing of my apartment."

"Jesus, Nick, sometimes it's hard to believe you made it through basic field operations training. Donna Low must have been sweet on you."

"Hey!" I protested. "I'm a damn good agent." Then I paused, looked down, and corrected myself. "*Was* a damn good agent."

"I know that, idiot. I just don't know how you can be so good at your job and so naive at the same time. If the professor killed and tortured those two Mossad agents, you have to assume he knows you're still alive. They might not have given up the girl, but you can be sure as hell they gave you up."

"If they gave me up, they gave Gabrielle up. That son of a bitch knows all about Gabrielle and me. He made that perfectly clear at our meeting in the café."

"If the bodies drop as I suspect, then you are going to have to hide her in the most secure, off-the-chart place you know, because unless he is stopped and put down, Gabrielle is in play. The weasel is pure evil. If there is such a thing as a Hell, he is a top lieutenant in Satan's army."

"What the hell am I going to do?" I pleaded, suddenly aware of the hopelessness of my situation.

"To start with, you need to be very fucking careful, and think like the professor. What makes him dangerous is his genius. But he's not perfect."

"How so?"

"From what I've heard, he has one big vulnerability. Like the self-important dick that he is, he takes a deep pride in his work and he likes to show it off to the world. The dude can't help himself. Abdul and the Mossad agents will show up dead with either their eyes burned out, or holding their castrated dicks, or beheaded with their heads sitting in their laps. Some sick signature move like that. If I am to believe the general, the professor likes to give a little lecture to his victims about his methods and successes, before torturing and killing them. A guy with that much ego is bound to make a mistake somewhere. His big fat head will be his downfall, and hopefully it'll also be our redemption."

"How long do you think I have to get Gabrielle to a safe place and come up with a plan to eliminate him?"

"Three or four days, tops. He won't leave Paris until he soaks up all the news about his ingenious exploits. I know a girl I used to see in the embassy. She's someone I can rely on. She will be able to tell me when he leaves and his destination."

"Do I meet him at the airport?" I asked.

"No, you don't meet him at the airport. He'll probably have a car waiting for him right on the tarmac with at least one or two trusted bodyguards. And if you think I am going to have you commit suicide by letting you take care of him, you're truly out of your mind. Not for nothing, but this is out of your league. You'll be the prop. The lure. I'll be the avenging angel."

"And how do you plan on doing this when you have to get that plane back to France?"

"The day after tomorrow, I will fly the plane back. The dickhead deserves that much. For all my bickering, he's treated me well. I'll tell him I have a family emergency and have to leave for the States. He'll have no problem getting another pilot to fly him around until I return. I will then take the first available flight out of Charles de Gaulle Airport, first class and courtesy of my rich friend, and be right back here. In the meantime, we will leave just enough breadcrumbs for the professor to follow, without him thinking it's a trap. What you need to do is get your little girlfriend to a safe place no later than the day after tomorrow, and don't tell anyone where she is. *Not even me.*"

That was Mike's way of telling me there was a chance this plan of his could backfire, and that we could become the professor's next victims. I asked, "And what do I owe you for doing all this?"

"A date with your baby sister," he replied as we both laughed.

Chapter Twenty-Eight

I opened the door to my suite and was met by my lovely Gabrielle. She threw her arms around me and we kissed and she said, "I love you so much, my handsome Nicky."

"And I love you so much, my lovely Gabrielle."

I did not have it in me to tell her anything about what Mike and I had discussed. That could wait another day. She seemed so happy, like a great burden had been lifted from her shoulders. She was the girl I met for the first time on the steps of the university, and I wasn't ready to derail that by telling her the ugly details of Mike's plan.

We had cleared a big hurdle this morning — sur*mounted* it, you could almost say — and I felt it was really important to build upon that progress. I knew it was very difficult for her. The scars and burns on her body were a constant reminder of the evil that exists in the world and the horrifying, life-altering tragedy she had experienced as a ten-year-old. I knew enough about trauma to know that I would probably be called to reassure Gabrielle a thousand times before she truly trusted me and no longer had flare-ups of insecurity and its more intense cousin, paranoia. I wanted more than anything to show her that she was safe with me, but Mike had just made it clear that this might not be true, unless I worked to make it so by getting rid of the professor.

Mike could pretend that what Gabrielle went through was not much different than what millions of other children throughout the world go through all the time, and because of that it wasn't such a mystery to me anymore why he so desperately wanted to meet my baby sister. She possesses the qualities that he admires in a person: resiliency, determination, and a refusal to cave into weakness or court pity. For all of his legendary womanizing, Mike actually held women to the same standards that he most admired in men, and it was this fact that made him more equitable than almost anyone I knew. He may have flirted with half the women he ever met, but any woman who stood a chance of winning him would have to show him that she had backbone and character. These were qualities that my little sister had in spades. And they were the same qualities that my father had always admired in her. For Mike, it also didn't hurt that she was adorable, played basketball, and controlled an arsenal of weapons larger than that held by most American police forces. I didn't quite understand his weakness for women who knew their way around firearms, but you couldn't hope to grasp everything about even your closest friends in this world.

The difference between Mike and my father was that Mike had a sense of morality and ethics. He had a line he would never cross, and I could not say that with any certainty about my father. Mike's concern for Gabrielle's safety was heartfelt. He knew that when men were tortured, the bravest of them could break, and that innocent lives could be put in jeopardy. That's why he didn't want to know where Gabrielle would be staying, and that's why I was trying to figure out a plan that would also keep *me* in the dark about her location.

Gabrielle really wanted to go out and buy new clothes. She had been wearing the same outfit for almost two days now and she couldn't stand it. She waited by the door as I went into the bedroom and took my handgun out of my backpack, along with my CIA credentials. The last thing I needed was for a cop to stop me and arrest me for carrying an unregistered firearm. After 9/11 the situation in Manhattan had changed drastically, and there were cops and undercover FBI agents everywhere. I placed my gun in its holster, which I attached to the back of my belt and kept hidden beneath a long spring coat that I had stashed in my backpack.

I walked out of the bedroom and took Gabrielle's hand. We left the suite and took the elevator down to the lobby. We walked outside and I immediately hailed a taxi that took us to Macy's department store on West 34th Street.

Chapter Twenty-Nine

Gabrielle held my hand tightly as we wove through the crowds and took the elevator up to Women's Apparel. Macy's was always a zoo in the middle of the day, and today was no exception. As we left the first floor and entered the world of women's blouses and lingerie and hosiery, I immediately felt like the only man for a thousand miles around, but I decided not to care. Gabrielle needed my help, and we were going to do this thing. We walked over to a section bursting with colorful spring and summer dresses of the kind Gabrielle liked to wear. Her eyes grew wide as she looked at an elegant, short-sleeved, A-line dress from StyleWe. She touched the fabric and pronounced it lovely and soft, but then looked at the prices and said, "It's much too expensive. Let's go look at other dresses."

I looked down at the price tags on the dresses that were between sixty and seventy dollars and told her, "Pick out ten in your size and go try them on."

"No, I told you, I don't want you spending a lot of money on me. I'm sure they have cheaper dresses that are just as nice."

"Do you really want to get married?" I asked.

"Yes, Nicky, you promised."

"Then pick out ten or twenty or fifty dresses that you like and go try them on, and if you bring up money one more time we will not be getting married. If I can't spoil the girl of my dreams, who can I spoil? I love you. Now please just do as I ask."

She looked at me, unable to come up with a reply, and silently began to pick out dresses in a range of colors. I thought I detected a small smile. When she had picked out ten dresses I walked with her to the ladies' fitting rooms and waited outside while she tried on the dresses. I had to be careful when speaking to Gabrielle, in English, because she didn't always pick up on the nuances in my speech. She would take things literally when I was just joking and playing with her. Before entering the fitting rooms, she turned to me and said, "Don't forget, you promised we were going to get married."

I looked at the panic in her eyes and reached out and grabbed her by the shoulders. "I have every intention of marrying you. I was only joking about the dresses, my beautiful Gabrielle. Do you understand? It was a joke."

She smiled and replied, "Yes, I understand. Thank you, Nicky. I love you so much."

"And I love you so much," I replied as I gently patted her on the butt and she giggled. A simple, playful action, like patting her on the behind would have been out of the question before this morning, but now she could giggle like a child and not feel like she was being molested all over again. The idea of me having to explain to her why we would have to be separated in just a few days was weighing heavy on my mind. It was now a dull ache, but would quickly become a throbbing pain.

I stood with my back against the wall of the dressing rooms … feeling safe that no one could come up from behind me and take me out with one shot to the head. I looked at all the ladies shopping and shook my head in amazement. How had it come to this? How was I standing in the ladies' changeroom in the middle of Macy's, in mid-town Manhattan, contemplating the real possibility that I could be the target of a hit at any moment? I had thought that once I was out of Afghanistan, this type of worry would no longer be relevant, but apparently I was very wrong. Maybe Mike was right, and I was as naive as a kid. I knew, in the way that we all know things about ourselves that can only be lived and not explained, that I harbored more contradictions than ever before. I was a capable agent, yes, but I was also stupidly in love, and had been just as stupidly convinced, until today, that I would be able to escape the likes of the professor just by running away from Paris. How had I ever thought this was possible? As I stood outside the dressing rooms, lost in thought, I could feel a leggy young attendant staring at me with concern. If I didn't know better, I would almost have said she was able to read my mind. I shot her a quick smile to put her at ease, and made a conscious effort to smooth out my brow and put my thoughts back where they belonged: inside my head.

After about half an hour Gabrielle came out holding all ten dresses and I asked, "Do they fit and do you like them?"

"Yes, Nicky, they are lovely ... so soft and comfortable. I have never worn dresses so nice."

I looked at her and said, "At times Gabrielle, I cannot believe how adorable you are, and how lucky I am to have you."

She smiled, and it was like every time she smiled, or laughed, or simply giggled I fell further in love with her ... if such a thing was possible. She replied, "Merci, Nicky," as she reached up, with the mound of dresses between us, and kissed me. I took the dresses off her hands and we shopped for a couple of hours. I bought her jeans and T-shirts, wool dress pants, an interesting jumper that I never would have guessed she would like, but which looked especially adorable on her, pajamas, comfortable shoes, two pairs of heels, a variety of simple undergarments and some truly lovely lingerie, spring jackets and sweaters, makeup, and grooming and hygiene accessories. We walked out with five full shopping bags for Gabrielle and one full shopping bag of clothes for me. The whole thing cost me less than five thousand dollars, or what my mother or older sister would spend on one outfit.

We left Macy's and stopped in at a pizzeria. I ordered four regular slices of cheese pizza, and two cream sodas. I showed Gabrielle how to eat a slice of NY pizza without a knife and fork, by folding it in half. After she let it cool for a minute, she took a tiny bite and said,

"Delicious, Nicky." I liked to think that she was calling me delicious, but that was a little joke I kept to myself. By the time I had finished my two slices, Gabrielle had finished maybe a third of her first slice. Occasionally, I had to clean her chin when a little oil from the pizza dripped down, but she was thoroughly enjoying the pizza.

It was nearly impossible to look at her in a setting like this and not think that at times she was living, for the first time, a childhood that had been robbed from her. I eventually ended up eating her other slice because she was too full, and it was great.

We got into a taxi and went back to the hotel. Gabrielle was very excited about wearing one of her new dresses to dinner tonight with Mike. We were going to meet at eight in the lobby and decide where to go and eat.

Chapter Thirty

I opened the door to the suite, and Gabrielle quickly walked into the bedroom and picked out the dress she was going to wear. She took it into the bathroom with her because she wanted to take a shower after wearing the clothes she had had on for nearly two days. The door to the bathroom was slightly ajar and I could see her undressing. I knocked on the door and entered. She was naked, except for her bra that she still had not unfastened. She looked at me and at first it was as though she was trying to cover up her body with her arms. I gently held onto her forearms and guided them down to her sides, as she looked up at me and blushed. I then reached around and undid her bra, which fell to the floor.

I picked her up and brought her to the bed. I got undressed and gently kissed and caressed nearly every part of her lovely body. We made love, and after we were finished I kept her in the bed beside me. She was certainly more relaxed than before, and after I reminded her that we had nearly three hours before meeting Mike, we made love again. She then ran off to pee and take a shower.

Chapter Thirty-One

I met Mike at the hotel bar at eight o'clock. Gabrielle needed a few more minutes to get ready, and then she would join us. Mike was drinking a Macallan 12-year-old scotch. I ordered the same and was kind of surprised to find Mike relatively sober. I asked him what he did all day.

"I took the train up to Parkchester and played ball."

"And did you kick ass on your old basketball court?"

"No, my old basketball court is no longer there. They paved over it, though God knows why, since it's just an empty space now. I walked a little further down and played on some other courts and yes, I kicked ass, but it wasn't the same." His voice was full of sadness. He then looked at me and asked, "And did Gabrielle get her new clothes?"

"Yes, she is very excited and will be down in a few minutes."

"And you got a little bit of something afterwards, or should I say a whole lot?"

"Let's just say Gabrielle and I had a good day."

He laughed as he looked up at the TV screen, which was turned to an international channel. Mike asked the bartender if he could turn up the sound and he did. The TV commentator said, "In Paris today, authorities have confirmed the identity of a man whose body was found yesterday in an abandoned warehouse. The body was that of Parisian graduate student and suspected terrorist, Abdul Haqq. Haqq is believed to have engineered and manufactured a large cache of explosive devices that were confiscated by Paris police from his apartment on the same day he was believed to have been killed.

"To our viewers, please be advised that the following report includes graphic details that some will find disturbing. Haqq was found beheaded, with his decapitated head sitting in his lap, and with the word 'Terrorist' written across his chest." They put up a picture of Abdul that they must have found in his apartment, with the words "Terrorist Suspect Beheaded" underneath his face. Before I could react I heard a gasp from behind me, and I turned to see Gabrielle running away from our table, toward the elevator.

I got up from the bar and told Mike to go get something to eat because there would be a good chance I might be gone for a long time. I downed my drink and slowly walked toward the elevator, feeling more like an executioner than a simple soldier in a fight to preserve innocent lives.

I opened the door to the suite and I heard loud sobbing from the bedroom. I walked into the bedroom and sat down next to Gabrielle, who was lying face down and crying, hard, into a pillow.

"I'm sorry, Gabrielle."

She didn't respond for a long time and then through a flood of tears and gasps she said, "They promised they wouldn't kill him. Those bastards, those bastards!"

"Who promised?" I asked.

"David and Elijah. I went to them when I discovered what Abdul was doing. I was too scared to go to the police. They promised they would take care of it without hurting him."

"And where were they when you got in touch with them?"

"They were in Paris. What does it matter where they were?" She continued to cry, and if it were any other person who had not been through the tragedy she had been through, I would have asked a hundred questions, such as, "Did you ever try to talk to Abdul when the two of you were growing up? Did you try to understand his situation, or did you just assume that because he was Muslim he was no good? Did you even consider telling him what you had been through so he could get a better understanding of why you reacted to him like you did? Did you even consider talking to your adopted brother when you found out what he was making, or did you just go straight to your first choice like always … David and Elijah? Two men who, you already knew, specialized in killing?" I kept all of those questions to myself.

She lifted her face up from the pillow and looked at me and said, "I need to talk to my parents."

"Not now, it's not safe," I said firmly.

"Then when?" she screamed at me.

"When I tell you, and if you even attempt to get in touch with them, both you and your parents will pay a heavy price. I don't need any more people getting killed because of your actions. Do you understand?"

She looked at me as if in total shock and said, "You don't really love me, do you?"

"If you still have to ask a question like that, Gabrielle, after all we've been through, you are more messed up than I ever could have imagined."

I got up off the bed and started walking toward the living room when she said, "Please don't leave me alone, Nicky. I'm so sorry."

"I'm not looking for an apology, Gabrielle. I'm just trying to protect you. When are you going to understand that?"

"Please Nicky, don't leave me. Please," She replied as I turned back around and pulled off my shoes and got on the bed. I wrapped my arms around her trembling body, and pushed her hair away from her ear and we sat there in silence.

Finally, I said, "I like the new dress on you. Is it comfortable and soft?"

She nodded her head and replied, "But it's not going to bring back Abdul."

"You informing on your brother to David and Elijah had very little, if anything, to do with him being killed."

"What are you talking about?"

"Do you think it was just a coincidence that when you got in touch with them that they just happened to be in Paris? They knew about Abdul's enterprise well before you mentioned it to them."

"But how could they?"

"Because they were in Paris trying to protect their business interest in Abdul's enterprise. It's not like Abdul went to any great lengths to hide his business venture. He thought that he was making these wallet-size explosives for legitimate reasons. That Americans, who love their guns, were lining up to buy these easy-to-conceal wallets for protection instead of carrying around guns. The explosives he made were not the type that caused major destruction. They were powerful enough to cause panic and hurt or kill one person, but not much more. David and Elijah and an intelligence officer in the US Embassy had him believing this lie. They were the ones making a huge profit off the devices, while helping the Russians undermine the democratic government of Ukraine."

"No, that can't be. David and Elijah would never do such a thing."

"When they learned that a CIA operative was assigned to find out about Abdul's business interests and his connection to possible terrorists, they and the intelligence officer knew they had to get rid of him. They knew that if he was captured alive by the French authorities and counter-terrorism squads, or alerted by the CIA operative, that it was all over for them, too, and that they would be hunted down. They were certain that Abdul's story would eventually ring true and that the authorities would piece together all the clues and that they would immediately be implicated."

"And that CIA operative was you, wasn't it, Nicky?" She asked this with a touch of disdain in her voice.

"I tried to save your brother. I violated a direct order not to get in touch with the French authorities. I called the police because I thought they would at least not kill Abdul, even if they ended up prosecuting him. The police were able to confiscate the weapons from your brother's apartment, but they were too late and too incompetent to save your brother."

Gabrielle was holding her head in her hands and I couldn't tell if she was hearing everything I was saying. I spoke softly to her now, saying, "I really liked Abdul. He was a good person, and a smart engineer, but he wasn't very worldly. Certainly not enough to understand the consequences of what he was involved in. When he brought me up to his apartment he showed me the wallets, and wanted to know if I would like to go into business with him. When I asked him if the weapons were being sold to terrorists, he got really mad and said, 'My parents and family were killed by terrorists. I would never sell anything to terrorists or be involved with such people.' He was a genius when it came to physics and math, but a good-hearted simpleton … easily persuaded when it came to matters of business. Don't think that you are the only person hurting right now because I can assure you that this whole matter, the murder of Abdul, is eating away at my very conscience."

Gabrielle had disappeared into herself by this point. I stopped trying to hold her and lay next to her on my back, looking at the ceiling. I had always had a sense that Gabrielle might be the informer. From the time I re-read the case files, I found it unusual that the sister and parents were not under suspicion. Gabrielle might be a basket case, but there was a touch of menace about her that made her dangerous.

Gabrielle stopped crying and turned to look down at me. I remained silent and then looked her directly in her eyes and said, "Maybe, Gabrielle, just maybe, if you had tried to talk to Abdul, you would have found out that he was a good person. Misguided, yes, but basically good. He loved your parents more than anything in this world, and I know he tried to get along with you, but you shut him out at every turn. You had to know that your Mossad buddies were killers, and yet you had no problem telling them about Abdul. You could have at least approached your brother first and tried to explain to him that his product was not being sold to innocent Americans, but to Russian agents trying to overthrow a democratic country."

"And how was I supposed to know that?"

"The same way you found out what he was working on … that's how."

"I found out by accident."

"Of course you did, Gabrielle, and even though at times you have a problem adding one plus one, you were easily able to figure out that those wallets were actually explosives."

"What are you trying to say, that I was somehow part of this insane business with David and Elijah and this intelligence officer?"

"No, you're too naive … too much of a liability to be trusted with the details of their business. But when they asked you to introduce yourself to me at the university, that was easy enough for you to do because you're really good at pretending."

She went to slap me across the face, but I stopped her and flung her hand back toward her body and said, "I don't like hitting girls, but I also don't like being hit by them."

She turned away from me and lay on her side and said, "I might be stupid, but never did I pretend to love you. I loved you from the beginning and all I have ever wanted was for us to get married and come to America … to be happy and in love, for just once in my life. I never wanted them to hurt Abdul, but I was confused and worried, and David and Elijah were the only two people who had ever helped and protected me. They promised they would not hurt him. They promised. And about this Russian thing, I have no idea what you are talking about. I'm lucky if I can find Russia on the map."

"And how did you find out about the wallets?"

"Abdul told me. I asked him where he was getting all this money from and he took me to his apartment and showed me the boxes of wallets, and described what they could do. Instead of telling him what they were probably being used for, I decided to let David and Elijah handle it. I was jealous of all the money and gifts he was giving to our parents while I had given them so little. But I was also worried about him. I'm sorry that I hurt you, Nicky. It was never my intention. I have never pretended to love you. Not for one second."

I remained silent for a long time, and yet when Gabrielle started to get up out of the bed I reached over and pulled her back and said, "I'm still in love with you, Gabrielle, and I still want to marry you and make you happy. Your decisions were misguided, but it didn't change the outcome. They had every intention of killing Abdul long before you told them what you found out. They used you. They had you divert my attention away from Abdul while they put their plan into effect. They were smart, corrupt agents, and I imagine by now they have both been killed and beheaded."

"What?" she asked.

"They knew that they had to get rid of Abdul, but in reality he was just a minor headache. Their true adversary was always the intelligence officer … their business partner. They knew it, but what they didn't realize was just how evil he is and how much more resourceful and intelligent."

"And is he after you now?"

"I don't know, but what I do know is that I have to get you to a safe place, and then Mike and I will take care of him."

"No, I will never leave you," she said forcefully as she folded her arms around my body.

"That's not the way it works, Gabrielle. The day after tomorrow I will have you taken to a safe place. Even I can't know the location. The less I know, the more secure you are."

Gabrielle looked at me with dawning alarm. "Why?"

"Well … if I don't know where you are, I can't tell anyone who might want to hurt you," I said.

"Why would you tell anyone where I am?"

"That's the whole point. I don't want to tell anyone. But … pain … does strange things to the human mind…"

"What are you talking about? Who is going to hurt you?" Her eyes went wild and she was grabbing onto my forearms.

"Gabrielle, please, calm down. It's just a precaution."

"A precaution against what?" she demanded to know. "You are not making sense."

"Darling, we have to face facts," I explained, as gently as I could. "David and Elijah were in business with a man who is so corrupt, and so evil, that we just don't know what he might do. We saw what he did to Abdul, may he rest in peace. We can't take any chances. Of course I'm going to do everything in my power to take the bastard down, and Mike has sworn to help me. But … if I'm captured first … I've never been in a … situation … like that before. I don't know how I'll react or what I might say."

Gabrielle buried her face in her hands and began sobbing. She climbed off the bed and began pacing across the hotel floor, still holding her face and crying. "What have I done? Why does this man want to hurt you? Nicky, I don't understand how this could have happened. My God."

I trailed after her in figure eights until I was finally able to wrap my arms around her. She finally stopped moving and collapsed against my chest, still standing. "I just want us to be married, to be happy … these monsters … I can't…" she was saying, her words only half audible.

"Shhhh," I said, holding her head and stroking her hair. "My love. We'll be all right. I'll be fine. I'll do everything in my power to make this right. But you have to trust me. Please—"

"I won't leave you, Nicky. Never!" she said, trying to hold me in place with her frail, petite body.

"Love, you have to," I said. "How can I make you understand?"

"You can't," she said. "You don't have to do this. We can run. We can go to, what do you call it, middle America. We can go to Kansas or one of those states where nobody will ever find us."

"They'll find us," I said. "No, we have to deal with this. You have to go to the safe place, and I can't know where it is. This is the life I chose … or more like the life my father chose for me … and I am not going to let anything happen to you because of a decision I made. You deserve a happy life, and if anything happens to me you will have plenty of money and a support system that will always be there for you and will always protect you. Mike will be there, and my little sister will love you. I know it. Even my father will be there for you, if you want him to be. You're so beautiful, Gabrielle, and you have so much to offer … if there is anything I am sure of, it's that you can do better than me."

"Better than you, is that what you think?" she said. "Well, I cannot do better than you because you are all that I have ever wanted ... all that I have ever dreamed about."

I'm not ashamed to admit that she had me crying at that point. We stood there, rocking on our bare feet and holding each other, weeping together.

I ran my hands across the beautiful contours of her face and said, "If we ever want a chance at a beautiful life together, you have to do what I tell you. If you stay with me, you become something else I have to worry about. Mike would never stand for it."

"And what is Mike's role in all this craziness?"

"He had no role. I reached out to him when I realized that both our lives were in danger if we waited at that hotel in Paris and took the flight to Tel Aviv in the morning. I did him a big favor once, and he has never forgotten that. Mike is better than that intelligence officer, and he always completes his missions once he takes them on. He's the best, and when he tells me you cannot hang around, he is dead serious."

She lowered her eyes, and ran her hands across my shirt and asked, "And your father, what type of man is he?"

"He was an absentee father who always managed to control his family from afar, or at least the two members of his family that he gave a damn about ... my baby sister and me. He was a US Army general before he was forced to resign. He was a hero, a brave warrior who fought alongside his men..."

"And now?"

"And now, he's a venture capitalist making a fortune off of the agony and suffering of the men he commanded and fought alongside."

"I don't understand."

I laughed and replied, "That makes two of us."

"What type of father wants their son to go into the business that you are in?"

"The type who puts country above all else ... until that country turned its back on him."

"And what did they do to him?" she asked.

I shook my head and said, "It really doesn't matter anymore, Gabrielle. I would rather not even talk about it. I've been blaming him much too long. I never had to sign any papers, or join the agency, but I didn't have the courage to go against the man. He would have preferred for me to join the army, or the marines, but I didn't want to get dirty like those service men and women do … splashing around in the mud and rain. I thought by joining the CIA I could at least stay clean, and use my mind at what I thought I was good at … analysis and intelligence gathering.

"When I told him about my decision to join the agency he simply looked at me and said, 'It's probably for the best. I never really thought you had what it takes to be a soldier.' From that moment on the man championed my decision. He probably thought that I might back out, but before I had a chance to blink my eyes he made sure I was in and then there was no turning back. When I told him I was being assigned to the embassy in Kabul, Afghanistan, he never looked happier in his whole life. Instead of saying you need to be careful and alert, and I'll be praying for you, he said, 'At least in Kabul, you will be serving your country in a meaningful way and in a strategic part of the world.' That was the last time I talked to him. His new line of work created a conflict of interest that wouldn't allow us to talk to each other. Everything I know about him up until now has come by way of my baby sister."

I walked Gabrielle back to the bed and we crawled onto the mattress together and snuggled against the headboard.

"I can't believe I don't know anything about your baby sister. Can you tell me about her?"

"Of course. You will love each other, I'm sure of it. She is amazing, and she happens to also be the only person, besides the men and women my father commanded, that I am certain he loves. She was born with a handicap, and has had to use a wheelchair and crutches throughout her life, but she has incredible determination and intelligence. She refuses to use her handicap as an excuse, and if you ever try to tell her that she can't do something, like play basketball, or climb Mount Everest, or shoot and hit a target at a hundred yards, she will prove you wrong and do it ten times better than you. She's adorable, and quite deadly. She could kill you with her bare arms from a wheelchair or wobbling around on crutches. She's a black belt in a number of the martial arts. She's my father's idea of the perfect soldier."

"She sounds amazing, like Wonder Woman," Gabrielle said as she smiled for the first time since learning about Abdul.

I laughed and said, "That's not a bad comparison. She's also the only one in my family that I could trust fully. When we were growing up we always told each other that we would never separate, that even if we got married our spouses would just have to get used to the idea that we were inseparable and would continue to live under the same roof. But then, as we got older, the real world intruded upon our grand plans. I went off to college and she went off to climb Mount Everest. I then joined the CIA and she went off to college and graduated a four-year college in two-and-a-half years. But once I am through with this business and we're married, she is going to once again be a big part of my life. I hope you don't object?"

"How could I object to living with Wonder Woman ... even though she will probably hate me because I am such a weakling!"

"She'll toughen you up."

"And is that what you would like ... for her to toughen me up?"

"No, I think you are perfect just the way you are," I said as I reached down and kissed her.

"Thank you, Nicky," she said as she rested her head on my chest. "I do need to be tougher. I don't want you to have to worry about me all the time."

"But I will worry about you all the time, whether you are tough or not. That's just part of being so in love with you. It's what married couples do."

"But your parents don't worry about each other, do they, Nicky?"

"No, but I don't think they were ever in love, or if they were, it was for a very brief moment in time. When my father would occasionally come home for a week or two it was like the house we lived in was partitioned … my mother and older sister on one side, and my baby sister and father on the other side and me somewhere in the middle, but leaning toward my baby sister. My parents didn't even sleep in the same room, and there were times I don't remember them exchanging more than a few words the whole time he was home … unless he felt the need to scold my mother for treating my baby sister too gingerly."

"That's so terrible, Nicky."

"My mother stopped talking to me nearly five years ago. Not a single word. She always knew that she had lost my baby sister to my father, but she had hoped she hadn't totally lost me to him also. She begged me not to go into the military or any government department, like the CIA, and when I did, she shut me out. Now, it's just her and my older sister, but at least they have a lot in common … my mother has been with enough men that she definitely qualifies as an unpaid prostitute … and my older sister is so in love with herself that even though she has had many boyfriends, none of them ever stick around. My baby sister and I always joked that once her boyfriends got her into bed and had sex with her, that was the end of the relationship. Even the most craven, sex-hungry guys couldn't stand listening to her talking about herself and always looking at her image in whatever mirror was closest. Once the relationship was consummated, it was over."

"That's disgusting. And your father allows this to go on?"

"He doesn't care, and he doesn't have any say. He gives them a healthy allowance each month and they're happy as hell, and he never has to talk to either of them. I doubt the man would shed a tear if anything happened to either one of them. He would just divert their allowances into the joint account he set up for my baby sister and me. I don't even know how many millions are in that account right now, but I'm certain there are many, many millions."

"And where does your baby sister live?"

"In her own house that my father bought for her when she graduated. It's a couple of hundred feet from the ocean. I cannot even imagine how much it costs. I imagine that the few times he makes it back to the States each year that he stays with her. You see … you are marrying into a very well-off family. Besides my baby sister, I doubt you will ever meet any of them, but it's probably better that way. If you ever did meet them that might give you real and significant reasons to divorce me."

"I would never divorce you. You are obviously nothing like them!"

"But I carry the same DNA as them. Aren't you a little bit worried that I might start exhibiting some of their traits?" I said jokingly.

"I don't understand," she replied.

"Don't worry. I'm just teasing. I'll never become like them. They're disgusting and you never have to worry about me or my baby sister turning into them."

"I know, Nicky," she said as she started unbuttoning my shirt and kissing my chest. She had come a long way, in a short time, after we broke down that first wall of resistance. Her initiating sex was as unlikely, just two days ago, as my older sister passing by a mirror and not stopping to admire herself.

After she finished undressing me, I was left with the pleasure of undressing her. Holding her and kissing her, I unzipped the back of her new dress and slipped it off her shoulders until it fell, a silky pool of fabric on the floor. I was so in love with her that for a time, I forgot all about that evil, decrepit freak, the professor, and about the fact that erasing him from the face of the earth was the last hurdle I had to overcome to be truly happy.

Chapter Thirty-Two

I woke up the following morning and walked into the living room to find Gabrielle sitting on the couch and looking at a French news channel. She was crying and as I looked at the screen I saw an incredibly grisly, partially obscured image of two headless bodies, tied in a seated position to the gates of the Israeli Embassy in Paris. Their heads were sitting in their laps, and across their chests were painted, in blood, the unbelievable words, "Dirty Jews."

"Oh my God," I said.

Gabrielle blew into a tissue and looked up at me, a pathetic mess of tears and fresh agony, piled on top of the mourning she had begun for Abdul the night before.

This horrific scene, staged so theatrically, was made to look like revenge killings for the death of Abdul. Two masked men are captured on surveillance footage from a nearby building. They're seen tying the bodies to the gates and then driving away in an unmarked car, with the only visible marking on the car being a sticker with the Islamic saying, "Allahu Akbar!" — Allah is great! — emblazoned on the bumper.

After consoling Gabrielle for a long time, I went down to see Mike. He let me into the suite, and told me he had already seen the French news. I asked him if he had been in contact with the woman he knew in the embassy and he replied, "Yes, the professor has plans to visit New York in three days with his regular body guards."

"You predicted his movements perfectly."

"It didn't take a genius to figure this one out. When dealing with a freak like him you bring your own food and silverware to the restaurant you are meeting at, and when you're meeting him in a warehouse, you wear a pair of gloves and don't shake hands."

"It says a lot about this bastard to be able to eliminate two Mossad agents so easily."

"They were compromised from the beginning … blinded by the money they were making, and at the same time trying to remain loyal to the Jewish state. Two conflicting interests is a lot to handle when dealing with a totally immoral and dangerous freak who easily picks up on the weaknesses of his enemies and spins them to his advantage."

"They squealed, just like you said."

"Yeah, well, I've heard the professor likes to use Agua Regia to get people to open up," said Mike.

"Royal water? I remember hearing about that stuff during training. Never encountered it in the field, thank God. That's hydrochloric acid and nitric acid, right?"

"Yup. It's one of the few acids that can dissolve noble metals like gold and platinum. Put a dab of that on the palm of someone's hand and see how long it takes him or her to speak up. Threaten to drop a dab into the eyes of the toughest Mossad agent, and see if he doesn't talk. Get Gabrielle to a safe place no later than tomorrow, and if by some chance you can keep from knowing the location, all the better."

"She'll be gone by tomorrow."

"Good! I know I joke about her, but believe me, I don't won't to see anything happen to her. What she went through as a child is horrible enough," he said, shaking his head.

"I wasn't sure *what* you made of that story," I said.

"Yeah, you stay too long in this business and you don't even see other people's suffering. If you'd have told me that story twenty years ago, it would have made me sick … twenty years later it barely registered and that's just not right." He opened the refrigerator and took out a beer. "I'll be flying back to France early tomorrow morning, and I should be back here early tomorrow night."

"That's going to be really tough on you."

"Not really, I'll be flying back first class and hopefully there'll be a nice-looking stewardess I can flirt with … otherwise I'll just sleep."

"What do I do while you're away?"

"Go out today and buy a laptop computer and set up a bogus account. After Gabrielle leaves tomorrow, search for a house to rent in a secluded area of Long Island … somewhere around Stony Brook … with a view of the seashore. If possible try not to go any further up than Port Jefferson, which is roughly the halfway point on the island. Tell the owners that you need to move in immediately, pay them six months' rent up front, in cash, and tell them to post on their website that the house has been rented for the next six months, to a newlywed couple that cherishes their privacy. Make sure the owner writes it out exactly like that. A newlywed couple that cherishes their privacy. Make him promise.

"Limit your search to four places, and put down the same information each time: married couple, no children, no pets, will pay the entire six months up front and in cash. No references, visiting from Italy. Phone … list one of your burner phones.

"But, you make the calls from different burner phones, immediately after filling out the information, and you make sure the calls go through to the agent in charge of the rental or to the actual people who own the home. Stress that you need to move in right away and that you're paying cash up front. If they say they can't accommodate an immediate move in, throw in an extra twenty thousand, as a bonus, if they can find a way to accommodate your clients. You can act as the couple's agent … that might take away some of their concerns."

"You will be living there with me?" I asked.

"No, I'll be camping out by the beach looking through a pair of binoculars like they do in the movies. Of course, I will be living there. I won't be going outside or standing by any windows, but I'll be there." He finished off his beer and opened another one. "Another thing, if you have time tomorrow, go into a camera shop that specializes in high-tech surveillance equipment and buy enough video and sound equipment to bug the entire house, and enough equipment to cover the entire outside, the street, and the beach. Tomorrow night, we will stay here at the hotel and the next day in the evening we'll go to our new home."

He sat down on the bed as he slowly sipped his beer and then he asked, "When you visited Dmitry, did he say anything about the professor?"

"He said that I had to be careful because the station chief in the embassy was dangerous and not to be trusted," I replied.

"Is that all?"

"Yes, why do you ask?"

"Just curious," he replied with a smile.

Chapter Thirty-Three

I opened the door to my suite to find Gabrielle sitting on the couch watching TV. I would have expected her to be glued to the news, but instead she was watching a Bugs Bunny cartoon that also featured Mr. Daffy Duck. I could not help thinking how nice it would be if I could just take Gabrielle by the hand and walk into the world of Bugs and Daffy. Their world seemed so much saner and more rational than the one I was presently living in. I sat on the couch and lay down with my head resting on Gabrielle's lap. She smelled so clean and pure and as she ran her fingers through my hair I closed my eyes and listened to the wonderful antics coming from the television, occasionally catching a giggle from Gabrielle.

I fell asleep as Abdul's disembodied head came floating toward me whispering, "I loved you like a brother. I loved you like a brother." I woke up in a sweat and looked up at Gabrielle who said, "It's okay, Nicky. It's okay."

I lifted my head up off her lap and asked, "How long was I asleep?"

"Just a few minutes," she replied as I looked at the television and saw the cartoons still playing. I walked into the bedroom and took a burner phone out of my backpack. I then walked into the bathroom, closed the door, and turned on the shower.

I called my baby sister, Athena, who was given that name by my father. I'd been told that her naming was one of the few occasions when my mother had the courage to stand up to him and disagree, before she simply bowed to his wish. Athena, in Greek mythology, is the goddess of wisdom, war strategy, and arts and crafts. She is often shown bearing a shield depicting the gorgon Medusa, which was given to her by her father Zeus.

My baby sister is gorgeous. She has long, dark wavy hair with a dark olive complexion, long eyelashes and mysterious, brown eyes. She suits her name perfectly in that she looks like a warrior, whether she's sitting in a wheelchair, walking on crutches, or simply sitting at the dinner table in a regular chair. If she and Gabrielle entered a room filled with men she would garner the attention of seventy-five percent of the men. Whereas Gabrielle looks like Audrey Hepburn, Athena looks like Hedy Lamarr. I have not agreed with my father on many things, but when it came to picking a name for my sister, he was right on the mark.

As much as I hated to admit it, I knew that she and Mike would make a handsome and compatible couple. The only problem would be that if he ever cheated on her, she would snap his neck and dispose of his body like a piece of trash without giving it a second thought, and there would go my best and most trusted friend.

My sister picked up the phone and I said, "Hey, Nick here. I need you to pick up my fiancée, Gabrielle, at four o'clock tomorrow morning at the corner of 46th Street and Second Ave. Take her to a *safe* place, and please, try not to kill her."

"I will do my best," she replied.

"I also need two-hundred thousand in cash."

"Okay!"

"I'll see you tomorrow. Love you."

"Love you, too."

She hung up, and I took the burner phone and smashed it to pieces.

I walked out of the bathroom and back into the living room. Gabrielle was still sitting on the couch watching cartoons. I sat down beside her and lowered the volume on the television.

"I just talked to my baby sister and she will be here at four o'clock in morning. She's going to take you to a safe place and stay with you. Neither Mike nor I will know the location, so it will be useless to even ask my sister where we are or how you can get in touch with us. You are not to make any phone calls. If you even try to she will break both your hands without blinking an eye."

"And how long do you think it will take?" Gabrielle asked.

"I have no idea, but in a case like this, no news is good news."

"So I am in the dark, as usual?"

"You put yourself in this situation, Gabrielle … if you hadn't called David and Elijah to tell them about Abdul, he would be alive and you wouldn't be in danger right now."

Gabrielle chewed on that idea for a moment before speaking. "And we never would have met, and you wouldn't have a hopeless child to worry about and complicate things."

"Now, you are just being stupid. Life does not go in a straight line. There are twists and turns, and after all is straightened out we will come out stronger for it. The past can either be your tutor or your poison. It's your choice."

"And is that supposed to make up for all the people who have been killed?"

"Neither you or I, are responsible for their deaths. I feel terrible about Abdul, but he chose to build those devices and get involved with the wrong people, and as for David and Elijah, the real possibility of getting killed is part of the profession they chose to be in."

"The same profession that you and Mike are in?"

"Yes, but neither of us is corrupt. That complicated their situation and compromised their mission and the allegiance they swore to their country."

"So I shouldn't feel sorry for them?" she asked with a touch of disgust.

"You can feel sorry for whoever you like, but don't expect any pity from my sister. She will protect you better than anybody I know, but if she feels that you might be compromising the lives of others, including Mike's or mine or hers, she will shut you down."

"I don't know what I will do if anything happens to you. I feel lost when you're away from me for even a few hours. I'm like a nomad wandering the desert, slowly burning to death beneath a merciless sun. I'm so lost, Nicky. So Lost!"

I took her hand and softly caressed the skin. I did not have time to be sentimental. I needed to stay focused on what had to be done. Mike and I were dealing with a psychopath who made mincemeat out of two veteran Mossad agents, and who was probably right now sitting in his office at the embassy, glowing at his handiwork as he looked at the news and read the newspapers. He was a creature without morals, a deformed, twisted genius with a superiority complex. You could rest assured that nothing would distract him from tying up this last loose end.

I got up from the couch and kissed Gabrielle and said, "I need to go out and pick up some things. Under no circumstances are you to open the door, or answer the phone." I handed her a burner phone. "If I need to get in touch with you this phone will ring. If you need to get in touch with me simply hit the enter button. The phone is programed to call me and no one else. Do you understand?"

"Yes. Please be careful," she replied as I smiled, opened the door, and left the suite.

Chapter Thirty-Four

I stepped off the elevator and walked through the lobby and out the door of the hotel. I could not get over that familiar feeling that I was being followed. It had started in Paris, and it had turned out to be true. David and Elijah had been following me from the moment I stepped foot on French soil, and when they finally pulled me into their car, it did not come as a surprise.

CIA operatives are trained to be alert and suspicious, especially when on an assignment. But here in New York, it was different. That depraved freak, the professor, had got into my head, and like a paranoid schizophrenic, I was sure that everyone coming toward me, or walking behind me, was a potential lethal threat. Such irrational thoughts can easily transform a superb operative into a dangerous threat to himself, and believe me, I was not a superb operative. Mike was not wrong, or kidding, when he called me naive at best, and Dmitry had warned me numerous times that this was not a game I belonged in, even saying that "the priesthood was better-suited to my talents" than the CIA.

I had made plenty of mistakes in Paris, none bigger than falling head over heels in love with the source's sister ... a woman who on her best day was irrational and who could use the help of a psychotherapist. She had been drawn to me because she said she didn't see "lust in my eyes," a fact that distinguished me from "all the other pigs" in Paris who looked at her like she was a snack. I hated to admit it, but she would have been better off if she did see lust in my eyes. She would certainly be safer. David and Elijah must have been shocked at how well she performed. They said she was good at pretending, but her performance on the stairs of the university and the first times we went out to eat were deserving of an Emmy and an Academy Award. Sometimes behaving like a gentleman could seriously backfire on you. If I had made any type of inappropriate sexual advances toward her, she would have peed her pants and run home to mommy and daddy. Instead, she initiated the encounter between us, totally clueless to the gravity of the situation. When I won her trust, I became totally responsible for her.

As I wove through foot traffic, convinced I was surrounded by assassins, it occurred to me that if anything were to happen to Gabrielle and I survived, I would never recover. That would be the thing that finally drove me crazy in a literal sense. I had escaped that fate in Afghanistan with Dmitry's help, but I might not be so lucky this time, and the stakes were even higher now than they were then. All that mattered now was protecting Gabrielle's life and safety, even if it meant sacrificing my own.

I walked toward Times Square where I knew there were plenty of electronics stores. It wasn't like I was bargain hunting, and getting ripped off was the least of my worries. Thanks to the old man, money was not an issue. If Athena had no problem with the money Daddy was throwing our way, I wasn't about to complain. But then, Athena probably knew a lot more about his activities than I did, or ever would. As I surveyed the businesses looking for just the right electronics store, I thought about how badly things could go for Gabrielle in her meeting with Athena. At a minimum, Gabrielle was in for a real shock … whereas she was able to use her charms on me and elicit my sympathy, that would not work with my baby sister. Athena did not play hostess to pity parties or tantrums, and she was not about to clean up anybody's vomit, if it ever came to that. If Gabrielle started acting up, my baby sister would have her outside digging ditches and every time she let out a sigh my sister would send the butt of a rifle across her butt.

Times Square had changed quite a bit since the last time I was here, about seven years ago. There were waves and waves of beautiful, blonde-haired teenagers and young women. It was like the place had been invaded by the Netherlands, and even I had a problem imagining that any of them posed a lethal threat. I walked into the first electronics store I came across and was greeted by an Arabic gentleman in his late twenties. I asked him if he carried any surveillance equipment.

"Yes, the very latest," he replied as he smiled and brought me over to an aisle and showed me equipment that the CIA stopped using thirty years ago.

I stopped him before he went into his spiel. "No, the very latest," I said as he turned to another gentleman who I imagine was his supervisor and said, in Arabic, that I was looking for the very latest surveillance equipment.

The supervisor looked at me and I spoke to him in Arabic, repeating exactly what the other employee had said, but adding, also in fluent Arabic, that what he had shown me already was about a generation out of date.

"You speak Arabic?" the supervisor asked.

"Yemen, special forces," I said.

He smiled as I followed him down a flight of stairs and into the basement. He turned on a light and there before us were the latest gadgets in high-tech surveillance ... including one that had just been introduced to agents at the CIA that fall. He said, "Expensive."

"Yes, I know." I went through Mike's list in my head and said, "I need enough outdoor surveillance, the least detectable kind you have, to cover every room of a ten-thousand-square-foot house and at least an acre around on all four sides."

He nodded and opened a case full of small devices, including cameras and microphones. "These are our smallest and best items. They're tiny, easy to install, and can be placed in plants, a water hose, a crack in the foundation of the house," he said. "A trained spy would have difficulty detecting such devices."

"Is it enough to cover the area I mentioned?" I asked

"Yes," he replied.

I then went through the entire list of what I needed for the interior of the house, including listening devices, audio and video recorders, and cameras. He had it all, and I told him to add a regular laptop computer to the order and two duffel bags for Gabrielle's clothes. I had him add up the entire transaction in the basement and I paid him in cash that I got out of my own account and with the codes I gave to Gabrielle. He remarked, "Yemen is a very dangerous place."

"Yes, but not nearly as dangerous as my next assignment." He ordered a taxi for me, and I had the driver drop me off two blocks from the hotel. I walked the rest of the way. I doubt the entire order weighed more than fifteen pounds.

Chapter Thirty-Five

I walked into the suite and looked across at Gabrielle who was sitting cross-legged on the couch right where I left her. She was perched there like a statue, staring at some American soap opera. I put my bag down and sat down beside her, but she didn't acknowledge me, so I grasped her by the hips and physically rotated her until we were facing each other.

"What," she said blankly.

"Everything is going to be okay."

"If you say so, Nicky," she replied in the same robotic tone. She scooched back around and fixed her eyes on the television.

"Are you just going to sit here all day?"

"Yes, I am trying not to think … otherwise I might scream and throw myself off the balcony."

"Stop talking stupid."

"I'm not talking stupid. If anything happens to you it will be my fault and I will kill myself … or even better I will have your sister kill me. It would be only right that she should get a measure of revenge against me for getting her brother killed, because I am so stupid." Switching to French, she said, "I am stupid, stupid, stupid, and I deserve to die."

I grabbed her by the arm, then let go. "Gabrielle, Jesus—"

"You can't deny any of it," she said, still not meeting my eyes.

"I can and I do deny all of it," I said. "Please don't ever say that you are stupid because you're not. And I have no intention of getting killed but I do have every intention of marrying the most gorgeous girl in the world and living happily ever after."

She buried her face in her hands for a long moment while I rested my hand on her back and just let it sit there. When she finally surfaced, her face was streaked with tears, but she was looking at me again. She ran her hand along the contours of my face and said, "You are so sweet and kind, Nicky. I don't know how someone like you could be part of this terrible world."

"This world is not so terrible, and after we are all settled in we are going to visit every place you have ever wanted to see."

"You promise?" she asked with a girlish charm.

"I promise ... starting with the Lincoln Memorial and the Statue of Liberty."

We held each other on the couch in silence, until it was time to get down to work. Gabrielle packed all of her clothes and essentials into the two duffel bags I bought at the electronics store. She asked me if she could borrow some money because she didn't have any and she felt strange having to totally rely on my sister. The request was kind of funny, but I passed on joking about it because she didn't always pick up on humor when I spoke in English and I didn't want to confuse and worry her any more than she already was. I gave her two thousand dollars and told her if she needed more to borrow it from of my sister and I would pay her back.

As I watched her pack, I was reminded of what the Mossad twins said about her — that she was "no warrior, but a fragile flower," and I knew they were right. The little bouts of indecision about what to bring and what to leave behind, the time she took to fold and refold a couple of items, all pointed to a nervous system that had been pushed to the brink and would probably be slowly recovering for decades to come, if not for the rest of her life. Gabrielle was vulnerable and soft. She was someone who needed protection. I feared for her, and I knew she needed all of the help that I was lining up for her, and some luck besides. Someone so damaged by her own history could not be expected to fight for her own survival, or at least not alone. She would need Athena, and I had no doubt that if anyone could keep Gabrielle safe, it was my sister.

After she finished packing, she came and sat on my lap and threw her arms around my neck and smiled. I asked, "Has anyone ever told you that you have the most beautiful dimples?"

"Yes, you and my maman et papa." She leaned in and we kissed.

"And has anyone ever told you that you have the softest and loveliest lips?"

"Yes, you."

I ran my finger along her lips and asked, "And only me."

"Yes. You are the only man I have ever kissed, but I am sure I am not the only woman you have kissed."

"No, but you are the only woman I intend to kiss from now and forever."

We kissed passionately and then we made love.

Chapter Thirty-Six

I woke up at around one in the morning and quietly got up from bed so as not to disturb Gabrielle, who was still asleep. Gabrielle when awake and smiling could pass for a carefree, lovely princess that one read about in fairy tales, but when asleep a true and defining picture of Gabrielle was revealed. She often trembled terribly when she slept, as though someone was poking her with a red-hot poker, occasionally letting out a scream that one might hear from a drowning person going down for the third time. I never mentioned any of this to her and when she did wake up in a panic I just gently wrapped my arms around her and said, "Everything is okay. I love you so much." She would then smile and fall back to sleep with her head resting on my chest.

I took one last look at Gabrielle and then I walked into the living room. She was reason enough to want to stay alive and put an end to this ugly business.

I have always loved my country. Of course I never had much of a choice, considering who my father is, but I seriously did love everything the United States stood for and its amazing history. My father, for all his shortcomings, is at least an educated man. He graduated college and even has a couple of postgraduate degrees. Throughout his military career, he taught at a number of the military academies for a semester or two, and despite what one might think, he believed that the humanities, especially literature, were essential for making of a good soldier and commander of troops.

He loved authors like Conrad, Dos Passos, Hemingway, and Tolstoy, and like the late Senator John McCain, his favorite book was Hemingway's *For Whom the Bell Tolls*. When at home, when not roughhousing with Athena — and to a lesser extent with his not so masculine son — he would read. Before departing, he would always leave five or six books on the edge of his desk in his study that he expected Athena and me to read. At first, they were mostly American history books. He was exceptionally fond of the Revolutionary period and men like Hamilton, Nathanael Greene, and Washington. After a healthy dose of history, he started leaving novels and books of poetry. At first, I was taken aback. My father, the old soldier, wanted us to read a bunch of sonnets? Surely he must be kidding. But we did as we were asked to do, and after spending time with his selections from Dante, Byron, Tennyson, and Yeats, it became clear that poetry was a route to understanding the dark side of humanity. He wanted us to have a working knowledge of the how the greatest poetic minds in history processed human history and experience.

Naturally, Athena read all the books he left behind three or four times, whereas I was just happy to get through them once, and so after he came home from his trips it was always my lovely sister who excelled at the pop quizzes he gave us, while I was a miserable failure. Athena would try to stand up for me by telling our father that I had read all the books he left behind, but in a strange way, that backfired. He would reply, "Well, apparently he doesn't possess the brain power of his baby sister." No denying it, the man was an inspiration and a role model.

I sat down at the table in the living room and wrote Athena a letter. A written letter, handed personally to the intended recipient, was the safest way to pass information. Emails, texts, and phone calls could always be intercepted, regardless of how many precautions you took.

I laid it all out for Athena … the entire situation I encountered in Paris, my friendship with the source, Abdul; the manufacture of the wallet size bombs and the fact that they were being shipped to Crimea and smuggled into Ukraine in the hope of causing unrest and upheaval; the role of the Mossad agents; the role of the man they called the professor; the CIA station chief in the Paris embassy; the torture and beheading of Abdul and the Mossad agents by the nefarious professor; and *me* being the final link … the last person … to know of the entire operation, and now being the target of the professor, who in a couple of days would be heading to New York to get rid of me. I told her of a house that Mike and I were looking to rent on a secluded stretch of Long Island's shoreline, with the hope of luring the professor and his bodyguards to the house where we would assassinate them. I explained the dangers we all faced. I told her about Gabrielle and about her having been raped by four terrorists when she was only ten years old, and about the scars and burns on her body. I gave her enough details to figure out where the rented house was, and when the professor and his minions were likely to show up. I told her that no one in top leadership positions in our government, especially the CIA director and the people around the president, could be trusted. That there was a good chance they had all been compromised by the Russians.

Mike had warned me not to get Athena involved, but what Mike didn't know was that my baby sister was extremely deadly and was a sharpshooter who could easily kill a target from five hundred yards away. Mike wanted to get a confession out of the professor, but I was hoping to eliminate the professor and his sycophants with one shot each to the head from long distance.

Chapter Thirty-Seven

Gabrielle and I took the elevator down to the lobby and exited the hotel, then walked along Lexington Avenue to 49th Street and headed toward Second Avenue. I carried one duffel bag and Gabrielle insisted on carrying the other bag. We turned right onto Second Avenue at 49th Street and kept going until I spotted Athena's black SUV parked on 46th Street.

I put the duffel bags in the back of the car and then opened the passenger's side door for Gabrielle, who slid into her seat. I walked over to the driver's side window and leaned in and kissed my sister on the cheek and said, "You're more beautiful than ever."

"Yeah! Yeah! Yeah! And you look shittier than ever."

I introduced her to Gabrielle and I could immediately tell that my sister intimidated her. Athena was wearing a shoulder-length holster and carrying a Magnum Desert Eagle .50 caliber piece — the type of handgun that could literally blow your head off.

I handed my sister the letter and asked, "Have you talked to Daddy?"

"Yes, he asked about you and I told him everything I knew." She handed me a manila envelope with the two hundred thousand in cash.

I slowly nodded my head as I looked across at Gabrielle and said, "I love you. And don't forget: no crying."

"And why not? You'll be crying once we drive off," Athena remarked.

I kissed my sister on the head and whispered, "I love you so much, and once this is over I am coming home for good."

"I know, and I love you so much." She drove off as I stood on the sidewalk and watched the two most important women in my life turn the corner and disappear. I started walking back to the hotel. The streets were relatively empty at this time and a cool breeze greeted me as I turned right on 48th Street. I once again had that feeling that someone was watching me … that motherfucker was inside my head, and the quicker I eliminated him the better.

Mike was already off to France, and I couldn't help feeling that his main objective was not simply to kill the professor but to get even with the agency that fucked him over. Mike and my sister were so much alike that it was scary … a job wasn't complete until all the dirt and slime that had infected the sanctuary of their mission was wiped clean, and they would go to great lengths to make sure that was the case.

I walked into the hotel and walked into a small bakery in the lobby that had just opened. I bought two heated bagels with cream cheese and a large coffee and then took the elevator up and walked into my suite. I placed the money in my backpack and then sat down at the small table with my food and coffee. I turned on the laptop and immediately started leaving breadcrumbs for the professor to eventually pick up on.

I picked a username that the average person would probably never figure out, but that someone like the professor, an experienced spy, would recognize, and feel clever deciphering. It was cryptic enough to appeal to his vanity as an expert at deciphering code. USERNAME: *hb76jjay89*. The *hb76*, short for George Herbert Walter Bush, director of the CIA in 1976, and *jjay89*, short for John Jay, first Chief Justice of the United States starting in 1789.

I then browsed through two French newspapers, *Le Monde* and *Le Figaro*, for the previous week, and the Jerusalem English language newspaper, *The Jerusalem Post*.

I then searched for beach houses on Long Island that offered a six-month lease, furnished, privacy, and immediate occupancy, and to my surprise a whole bunch showed up. I looked at four houses, and even went on Google Maps to check out the immediate vicinity of each one. I decided on a house, just below Stony Brook, with its own private beach and what passes for wilderness on each side. The house was renting for $12,000 a month with a six-month lease. At about eight o'clock, I called up the agent representing the property and told him I was very interested, and he naturally said that at present they were looking at two other offers but would be glad to also take a look at my offer. I told him that I would give him $15,000 a month, ninety thousand up front in cash, and ten thousand in cash on the side for him if he could get it done today. I told him I was representing an Italian couple, royalty, who just got married and wanted to immediately move in, that money was not a problem, and that they had no kids and no pets.

We agreed to meet at the property at one o'clock and he would bring along all the documents and contracts I had to sign. When he asked for references, I told him they were friends of the Pope. I gave him the phone number to a burner phone.

I called up a limousine service, using the same burner phone and number that I gave the agent, and told them I needed a limo and a driver for the day and to pick me up at ten o'clock at the hotel. I wanted to get there in plenty of time to check out the area before the agent showed up.

I left a hundred thousand dollars in the envelope that Athena gave me and stuffed another ten thousand in my wallet. I put the left over ninety thousand in the safe that was in the suite. I put my gun in its holster and covered it up with a sports coat that I put on over my shirt. I looked around the bedroom and could still smell the subtle scent of the little bit of perfume Gabrielle wore. It seemed to radiate through my body like an electric shock. I left the suite and took the elevator down to the lobby.

Chapter Thirty-Eight

I got into the back seat of the limo, a small limo that seats between six and eight passengers, and reached over and handed the driver the address of the house, along with a two hundred dollar tip upfront and a promise of more to come. The driver, Andres, was in his late twenties and said he knew the area really well. He had graduated from Stony Brook University a few years earlier and was currently pursuing his master's degree in English literature at NYU right here in the city. He said that working as a limo driver was great because he loved to drive and made good enough money that he didn't have to take out any student loans.

He turned onto the Long Island Expressway (I-495) and took it straight up to exit 58 where he got off, a few exits down from the university. He drove south and turned onto a street that ran parallel to the beach. The area was very upscale, quiet, and picturesque. He stopped before the house I was hoping to rent and from the outside it looked perfect. It was modest in size, with two storeys, and probably perfect for a family of five, or in this case a family of two. It was set about a hundred and fifty feet back from the street, and on both sides a small forest provided extra privacy. The beach was no further than two hundred feet from the back entrance, and the driveway curved all the way around to the back of the house so guests could park their cars and walk straight down to the beach. It was perfect!

I had Andres drive around the area a number of times, and I don't know if we saw a dozen people walking around. The house was on a long street, which made surveillance fairly easy. Individuals doing reconnaissance could easily park four or five houses down and still get a good view of the front of the house, and that is exactly what Mike and I wanted. We wanted the professor to know that I was living there, and to monitor my day-to-day routine.

The renting agent called my burner phone at ten minutes to one and said he would be at the house in just a few minutes. I had Andres park a few houses down, and I got out of the limo, holding the manila envelope with the money. I walked over to the agent, who had just stepped out of his car and was waiting out front. He was a young guy, early thirties, and well dressed. I shook his hand and we entered the house for a tour. At about three thousand square feet, the house was big, but not the type of place one could get lost in. There were three bedrooms and two bathrooms on the top floor and one bedroom and one bathroom downstairs. The kitchen was large and so was the dining area. It also had plenty of windows. This was not necessarily a good thing, but apart from one large bay window in the living room, they all had plantation shutters that one could easily close. On the plus side, it was the type of house that one could easily *bug*, especially since it was filled with overhanging chandeliers, nooks and crannies, and high ceilings.

We walked outside and down to the beach. It was a beautiful day, and the ocean was calm, and as I looked out across the water the only thing I could think of was blowing the professor's motherfucking head off. Dmitry would be proud!

We walked back into the house and sat down at the dining table. The agent handed me a short stack of papers to read and sign, and I handed him ninety thousand in cash to cover the rent, and an additional ten thousand for himself. He gave me two identical key chains with the same six keys on each chain. The keys were labeled, which made it easy.

He remarked, "I have never done a transaction like this before."

"There's always a first," I replied.

"This couple … they really like their privacy."

"Yes, sometimes the spotlight gets a little too bright, and you just need to disappear."

He nodded his head and then I remarked, "Don't forget to take the house immediately off the market."

"It'll be the first thing I do when I go back to the office right now. Don't want to be carrying this amount of cash around."

"No, you don't … at least not without an armed bodyguard." I folded the copy of the papers I had signed and put them into the inside pocket of my jacket. I slipped the keys into my pants pocket.

We walked out of the house, shook hands, and then I walked back to the limo and slid into the back seat.

"So how did it go?" Andres asked.

"It's a nice house, but a little too small, and they're asking way too much for it."

I had Andres drop me off at a deli where I picked up roast beef heroes for both of us, and a couple of sodas. We ate in the limo. I tried as much as possible not to have him seen with me. It was amazing how many innocent people, taxi drivers, bartenders, girlfriends, and hookers, turned into collateral damage just because they were seen with a target … often tortured and then killed just on the off chance they could provide information. Life was cheap and morals were too often thrown to the wind in the world of espionage.

I knew all this and yet I still got involved with Gabrielle. Yes, she informed on her brother to the Mossad twins, but as it turned out they were ten miles ahead of her when it came to Abdul. I made her a potential target because I didn't have the willpower to resist her charms and beauty.

The Mossad twins used Gabrielle to distract me, and I took it a step further and threw her smack into the ring. It was an unpardonable sin, and if anything were to happen to her and I was still alive, I could never forgive myself.

We finished our sandwiches and Andres turned back onto the Long Island Expressway and headed back to the city. He told me that after he got his master's degree he intended to go for his PhD and hopefully get a job in a college or university teaching literature and at the same time finish writing the novel he was working on. I asked him what his novel was about and he replied, "About a girl I am in love with, and because of my insane jealousy, I lost." He laughed, "What else? Always girls."

"You said you were still in love."

"She is the girl of my dreams, and I doubt a day in my life will go by in which I don't think of her."

"Do you know if she has moved on … meaning, do you know if she has a steady boyfriend, or got married and had children?"

He laughed and shook his head, "I don't know about any boyfriend or husband but I'm fairly certain she doesn't have any children. She was career oriented, and she made it abundantly clear that children were a long way off."

"And how long ago did you two break up?"

"Three years ago."

"With all those uncertainties and if she is the girl of your dreams, I would try to track her down, accidently bump into her at a place where she might be working and start up a casual conversation and see where it goes from there. Three years is a fairly long time in a young couple's life. You be surprised what compromises might suddenly be available that seemed totally out of reach when you broke up. What is her name?"

"Selma," he replied.

"Selma," I repeated and continued, "That's of German origin, and if am not mistaken, means, *Godly Helmet.*"

Andres parked in front of the hotel and I paid him what I owed him for the ride and gave him an extra five-hundred-dollar tip. In the last few days, I had thrown around more money than I had spent in my entire life. I might be dead in a day or two, and since you can't take it with you, why not give it to a kid who I was certain had a bright future ahead of him?

As I was getting out of the limo, Andres asked me, "What's your favorite novel?"

I thought about it for a few moments and then replied, "Conrad's *Heart of Darkness*, followed by Hemingway's *For Whom the Bell Tolls*."

"You have amazing taste."

"I have my father to thank for that. He is a man of many faults, but his love and appreciation for great literature is one of the few good things he passed along to his children."

Andres handed me his business card, we shook hands, and he drove off as I walked into the hotel. I looked down at his card, and tore it up and threw it into the trash. You'd be surprised at the type of information one might get off a dead body and how far a freak like the professor might go to be sure he had left nothing to chance.

Chapter Thirty-Nine

I walked into the suite, took off my sports coat with the rental papers in the pocket and put the keys next to the laptop, along with my gun. I opened a beer and drank it down in a couple of gulps. I wasn't expecting Mike back for a number of hours. I took a walk around the suite to make sure that nothing was disturbed while I was gone. I then opened another beer, turned on the computer, and started leaving more bread crumbs. The biggest one I left was a search of the Paris embassy website. I clicked around for several minutes, making sure to open a few security updates and other news items, knowing that the professor would track my search history.

I then picked up my gun and walked back into the bedroom. I put the gun on the nightstand by the bed and lay down. Gabrielle's scent was everywhere and in my head I could hear her lovely French accent, and see her beautiful face with those adorable dimples when she smiled.

I fell asleep, and Gabrielle's face and voice were replaced with the floating head of Abdul, who was repeating the words, "I love you like a brother. I love you like a brother."

I woke up in a sweat, and looked down at my gun. It wasn't the first time I had contemplated the unthinkable. It had only been a few days, but I couldn't help wondering if I would ever know what it felt like again to close my eyes and sleep peacefully. I had seen plenty of death in Afghanistan, but it was always through the eyes of an analyst … looking at photos, walking through regions of a recent firefight where the bodies of soldiers were still being carried off. I had never been in any type of situation where I had to fire a gun in self-defense. I could not even begin to imagine the traumatic effects on the soldiers fighting on the border alongside Pakistan where the fighting was the most intense, and where the enemy was allowed to simply jump over the border and we couldn't do anything about it but stand down. Was it any wonder that the suicide rate was so high for returning soldiers? There wasn't enough medication in the world to alleviate all of the mental stress they endured, and there were so few doctors or psychiatrists with wartime experience that could treat and sympathize with and truly understand the traumatic aftereffects these soldiers were feeling.

I felt helpless, and I had not been through anything like what they had experienced. I couldn't talk to anyone about how I was feeling … my fiancée trembled when she slept, and Mike would just shake his head and say, "It will pass with time." My mother wasn't speaking to me, and my older sister didn't know the meaning of empathy, not that I would ever confide in either of them. Athena had always been the one I could turn to, but I could even sense a change in her … or maybe I was just imagining it? I don't know anymore, but it was like my father's influence over her was complete. The man finally had what he always wanted from at least one of his children, a clone of himself in the form of my baby sister. She was fearless and dangerous, and whereas I knew she would do anything for me and that I could always count on her, I wasn't sure how far our loving father had compromised her moral compass.

For all that I knew, Gabrielle might have been safer staying with me and taking on the professor. A few days of her whining and complaining, and Athena might actually kill her. I could see it now: "Athena, where's Gabrielle?"

"She's gone, get over it."

"What do you mean by she's gone?"

"You know, gone … singing with the angels."

"You literally got rid of her?"

"Yeah, you can thank me later. My God, Nicky, if you can't do better than that snivelling mess, you really are as pathetic as Dad says you are."

***

I walked into the living room and took out another beer and downed it in two gulps. This was a habit I had picked up from Mike. I quickly opened another. I wasn't thinking rationally. Being alone could be an operative's best friend, giving him time to think clearly, or it could be his worst friend … giving his mind time to shift to probabilities and to dangers that did not exist. I think I was stuck somewhere in the middle. Thinking my baby sister could literally kill Gabrielle was way out there … locking her in a closet with a bucket for a toilet and passing food under the door was a lot more probable.

The burner phone that Mike used to call me beeped. I checked it and found a text from him saying he would be there in ten minutes and asking if I needed him to pick up any food. I texted back and told him yes, and that there was a deli in the hotel lobby.

We could have ordered room service, but I didn't want anyone near us who didn't absolutely need to be around. This was not like the movies, where actors playing waiters and maids were collateral damage, and after the director called *cut* they were able to get up and walk away. In Afghanistan innocent bystanders were being killed all the time. They could be eating in a café or shopping in the market and get hit by crossfire. It didn't matter to the Taliban or other terrorist groups how many innocent lives were lost, as long as they struck their target.

The only time it mattered was when Americans killed innocent civilians, or when Americans were used as scapegoats and guinea pigs to further the nefarious ends of the corrupt government in Kabul. Mike was used as a scapegoat, and we had all the intelligence, communications, and information about his whereabouts at the time the civilians were killed. He was nowhere near the scene, and did not have the fire power to hit a target that far away, and yet our embassy chief, the military, and our spineless government were willing to ignore the facts just to keep the Kabul leadership content.

Mike had been out for revenge ever since then, and little did I know that I would be the one to give him the opportunity he'd been waiting for. Moreover, Mike wasn't the type of guy who believed in *tit for tat*. The type of revenge he would seek would be ten times worse than what they did to him.

I was pondering how bad this could get when Mike gave his signature knock on the door: two quick taps and a beat, followed by a third tap. I checked the spyhole to be sure it was him, then opened the door and in he came, carrying a large duffel bag and a deli bag with the sandwiches. He had brought along surveillance monitors as small as cell phones and iPads that would send off a signal anytime someone or something was in the vicinity of the house or property. You simply touched a button, and the intruder's image, vehicle, and location would immediately show up. If multiple intruders were on the property and coming at you from different directions it would split off into multiple screens and you would see the intruders' images, their locations, and how they were coming at you. It allowed you the freedom to move around without being stuck in a room looking at a bunch of monitors the size of small televisions.

I could tell from the moment that Mike walked into the room that he had been using, and since he was not one to hide or deny a guilty pleasure, he threw a bag of cocaine on the table and said, "Help yourself."

"I think I'll pass."

"We're not going to be leaving this room until late tomorrow afternoon. If you can't get straight by then you're a bigger pussy than I thought."

And like the pussy I am, I took a number of hits of the cocaine.

"Gabrielle gone?" Mike asked.

"Yeah, I had my sister take her away."

Mike came at me like a bull and I was certain a punch to the face or stomach was coming my way, but he stopped short and yelled, "After everything I told you, you still go out and get her involved. What type of idiot are you?"

"She's the only one I could trust."

"Don't give me that shit! There's numerous locations you could have sent her off to where she would be safe."

"My sister is as dangerous and smart as anyone I have ever known. Do you really think I would jeopardize her safety if I didn't think she could handle it?"

"If anything happens to her, I swear to the Almighty that I will kill you."

"If anything happened to her and I was alive I would kill myself and save you the trouble. I don't understand, what is this fascination with my sister? You don't even know what she looks like."

"She looks like a warrior Goddess."

"How do you know that?"

"Because you showed me a picture of her at the embassy a couple of years back when we were partying. She has a face you never forget and her eyes and her hair ... my God, she's perfect. In a wheelchair or on crutches, I'm quite sure she could take you down in thirty seconds."

"Probably ten; you in thirty."

"Even more perfect. I swear, I can't believe you two come from the same parents. Are you sure you're not the bastard son of one of your father's dalliances?"

"One can never be sure ... maybe after all this is over I'll take a DNA test."

"It would explain a lot," he replied with a laugh.

"Hey, who knows? Maybe this week or so Gabrielle spends with my sister might toughen her up."

"That would be miracle. I mean, don't get me wrong; I am very happy you found the girl of your dreams. She's petite, cute, and helpless. You make a perfect couple."

"Seriously, that's how you see her?"

"Okay, let me rephrase … She's petite, very pretty, and utterly helpless. Is that better?"

"Yeah, I personally think she's gorgeous and not quite as helpless as you think."

"Of course you do. Maybe after all this is all over, you can have Daddy buy you a small island where the two of you could go live and feed each other grapes all day and night."

I handed Mike a beer as he snorted a few lines of coke and said, "Not bad, but not nearly as good as the stuff your friend got you."

I shook my head and Mike asked, "What's wrong?"

"Just before you got in touch with me, I took a nap and I had a dream about Abdul … the same dream I have been having for the last few days."

"Oh, the guilt dream," Mike said, laughing and snorting another line. "A classic. Lemme guess. He's coming at you, dragging chains…"

"No chains, but it's a pretty fucking horrible dream." I drew my finger across my throat and waved my hands beside my ears. Mike just stared at me and laughed once more, but quieter.

"It'll pass," he said. "You did the best you could to save him … so get over it." I sat for a moment and thought about that. There was nothing else to say. Abdul was history and Mike was right. I needed to move on.

"Did you talk to your girl in the embassy?" I asked.

"Yeah, nothing has changed. The freak, and his entourage of assistant freaks, is still planning on leaving in another two days."

"How big is the entourage?"

"Three or four. It was unrealistic to think that someone as physically deformed as him would have only one bodyguard. No big deal, just a few extra scumbags that will be erased from the planet, and I don't want to hear any shit. I don't care if one of them is still alive and begging to be spared; he still gets a bullet to his head. That's a lot kinder than the way their boss treats his captives before beheading them."

"I understand," I said, as I snorted two big lines of coke and downed a beer. Suddenly, my appetite was gone and those sandwiches

Mike bought us were an afterthought. No better appetite suppressant than cocaine.

"So, how was the flight over? Any good-looking stewardesses to tease, flirt, and mess around with?"

"A few good-looking ones, but they were more your type. One actually spilled a drink on the passenger sitting across from me."

"So, no wild sex in the bathroom of the plane?"

"I would have to go without sex as long as you do before I would even think of having sex in a bathroom on a commercial plane."

"And what makes you an expert on my sex life?"

"The fact that I spent two years working with you in Kabul and you were the only single guy I know of who did not have sex at least once with a female employee of the agency or embassy."

"It was against regulations," I said, and he laughed.

"In a war zone those regulations don't apply. For God's sake, in Switzerland they don't apply … never mind a war zone. A few of the girls asked me if you were gay."

"You're joking, right?"

"Yes, I'm joking. You're an amazing piece of work. You refuse to get involved with any of the girls working in the embassy, and there were a few hot ones, or any of the Afghan girls attending the university, and there were plenty of hot, non-religious ones who were as horny as fifty-year-old virgins, and yet at the drop of a hat you start up a serious relationship with the sister of the man you are spying on. Explain that one to me?"

"It's like I told you, she's the girl of my dreams. We all have a type, and except for the baggage, Gabrielle fits that type perfectly … right down to her cute little butt and her tiny toes."

Mike shook his head, and then snorted two big lines of coke and handed me the straw. I did the same, and then walked over to the refrigerator and took out two beers and handed one to Mike.

"And everything went well with getting the house?"

"Yeah, better than I expected. It's on the south shore, a couple of exits down from the university, with its own private beach and wooded areas on both sides. Not too big, but just right, with a driveway that curves right into the garage that is attached to the back of the house."

I opened the computer and showed Mike the house and the property. At this stage, we wanted to leave a trail that would pique the professor's interest. Mike looked impressed. "The house is perfect," he said. "I don't know if we could have designed a house more suitable for our purpose. How long did you have to take the lease out for?"

"Six months," I replied.

"Should I even ask how much?"

"Over a hundred."

"Wow! Hopefully, this is the last major expense."

"If everything goes as planned it will have been worth every penny and then some."

"Oh, you're thinking small," Mike said, a gleam in his eye. "This operation is worth a thousand times your investment."

"How do you mean?"

"I'm talking saving the whole damn country."

"I get it," I said, although I wasn't totally sure I did. "Taking down the professor could be the start of something big."

"You're damn right. When I think about the trickle-up effects of this one operation, I get giddy. Fucking criminals, think they can steal our country. We shouldn't have to worry about taking out rogue agents, or the fact that our government — *our government* — is responsible for putting thugs into these top-level positions. We shouldn't have to do any of this at our own risk and expense. Don't you worry; I plan on us being reimbursed, and with a corporate executive's bonus on top of it all. But the other payday is a change in Washington. These motherfucking lowlife snakes … I'd like to take a bat to each one of them and teach them a lesson that they would never forget."

If I had any doubts that Mike's plan went way beyond killing the professor and his entourage, he had just put them to rest. I then showed Mike the surveillance equipment I bought at the electronics store, and after looking at just about every piece, he remarked, "Very nice. It shouldn't take much time to set all this up. Tomorrow afternoon we'll rent a car, go grocery shopping, pack the car with all our stuff, check out of the hotel, and head up to the house and pull into the garage just after nine o'clock."

"How did it all come to this? This is the type of shit that takes place in developing countries."

"It's what happens when naive people vote in an incompetent, greedy, clueless leader and spineless minions who follow his every directive as though it was coming from the mouth of God. The same people who are screaming and yelling and rejoicing at his rallies are the same people who wouldn't be allowed within a hundred yards of his golf courses, resorts, and hotels. The late congressman from Baltimore summarized it beautifully, when he said, 'When we're dancing with the angels, the question will be asked, What did we do to make sure we kept our democracy intact? Did we stand on the sidelines and say nothing?' The answer to that question is that on one side of the aisle not only did they do nothing but they encouraged the deranged lunatic at every turn."

He picked up the straw and snorted two huge hits of the coke and then he handed the straw to me and I did the same. He then continued as he sat back and downed a beer, saying, "I'm going to truly enjoy retirement, and I might even throw a party where everyone has to bring an American flag, and we make one big pile with all the flags, and then we burn them all and celebrate our liberation from the corruption in Washington. We could even roast marshmallows and hot dogs if we can keep the fire going."

"If you want any chance with my sister, I wouldn't invite her to that party."

"Why, would she be offended?"

"Probably, and the scene might get really bloody."

"Wow! The more I learn about this girl the more perfect she seems. Well, I'll just have to compromise and pick another symbol to burn. Have any ideas?"

"Yeah, how about banners of your favorite basketball team, the New York Knicks. You're always complaining about how bad they are and what a disgrace they are to the great city of New York."

"Okay, no need to get personal. Yeah, they haven't had a winning season in nearly twenty years or won a championship in forty-five years, but I haven't given up."

"Well, maybe it's time you did. My sister would love a party like that. She hates losers."

"You know, you're right. Fuck the Knicks! I've spent a lifetime rooting for that bunch of losers. They don't deserve my loyalty."

"Absolutely, and why waste any more of your precious time rooting for that bunch of losers, when you and my sister can be kicking each other's asses, and shooting helpless animals, and plotting the assassination of world leaders?"

"I don't shoot helpless animals."

"Well, neither does she. I was thinking of the human type, and don't you dare go there…"

He started to laugh as he lowered his head and snorted a couple of more lines and then passed the straw to me.

"How did the general take the news about you taking time off to treat a sick relative?"

"He was cool about it, and said all the right things. It was easy enough to get him another pilot to fly him around on the taxpayers' dime." He laughed as he downed another beer and said, "It's amazing how we boast about not having a monarchy, like the British, and yet we have dickheads like the general flying around the world, with his own personal pilot, on luxury Gulfstream jets, with unlimited charge accounts and a string of hookers to greet him wherever we touch down … and yet in his forty-year career he has never spent a day on a battlefield."

"At least my dad was always beside his soldiers."

"And how many Purple Hearts?"

"Probably as many as Audie Murphy. Not for nothing, but I have to admire the son of a bitch for his courage and commitment to his troops. He would curse out my mother and older sister with a viciousness that almost made me feel sorry for them, but never did I hear him say a bad word about his men. Athena once asked him if any of his men ever acted cowardly during a battle and he replied, 'Yes, but one should never pass judgment unless one has been in the same situation and under the same conditions.' She could get away with asking him such a question, whereas if I asked the same question he would have ripped me a new asshole."

"And if he knew that you got her involved in this mess?"

"If everything turns out right like I fully expect it to, he wouldn't do a thing. He would probably slap me on the shoulder and tell me that I showed sound judgment in consulting my sister. God forbid anything were to go wrong, the man would kill me. I have no doubt about that. He would make me wish the professor got to me first."

"What would he think of me?"

"Oh, he would love you ... tough guy flying combat missions, a womanizer…"

"So he would have no problem if I married the girl of my dreams and cheated on her?"

"Oh no, God no. The son of a bitch would kill you. But you wouldn't have to worry about him because before he ever got hold of you, Athena would dispose of you by throwing your sawed-off body parts in the nearest dumpster."

"Oh, so very perfect. It's hard to believe such a creature exists." He bowed his head and snorted two more lines of coke and handed me the straw as he continued. "Just out of curiosity, what do you think your father will make of Gabrielle?"

I shook my head as I took two more beers out of the refrigerator and handed one to Mike. "I don't even want to think about what his first impression might be. The only thing that might save her at first is if he finds out from my sister what she has been through. That might give her a short reprieve before he shows his unabashed and complete disdain for her weak nature."

"And how do you think Gabrielle will react to your father?"

"She'll probably poop and pee all over herself."

Mike laughed as he took a big gulp of beer and asked, "You're joking?"

"Yeah, I'm joking. She'll probably only pee on herself," I replied with a laugh. "My real concern is Gabrielle surviving her time with my sister. I warned her not to whine and complain to Athena because my sister's patience is limited and her wrath can strike as quick as a tornado. I will not be surprised if Athena winds up locking Gabrielle in a closet, with a bucket for a toilet, and passing her food to her under the door. That's probably the best we can hope for."

Mike laughed, once again, as he downed the remainder of his beer and took a couple more hits of the coke. He left at a little past two in the morning and gave me two tranquilizers to take so I wouldn't be up all night tossing and turning because of the coke. The sandwiches he picked up were still on the counter where he left them when he first arrived.

Chapter Forty

I met Mike in the lobby of the hotel at eleven o'clock, and after having a late breakfast in a nearby restaurant and two large cups of coffee, we took a cab to a car rental place and rented a large black SUV with tinted windows and plenty of trunk space. Mike insisted on this type of vehicle. I imagined he was already counting the number of bodies we would be transporting to the crematory when this was all over.

We then went back to the hotel and lay down for a couple of hours. This was going to be a very long night. At four o'clock, we checked out of the hotel and packed the SUV with all our equipment, clothes, and an assortment of weapons ... Austrian-made sniper rifles with silencers, American-made Barrett M82 rifles — the type of weapon that would wipe away half a person's body — and Desert Eagle .50 caliber Magnum handguns. Mike was preparing for a war against a twisted, deformed genius, and I wasn't about to say anything. Mike might not have a degree in physics and chemistry, but he knew what was needed to take out enemy combatants, and he would not take any chances. There was little doubt in my mind that he and my baby sister would make a perfect pair ... if only he could control a few of his other vices, it would be a marriage made in heaven ... or maybe in hell.

At six o'clock we sat down to a wonderful dinner at a high-end steak house on the lower east side of Manhattan. We split a bottle of fine wine, and that was it for the booze.

At a little after seven-thirty we turned onto the Long Island Expressway and headed toward the house, making one stop at Huntington Station to visit a supermarket. We picked up enough groceries and provisions to last us a week and a couple of cases of beer, which was nothing for the two of us. At a little after nine, we turned into the driveway of the house and parked in the garage.

Once we hauled all of the supplies into the house, Mike got to work studying the interior. He examined every inch of the place, including the attic, looking for any existing bugs and scoping out the best places to put the ones we had brought in. We then repeated the process outside, going over every square foot of the property and the surrounding area from all different angles. When we finished checking the grounds, Mike looked at me and said, "You did real good."

I felt a little guilty because my inspection was nothing compared to his. We wired the exterior of the house first because any threat would naturally come from outside first. Thankfully, there was a full moon, which provided us with extra light that came in handy when we had to place surveillance equipment in the shrubs by the beach, and in the wooded areas on both sides of the house. The entire time we were outside we did not see one neighbor walk by, but as Mike pointed out, that didn't mean they weren't watching. In rich, upscale neighborhoods like this, almost every home had specialized surveillance equipment that easily tracked individuals close to their property. What was strange was that the house I rented had no surveillance installed at all, except for an antiquated alarm system.

After we finished wiring the exterior, we got to work on the interior. This job was relatively easy because of all the overhanging fixtures and the nooks and crannies built into the house. Mike insisted that every room and bathroom be equipped with cameras and listening and recording devices. After we finished with the installation, he checked all the monitoring equipment, and everything seemed to be working perfectly. He walked through the house over and over again, occasionally standing in the middle of a room for minutes at a time, like a movie director setting up a shot. He was in charge, and I could sense that he did not trust my judgment or my ability to act appropriately if a situation arose. To drive the point home, he said, "Your baby sister would appreciate this set-up."

"Yes, she would," I replied. "Maybe you'd like to call her in to replace me?"

"That would be ideal, except for the fact that I don't want to put the girl of my dreams at risk. You understand, don't you?"

"She thrives on adventures like this," I replied as he started checking the arsenal he brought along. He picked up the sniper rifles and looked through the scopes and asked, "Have you ever fired rifles like this?"

"Only during training, and I wasn't very good at hitting the targets."

"Few are ... it's a real skill," he remarked. I waited for him to compare me to Athena, but he just stood there smiling as he picked up the Magnum handguns and loaded the cartridges into each one. He handed one of the guns to me along with a few extra cartridges and remarked, "You'd be wise to carry that around, along with the toy gun you're used to."

He reached over and put me in a loose headlock and said, "I love you, Nick."

"Despite my many deficiencies?" I asked jokingly.

"Despite everything, you are the one person I can trust and whose loyalty is never in doubt. Dmitry knew that about you, and he loved you for it. Even though it was the wrong move to go see him at the end, I'm sure that having you beside him as he died was more than he ever could have hoped for. The Russians got to him, and in a strange way we're going to get back at them."

We finished at around five in the morning and Mike went upstairs to stake out a spot in one of the bedrooms while I fetched a couple of beers from the kitchen. I went up to find him sitting next to a window in the dark, looking out at the grounds and the ocean beyond. The moon beamed down on the water and left a strip of white light that narrowed and disappeared in the distance. I handed Mike his beer and sat down next to him. He thanked me and stared out the window as he talked.

"I've probably flown over every major body of water on this earth, and yet I can't remember the last time I looked out the cockpit or the window of a plane and thought about how beautiful, mysterious, and alluring it all was, and how much we still didn't know about the life beneath the water."

"Maybe, it's better we never find out."

"You're right. Once we take away the mystery, we tend to destroy the beauty."

"Have you been in touch with your contact in the embassy?"

"Yes, the scumbag is still there and the French news outlets have the story about the wallet bombs, your friend, and the two Mossad agents all wrong."

"And the French authorities and anti-terrorist units?"

"Who knows … it's not like they are going to share any information with us. We have fucked our allies, over the last couple of years, more times than a dollar-and-ninety-nine-cent hooker walking the streets of Sunset Boulevard. They simply can't trust us, and who can blame them."

"You think they know about the professor?"

"Of course they do, but what are they going to do, take him out?"

"It would be nice," I replied as I took a sip of beer.

"The Europeans and our allies around the world have waited three and a half years, and now they are all down on their knees praying that the American people don't re-elect him. Imagine that, putting your hopes on the people who elected the bastard. The media couldn't take him down, the Dems were so sure he would lose that they didn't bother to show up to vote, and the Russians handed him the election with a little help from the FBI. Who could have imagined? Who was it that said, 'You can never underestimate the stupidity of the general public?'"

"A gentleman named Scott Adams. He's a cartoonist and an author."

"My God, he must be having the laugh of his lifetime. I thought it might be Mark Twain. He's pretty famous for saying stuff like that."

"Like, 'Suppose you were an idiot and suppose you were a member of Congress. But I repeat myself.'"

"Exactly. He's probably laughing hard enough to wake up the corpses next door." He laughed as he drank from his can of beer.

"Do you think the European anti-terrorist units and Mossad know that those baby-sized bombs were being built for the Russians and shipped to Crimea with the sole purpose of destabilizing the democratic country of Ukraine?"

"If they didn't a few days ago, I'm fairly sure they've figured it out by now. When you put it all together, it makes perfect sense. The Russians want to destabilize the government in Ukraine and install a puppet regime like they had before. The Russians' strongest supporter is the current administration in Washington and its toadies in the Congress and the Senate. The current administration is all about making money and using the 'office' of the president to enhance the personal fortunes of a small group of people. Ordinary Russians might be living in poverty, but the Russian government is more than willing to throw millions of dollars into the accounts of our fearless leader. Why else do you think he's refusing to release his tax returns? Every president for the last fifty years has released his returns, and this joker just keeps saying his hands are tied, that he's being audited. Bullshit. I keep wondering when Congress is going to force him to open his books, or at the very least come out and say that he should."

"Amen," I said, and gulped down the last of my beer. "But what about the professor? Do you think he's in it for the money or the politics?"

"Both, probably. At the very least, he knows about it. Whether he's cashing in or not, I couldn't say for sure. The guy has no prior experience and is most likely a Russian mole. And if he's not a mole, he's a useful idiot who's promised to look the other way. Why in the world is Paris the production hub and the port of transfer for weapons to Crimea, when there are plenty of other countries that would be more logical ports of transfer? I'll tell you why. Because the professor is directing and managing the operation. And now that you've alerted the authorities, he's cleaning up every link to himself. You're the last person that could link him to the operation, so he's coming after you. The Mossad agents were first, but unlike them, we're ready."

"You seem to have it all figured out," I said, hoping to hell it was true.

"Not quite, but soon enough," Mike replied, as he stared out the window at the crashing waves, illuminated by a descending moon.

Chapter Forty-One

The next two days were suspiciously calm. Mike stayed inside the whole time and made sure never to stand by a window. I knew he was in touch with people, but exactly who, I did not know, except for his friend in the embassy, who alerted him that the professor and his entourage had arrived in New York. I went outside a few times each day, pretending to water the flowers and stroll along the beach. Of course, I was armed at all times with the Magnum and what Mike had referred to as my toy gun.

I spoke to the mailman on one occasion, and he asked me if I was expecting any mail during my stay. I told him I had all my mail delivered to a post office box. He told me that he had been on the job nearly twenty-five years, and on this route for fifteen.

I asked, "Do you ever have any contact with the people who live around here?"

"Not much. Some I have never met, others only when I have a package that needs someone to sign for it."

"That must suck around Christmas time?"

He laughed, "I do quite well, and the area around here is like paradise, so I have no complaints."

"Yes, I can't argue with you there."

The day after we were alerted about the professor, I noticed a big brown delivery truck stopping at a few of the houses and dropping off packages. The driver drove past me and waved and I waved back. He was a big, muscular guy wearing a brown uniform.

At first I didn't think anything of it, but later I told Mike about it and he nonchalantly remarked, "Yeah, I saw him, but I doubt it's anything." It was his attitude that surprised me because Mike suspected everyone and everything, and to just blow off the truck and the driver was unusual, but I didn't pursue the topic any further. I figured he was probably getting tired like me. Stakeouts could be draining, and even more so in a neighborhood like this, where houses are far apart and sightlines are long.

The following day, I looked out the front window and I saw the delivery truck park across the street. I turned to go alert Mike and that's when Mike suddenly showed up and punched me square in the face. I stumbled backward and then he punched me again and the lights went out.

Chapter Forty-Two

I don't know how long I was out, but when I came to I was sitting in a chair with my hands and feet tied tightly and my torso wrapped in packing tape around the chair. The professor sat in a chair across from me, his withered legs crossed like he was at some kind of tea party. He smiled and rubbed his chin with his twisted hand as though he was studying a specimen he was about to operate on. I could feel my jaw and the right side of my head throbbing, and I could sense someone else nearby. I turned my head and saw the delivery truck driver standing behind me, his beefy arms crossed over his chest.

As my mind cleared, I remembered Mike. Fuck! Not possible! I looked around for him, half expecting him to appear behind the professor and do his bidding. On top of everything, beyond the immediate danger I was in, the crushing weight of having been duped, betrayed, by the man I thought of as my closest friend, roared into my mind and took over. I stared at the professor as coolly as I could, but I had never scored very well on the agency's deception tests. My poker face was mediocre at best. Back at the academy, Donna Low used to call it my "Resting Flush face." She warned me that I couldn't rely on it. I tried desperately to channel calm, controlled energy and willed my face to follow the program.

"What the hell happened? What the hell are you doing here?" I asked, still sounding panicked.

The professor laughed as he watched me wriggle around and try to put a little space between myself and the chair.

"Don't play coy with me, Nicky. You've been expecting me all along, but I don't think this is exactly how you expected things to turn out. You're an amateur at best, and how a simpleton like you has managed to stay alive this long is … an affront to the theory of evolution."

"What do you want?"

"Again, you insult my intelligence. Where is that lovely creature you escaped from Paris with?"

"We broke up. She took off with another guy."

"Of course she did. I am going to have such a wonderful time slicing her up. Beauty like hers has such an adverse effect on me."

"I guess so, you diseased, twisted freak."

"Please, keep on talking. It will make my dissection of her so much more pleasurable. I might even take a bite right out of her face, just before removing her eyes."

"How in the world did a psychopath like you become the station chief in the Paris embassy?"

"Oh, Nicky, you disappoint me. I thought you knew how the world worked. A million dollars to the campaign fund, another million to the inauguration committee, and voila. No background check, no documentation, just a little squeeze here and a little squeeze there. I imagine if I offered a few more million he might have made me director of the agency, but then it would have been tricky getting through the confirmation hearings."

"Not for a genius like you," I remarked, trying to sound sarcastic, but coming across pathetic, I was certain.

"That's true enough," he said with a weird giggle.

I felt my heart rate coming down. What did I have to lose? Everything, of course, but at least Gabrielle was safe. And Mike — if he was in on this, wouldn't he be standing behind the professor, sharpening a knife and getting ready to slit my throat? I began to take heart, and with it, my confidence returned.

"And is our fearless leader also making a profit off the arms sales to the Russians?"

"One has to feed the dog a few treats to keep him happy."

"And his litter?"

"But of course, and the director and a few influential congressmen and senators. You don't get such blind loyalty without showing your appreciation."

"I guess not."

"But sadly, all good things must come to an end. I gave a pen to your delightful president, at a White House function not too long ago, and told him that I would really appreciate it if he would use it whenever signing important documents, bills, treaties, and so forth. I assured him that I would be paying attention when they showed him on TV signing such consequential legislation, and made sure he understood that I'm not easily fooled. Another million to his now-defunct charity and he hasn't missed an opportunity to show off the pen."

"And so, what is the pen filled with, invisible ink?"

"Nothing so basic. My god, Nicky, you really do lack imagination."

I forced a small smile to let him know he couldn't get to me, and he continued, egotist that he was, unable to stop boasting of his accomplishments.

"You know how the idiot likes to suck on the ends of his pens like a piglet at a mother's nipple? Well, every time the pig sucks on the end of that pen a poison is released, a sweet-tasting poison, that in his case seeps into the bloodstream very slowly, over a period of months. First, he will start acting more erratic than usual and making outrageous statements that only his cronies in Congress will back up with no evidence. Then he'll start to experience intense headaches, and who knows, maybe he'll start a nuclear war with Greenland. Finally, he will be admitted to the Walter Reed Army Medical Center where they will try to alleviate the pain by inducing a coma-like state to help with the intense pain, but not even that will work ... and then one day his head will simply explode like an overripe pumpkin that has been left out too long in the sun."

"That's insane," I remarked.

"You think so? Have you looked at your Secretary of State lately, with those bulging eyes, and those conspiracy theories he's sprouting, wild stories that have everyone shaking their heads? He was my guinea pig, and so far the results have been very encouraging. It's a shame you won't be around to see the completion of my plan. My crowning achievement, the elimination of half of humanity ... an invisible virus that will spread like wildfire from continent to continent, overburdening health care systems, destroying the world economy, stewing unrest and discontent among the populace."

I recoiled from this bizarre statement but tried not to look too worried. "Who do you work for?"

"I'm a free agent, like your late friend Dmitry."

"You're a Russian mole."

"If you say so, but enough with the small talk ... now it's time to get down to the fun stuff." He retrieved a briefcase that had been sitting by his foot and placed it on his lap, then opened it and took out a large metal syringe.

"Do you know what is inside this syringe? Of course you do. Like a good boy, you have done your homework. One drop will eat through your eyeballs in minutes and you will suffer unbearable pain before it reaches your brain and eventually kills you. On the other hand, if you tell me where the girl is I will simply have my friend slice your head off with one mighty swing of his sword." He looked at the driver and said, "Please go get your weapon to show our friend."

The driver left the room as the professor fixed me with a deranged stare and said, "The agency should give me an award for getting rid of its trash."

"You think so, you sick motherfucker?"

"Now, now," he said, coolly. "There's really no reason to get nasty after such a civilized conversation. Now, where has that fool disappeared to?" The professor stood up, with the syringe in hand, and walked to the bay window overlooking the beach. Suddenly there was an explosion of glass and the mournful cry, "No! No! Not me."

Mike burst through the door, with his sniper rifle raised. Right behind him was my baby sister, in a wheelchair, with a sniper rifle across her lap. The professor continued to groan on the floor as my sister yelled, "You should have let me take the shot. What, did you get the bastard in the gut?"

Mike looked down at the professor and replied, "But the freak is getting exactly what he deserved — the same type of pain and misery he dished out. Not only did I shoot him in the gut, but look," he said, pointing to the professor's chest, which was wet and smoldering. "The bastard sprayed himself with the acid."

Athena got to work untying me and we all looked down at the professor, who was howling like a deranged dog, as the acid ate through his chest and barreled straight toward his heart ... dissolving the muscle just as his syphilitic mind had eaten away at his soul many years ago.

I have to admit ... I was kind of disappointed ... I was expecting at least some sort of mysterious, ominous final words from the mad genius like "The horror, the horror," something that I would be able to use in a book at some later date, but he died in front of us with no more than a burp and a gurgle and then silence.

Chapter Forty-Three

I looked at my warrior sister and then at Mike and rubbed my chin where Mike had clocked me.

"Did you really have to knock me out?" I asked.

"Sorry about that, buddy," Mike said, moving closer to me and putting his arm around my shoulder. "I couldn't take a chance."

"What, that I would screw up the entire operation?"

"No…" he said, unconvincingly. "There were just a lot of moving parts. I needed you there as bait for the professor, and you did a stand-up job."

"More like a flat on my back job," I said, still not sure how I felt about how everything went down.

Mike laughed and said, "I knew your sister was on her way, and I really just needed you with your lights out so I could be sure everything went down as planned. I hope you won't hold it against me."

"Nah," I said. "How could I? You saved my life."

"Oh, get a room, you two," Athena said. She'd been watching us with mounting irritation mixed with mirth. I walked over to her and kissed her on the head.

"Very funny, sis. Good to see you. And may I say, you're looking exceptionally beautiful today, Athena."

"Thank you, Nicky. Sorry I can't say the same for you," she replied as the taste of blood was still swirling around in my mouth.

"What are you talking about?" Mike interrupted. "He's never looked more manly in his life."

Athena looked at Mike and then back at me. "Does he ever shut up or am I going to have to put up with this my whole life?"

"I don't know what agreement you two have come to, but if I were you, Athena, I would think seriously before signing on the dotted line."

"Either that, or I could just cut off his tongue. The rest of him is too yummy to mess with."

"Oh please, just shut up. I'm ready to vomit."

"Your brother is the best, but he's a little bit on the sensitive side," said Mike.

I ignored that, but turned to him with my best *j'accuse* look and said, "I thought you didn't want her involved in the mission, Mike? What changed your mind?"

"The fact that *you* got her involved. Besides, she had already figured out the location of the house, and who do you think alerted me to the delivery truck?"

"Daddy's little girl," I replied jokingly as Athena looked at me with rage in her eyes.

"How would you like to have the rest of your face rearranged … at no extra charge?" she asked.

"That wouldn't be very nice, Athena."

"Maybe not, but it'd be a whole lot of fun," she said as she reached over and slapped me across the face, hard.

"Holy shit, that really hurt."

"Good," she said, looking pleased with herself and not even a little apologetic.

"Wow! A brother and sister fight. I know who I'm putting my money on," Mike said as Athena looked at him and said, "If you don't shut up, I swear, I will send both of you to the emergency room."

"Yes, sweetheart … whatever you say."

"Uh-oh," I said under my breath, and waited for Athena's reaction.

"What did you just call me?" she asked.

"Um … sweetheart?" Mike looked worried.

"Yeah, you can just deep-six that nickname right now. I am nobody's sweetheart and nobody's honey. You'll have to do better than that."

"Okay, okay! How am I supposed to know these things? You need to write down a list of dos and don'ts."

"Don't worry, you'll be getting that list. I'll be pinning it right to your ass."

"And how I'm I suppose to see it from back there?"

"I'm sure an asshole like you will figure it out."

"I warned you, Mike."

Athena turned on me with barely contained wrath. "Warned him about what?"

"About how you are so much more than just a beautiful face," I replied to my sister, who relaxed her guard and laughed.

"She's perfect," Mike said. "The most perfect creature I have ever met."

"Flattery won't get you anywhere, but I give you permission to continue."

I laughed and then asked, "Hey, where's Gabrielle?"

"Oh, you mean the crybaby?"

"Uh-oh," I said.

"I stuck that snivelling mess in a broom closet on the first day, with a bucket to use as a toilet, and I passed her meals to her through a slot in the bottom of the door. At what asylum did you run into her?"

"You're joking?"

"No, I'm not joking," she replied as she held two fingers very close together and continued. "I came this close to killing that hysterical bitch and dumping her body in a dumpster. That probably would have been the best thing I could have done for you…"

Suddenly, I heard, "Nicky, my sweet Nicky," and when I turned around my lovely Gabrielle jumped into my arms and we kissed over and over again, and I asked, "And how did my sister treat you?"

"Very well, Nicky, and she toughened me up," she replied as she made a fist and showed me the beginning of a little muscle. "I practiced with a bunch of guns, and I almost came close to the target a few times. Didn't I, Athena?"

"Yes you did, my little warrior," my sister replied with a smile. Then she and Mike left us to get reacquainted while they went around the house and gathered all the surveillance equipment and checked the quality of the recordings and the images. According to them, everything came out perfect. The proof was in the bag.

About an hour later, we all gathered in the long driveway to see Athena and Gabrielle off. Mike gave Athena a bunch of evidence to take back with her and as he leaned into her car to say goodbye they kissed, passionately. It was quite a sight: my baby sister and my best friend, locking lips. What can I say? I warned him. He got himself a gem, with claws, and if he thought the professor was a tough opponent, he was in for the surprise of his life if he ever pissed off his sweetheart.

After the two lovebirds were finished, I leaned into the car and kissed Athena on the head twice. "I love you so much, so much," I whispered.

"I know, and I love you so much."

"How can I ever repay you?"

"I'll think of something, don't you worry," she replied as I walked over to Gabrielle's side and leaned in and kissed her passionately and said, "I am so proud of you, Gabrielle."

"Thank you, Nicky," she replied as she held onto my hand through the open window. "I love you so much."

I smiled at her and planted one more soft kiss on her lips, as a kind of reply. Her eyes fluttered closed and only opened as I struggled to pull myself away. It was hard to let her go, but Mike and I had work to do. We watched as the girls drove away, and then we turned to the grisly task of cleaning up.

With the cleanup came the full story. Mike explained that the professor had shown up with four thugs, and that my amazing sister had taken all four of them out with a single bullet to the head.

"Nick, it was incredible. She was two steps ahead of me the whole time. It took her maybe three minutes to deal with that bastard's whole entourage. I know you told me all of this, but I'm seriously humbled by her capabilities. She was so calm the whole time. I've never seen anything like it."

"I know, right?" I said. "She's the first to react, the quickest to draw, and the most accurate shot in any group she's in."

Mike was still rhapsodizing about her skills while we lifted the bodies of the men and loaded them into the back of the delivery truck. Then we put gloves on to go back and deal with the mangled wreck that used to be the professor. We were lucky that he happened to fall onto an area rug near the window, since it would have been a hell of a job trying to scrape his partially dissolved body off the floor. Instead we rolled what was left of him up in the rug, put his remains into a wrought iron box the size of a coffin, and loaded him into the back of the delivery truck with his four comrades, slamming the door shut.

Mike then asked me if I had ten thousand dollars on me and I said, "Yes."

"Great. I've got a crew coming over here to clean this place up and fix everything that is broken. I sent them pictures, and a warning about the dropped acid, and they said it'll be no problem. By late tomorrow morning they'll have the place looking like new. I told them not to go into the garage because I stashed all the evidence in the back of the SUV, except for this one recording with everything on it." He put that into his coat pocket, while I placed the money in the cabinet above the stove in the kitchen.

We got into the truck, and Mike drove. I asked, "Where are we going?"

"To the end of Staten Island where one of our guys own a funeral parlor and a crematory. He's expecting us."

The drive to Staten Island was long, and by the time we got there it was after midnight. We pulled into the driveway of the funeral home and were met by the owner. Mike asked, "You got it all fired up?"

"At fourteen hundred degrees and rising," the owner said as we lifted the box and brought it down to the crematory. We lifted the body, wrapped in the rug, and placed it on a slab, and the owner slid it into the fire and closed the door. "I gather that's the infamous professor?"

"You guessed right," Mike replied as we carried the box back out to the truck and threw it in the back with the other corpses. The owner handed us a couple of beers as we watched the remains of the professor reduced to white ash. It took about an hour and a half and then the owner swept the ashes into a large urn.

We then went back to the truck and lifted two bodies onto gurneys, placed them on a large slab, and the owner slid their bodies into the oven and closed the door. It was against the law to cremate two bodies at once, but since no one would be asking for their remains it didn't make much of a difference. It took nearly four hours to reduce the muscular thugs to white ash, and then the owner swept their ashes into the large urn with the professor's remains.

The final two bodies were placed into the chamber, and while they were burning I borrowed the owner's car and followed Mike, who was driving the truck, to furthest point on Staten Island. We doused the truck with gasoline and watched it burn. We then drove back to the crematory as the owner was sweeping the remains of the last two thugs into the large urn. Mike took the urn into the bathroom and flushed the final remains of the professor and his entourage down several different toilets, taking care to distribute it evenly and pour the contents in slowly to avoid causing a backup. He then threw the urn into the dumpster and dropped a large rock on it and it shattered it into a thousand pieces. I gave the owner five thousand dollars, and he called a taxi for us. We arrived back at the house on Long Island a little after noon.

We walked into the house and it looked exactly like it did the first day I inspected the home. The shattered bay window was replaced with an identical window, the throw rug was replaced with a duplicate, and the landscape looked pristine. I said, "They did an amazing job."

"They're professionals," Mike replied. We gathered all our stuff, placed it into the SUV, and drove out of the garage toward Washington, DC.

Chapter Forty-Four

After settling into a cheap hotel just outside the city, we went through the footage and the recordings of the professor at the house. They could not have come out any better than they did. As an added bonus, we also got about six months' worth of material collected by Mike's contact at the embassy with help from several other staffers who hated their boss enough to risk their careers on a surveillance operation against one of their own. The recordings were all the same ... the professor telling the story of a government paid off, and profiteering from the sale of arms to a foreign adversary. The president, the director of the CIA, the secretary of state, congressmen and senators had all earned big bucks off the deal.

We made multiple copies of the evidence, saved two of them in different places on the cloud, and put four bundles of material — data keys, documents, and photographs — into four separate packages. We took two of the packages and first drove to *The New York Times* office in DC and asked for a certain reporter who came out and greeted us. He led us to a private room where I showed him my CIA credentials and we handed him the package. Mike remarked, "There is enough evidence in there to bring down the whole government."

The reporter opened the package, flipped through the photos, and plugged the data key into his laptop. He listened to a couple of the recordings and watched a few minutes of the video footage. He just kept saying "Holy Shit!" under his breath and finally asked us how we wanted him to handle this explosive material.

We told him that if he did not hear back from us in three days to run the story.

We then went over to *The Washington Post* building and told another trusted reporter the same story, and after he listened to the recordings and watched the footage he uttered the same amazed oath: "Holy Shit!" Once again, we told him that if he didn't hear from us in three days, he should run with the story.

We then went back to the hotel and Mike sent a message to his contact in the embassy and told her to immediately pass it on to the director of the CIA in Washington, DC.

The message read: "We are two CIA employees that have uncovered top-secret information clearly implicating top government employees in a scheme to profiteer off the sales of arms to Russian separatists in Crimea. We have further evidence that links these actions to a political conspiracy to overthrow the democratic government of Ukraine. Copies of the recordings and footage of the operation have been shared with *The New York Times* and *The Washington Post* and reporters have been told to run the story if they do not hear back from us by 4 p.m. tomorrow. Meet at Rock Creek Park at 10 a.m., by the benches overlooking the waterfalls. The professor sends his regards."

Mike's embassy contact sent the message, and in less than a half an hour the director got back to her with a message that simply read, "I'll be there at 10 a.m."

"So what exactly is our plan?" I asked Mike, who sat on the bed drinking a beer.

"Simply to get back what is due to us, and a little extra," Mike replied.

***

After a good night's sleep and a waffle breakfast at the hotel, we bundled ourselves into the car and headed for Rock Creek. We got to the park about fifteen minutes early and scouted the area for any agents who might be looking out for us, but we didn't see anyone suspicious. Even so, we knew that didn't really mean anything. Agents who didn't want to be seen knew how to escape notice, even by other agents. We were fully armed, and Mike was holding the package. The director arrived promptly at 10 a.m., and sat down on the bench and pretended to read a newspaper. He was a heavyset man, impeccably dressed in a dark blue Brooks Brothers suit and brown loafers.

Mike sat on one side of him and I sat on the other. He looked at each of us as Mike asked, "Remember us?"

"No!"

"Well, let me help you recall. You signed off on an order to dismiss me from the agency on the false charge that I killed innocent civilians in Afghanistan when the record showed that I was actually surveying territory in a helicopter a hundred miles away from the massacre. Is that ringing any bells?"

The director pursed his lips and stared at Mike unapologetically. "I do remember that, and I remember that your dismissal came as the direct result of a recommendation by the station chief. I was following his request."

"Of course you were," Mike said coolly. "It's always good to know that the director has the backs of his agents in the field. And my friend over here," he said, pointing at me and continuing, "You gave the professor the go-ahead to kill him. Were you following orders then too?"

"I—"

"Shut up, you piece of shit! And talking about pieces of shit, the professor says hi from above, or in his case probably from below ... a real asset to the agency, that guy. I'm sure he'll be greatly missed. Did you know he was a Russian mole, or did our fearless leader forget to mention that to you?" Mike shoved the package into the director's ample stomach.

He opened it, pulled out the data key and a digital tape recorder, and said, "What do you expect me to do with this?"

"Listen to the recording, and when you go back to your office you can watch the footage. The professor had a face that simply loved the camera."

Mike turned on the recording and the director listened. He clicked it off halfway through as though he'd heard enough, and said, "What do you want?"

"Five and a half million dollars," Mike said, letting the number sink in. "Five million for pain and suffering, and to compensate us both for lost income, since I don't expect you to be hiring my friend back anytime soon. Half a million for the expenses we incurred fending off an attack on our lives by your buddy, the professor. Did you know that he came all the way over here to try to kill us? Oh wait, you were probably behind it all. Yes, I'm quite sure of that."

The director shot Mike a look of disgust. "And where do you expect me to get that type of money?"

"Hmm, let's see," Mike said, obviously enjoying himself. "How about from your share of the profits from the arms sale? That would work. Or … you could dip into that top-secret account that the agency uses whenever an alarming situation comes up and there is an urgent need for huge amounts of cash. Either would be fine. You choose." Mike handed the director a piece of paper with a long number written on it for a bank in the Cayman Islands. "You can send the money here," he told the director. "You have until 3:45 p.m. today. Also, I would like to receive my full pension and a little extra bonus for the nightmare you put me through, and that can all go into the same account."

"Is that it?" the director asked as he started to get up and Mike shoved him back down.

"Not so quick, big boy. If by some chance the reporters at the *Times* and the *Post* don't hear from my friend and I for longer than a month, things will get a lot worse for you. We have arranged for a further shipment of information to be sent to both reporters, and only we can call it off."

"What information? You have nothing on me that isn't shared with a half-dozen other officials…"

"Wow, you really believe your own crap, don't you? That's almost impressive," Mike said. "Let me take you on a little tour of recent events. Do you remember where you were last October 24? Do you remember you caught a ride to Paris on Air Force One, and you had that little face-to-face meeting with the professor in a supposedly secure satellite building of the Paris embassy? From the looks of the video we received from our contact, you had a lovely piece of chocolate cake and a nice, foamy latte during your *tête-à-tête* with the professor. What was it you were going to personally receive in exchange for looking the other way on those Crimea arms shipments? Two million and change? Tsk-tsk. Naughty boy."

The director glared at Mike, trying unsuccessfully to hide his shock. He thought for a long moment before launching a pathetic attack.

"How the hell do you know the fake news won't just run with these stories anyway?"

"Oh, the fake news. That's rich. Well, we can't say for sure, can we? You never can tell what lengths a truly independent investigative reporter will go to in order to speak truth to power, as they like to say. And more power to them. But the journalists we dealt with are well known to us, and well aware that the lives of two former agents depend on their discretion. More importantly, the full extent of your own profiteering will only be made known to them if you lay a hand on us. That's the best I can do. Give us what we want and you *might* stay out of federal prison."

"You'll never work intel again, and no one who supports the president will believe a word of anything that's written about this," the director spat. "Hell, they won't even read it. That's the part you don't get. No one's listening, and no one cares."

"Oh, I think your math is off, sir. Thirty, maybe thirty-five percent of the country has been brainwashed, yes, but the sixty-five to seventy percent of Americans who can still think for themselves are sick to death of this administration, and they're not going to stand down. Those are the people who will help us wake up from this collective nightmare. Do you really want to risk your job and reputation? If there's a full exposé of the agency's involvement in the Russia–Crimea conspiracy, even President Pumpkin won't be able to save you. He has his ratings to consider, after all..."

The director was somewhere else, not even listening. Mike snapped his fingers in front of the man's eyes and he shot us both a look of profound irritation mixed with defeat.

"One last thing," Mike said. "I leave it to you to decide what to do about our fearless leader and his wacky secretary of state. The professor was not one to joke, and if you need a reminder, just turn on the news and listen to the bizarre ramblings of his test subject ... that will be the leader of the free world in a few months — the man with the power to start a nuclear war. For once, it might be a good idea to put your country above your personal greed and self-preservation."

After Mike dismissed him, the director shuffled off to his SUV and left the park.

***

At exactly 3:30 p.m. five and a half million dollars were transferred into Mike's offshore account, and he was awarded his full pension and a fifty-thousand-dollar bonus for his outstanding service to our country. The agency accepted my resignation, and made arrangements to forward a couple of back paychecks they owed me.

Mike was sitting on the bed in our run-down motel room, enjoying a cold beer, when his contact in the Cayman Islands texted his burner phone to confirm that the money had landed in his account.

"Woo hoo!" I yelped. "Why don't we go out and celebrate?"

"No thanks," he replied.

"Why not? We're free, and now you're also rich."

"Yeah, but now I'm spoken for."

"What the hell does that mean?"

"Your beautiful sister and I are engaged," he replied, with the biggest, dumbest smile on his face.

"Congratulations, but we still have to eat, and it's not like Athena has anything against booze."

Mike's phone rang. It was Athena. "Yes, my lovely, heart-throbbing warrior, everything went perfect."

I looked at him and couldn't believe what was coming out of his mouth … this, from the same guy who never missed an opportunity to flirt or go further — often much further — with any babe who caught his eye.

"Yes," he continued, "If I can get your brother off his lazy ass we will be there as quick as possible. The cabin — great! Love you." He hung up the phone and simply looked at me and asked, "What's wrong?"

"Nothing," I replied as I shook my head in disbelief.

"The cabin … she said you knew where it was."

"It's all the way up in Cooperstown."

"Great. I've never been up that way. Now I can visit the Hall of Fame."

We picked up a few sandwiches, got into the SUV, and drove to Manhattan to drop off the car. We then rented a plane and flew up to Cooperstown. There was no way Mike was going to drive seven hours to see his heart-throbbing, warrior fiancée when he could get there in less than an hour as the crow flies.

Chapter Forty-Five

In some respects it seemed like I had known Gabrielle my whole life, even if ninety-nine percent of that time was in my head. I held onto her tightly, as we stood beside Otsego Lake, across from the lovely village of Cooperstown, near the cabin that Athena and I had purchased about three years ago. Despite the blossoming scent of a thousand different varieties of plant life, the only fragrance that I was able to detect was the clean and fresh aroma emanating from the lovely lady in my arms. I sniffed deeply at her neck and hair, wrapped my arms around her petite body, and lifted her a couple of inches off the ground before kissing her softly on the lips. I couldn't believe how light she was. Even with the weight training exercises that Athena had her doing, she would always be petite … that was just the way nature and God intended her to be.

Athena was tough, and dangerous and at times quite intimidating, but all I had to do was look back to our teenage years growing up together, and remember what a big heart she had, and how caring she was. She was the only one in my family who stood up to my father when he stood there screaming and berating me like I was no better than an insect. She was, and would always be, the one person I loved more than anyone in the world.

She worked her hide off to find creative workarounds and ways of compensating for her disability, and she had my father pushing her to succeed. He kept on pushing her to reach her full potential. He might have been an absentee parent, but his presence was always felt, and his incredible work ethic, and his code of honor, were stamped into my sister's brain.

At first the coupling of my sister and Gabrielle might have seemed like a disaster in the making, but once Athena learned of Gabrielle's tragic past she realized that, unlike her, Gabrielle did not have a person in her life to guide and push her past the hideous rape … to help to remake and reshape her life and ensure that she was never again the victim. The Mossad twins cared about her, undeniably, but they also treated her with kid gloves, in a way that was somewhat disabling. They never taught or encouraged her to take that hideous experience and to remake herself into a person with expert self-defense skills and the mindset of a conqueror instead of a victim. In the eyes of those two burly men, Gabrielle had always been a fragile flower.

In the short time she had spent with Athena, I could see the difference in Gabrielle. She didn't stick to me like glue, like I was the only barrier between her and all the evil of the world that was trying to get at her. When we were alone her scars and burns were no longer a source of shame. She would walk out of the shower with her bathrobe loosely tied and with her burned breasts and scars visible. She laughed and smiled and moved her nimble body around like a dancer, and for the first time since meeting her I didn't sense that she was putting on a show or pretending to be anything or anyone other than herself. She was a fledgling bird learning to fly.

Mike had stopped kidding me about her. I think even he had noticed a difference in her. Either that, or Athena had warned him that if she heard one more wisecrack about her friend she would personally kick his ass. Mike had finally got the revenge he sought against the agency that turned its back on him, and the transformation from ruggedly handsome playboy to love-stricken and loyal boyfriend was striking. Mike and I had both found the girl of our dreams, and anyone watching us from the outside would probably have said that all four of us seemed disgustingly happy. Athena and Mike started each morning in the gym that we built below the cabin, lifting weights, doing hand and leg exercises, hitting the punching bag, and wrestling on the mats. Athena's upper body strength was seriously impressive, and I never saw her lose a match to Mike, who was no slouch, and not the type to let her win. It was hard to feel sorry for him. Being pinned to the mat by a woman as gorgeous as my sister would be a fantasy come true for most guys.

What really frustrated Mike was losing to my sister on the basketball court. Naturally, they couldn't play a normal game, but man, did they compensate. They would spend hours competing against each other, playing games like "horse," where if one hit a foul shot, the other would have to hit the same shot, and if they didn't hit the shot they would get a letter and the first one to spell out "horse" was the loser.

Mike and Athena were both right-handed, but my sister had practiced so much with her left hand that she had become ambidextrous. So she would take shots from twenty feet out with her left hand and hit her mark, and when Mike tried to match the shot he would fail miserably, barely able to reach the basket. My sister would taunt him and ask, "Are you sure you've played this game before, because you shoot like a Beverly Hills debutante?"

I would walk past him and remark, "I warned you."

"My God, she is the most perfect creature I have ever met," and he would look at her with admiration and unbridled love.

After beating him, she would treat him to a drink. "Can I get you a beer, handsome?" she would ask.

"Yes, MJ," he said — short for Michael Jordan, his nickname for her at the time, "that would be great."

***

After two weeks at the cabin, Gabrielle and I decided it was time to get married. She wanted to invite her parents, who she was talking to every day, and who were still in mourning, as one might suspect, after losing their son. I told her I thought it would be better if we invited them to come and stay with us in the autumn after they were feeling better. The ceremony was going to be no more than a few minutes, and since it was only going to be us, Mike, and Athena, I didn't think the pressure and anxiety of traveling so far was the best thing at this time for them. She agreed but it would be the first phone call we made after being officially married.

The night before the wedding, I was sitting alone with Athena in the kitchen and she said, "I invited Dad to the ceremony and he said he would be there. I hope that is okay?"

I looked at her, somewhat taken aback at first, and then replied, "He definitely deserves to be there. Thank you."

"Don't worry, I didn't invite the other two. You can call them up and tell them the good news."

The next morning, the four of us drove to the church in Cooperstown. Mike was my best man, and Athena was Gabrielle's maid of honor. Gabrielle was dressed in a simple white dress, with a black belt tied around her waist, and a matching pair of white flats. She looked just like she did the first time I saw her on the steps of the university, except that she had traded cheap cotton for crisp linen. My beautiful sister, who had always despised dresses, wore an elegant pantsuit. Mike was rocking a light blue suit, and I went for a basic black suit, but with a little sheen.

My father was supposed to meet us at the church, but when we arrived at a few minutes to ten there was not a soul in the church besides the priest. We waited for about fifteen minutes until Athena finally said, "Let's get the show on the road. Dad's probably lost somewhere in the Baseball Hall of Fame."

In a simple five-minute ceremony, the priest pronounced us husband and wife and told me I could kiss the bride. We kissed, and like always, it was heavenly, but a little more so on such a beautiful and momentous day.

Mike and Athena clapped, and we all kissed and then the priest, who was a sweet man but a poor keeper of secrets, started shuffling and smiling and said, "Shall we get on with the next order of business?"

Athena and Mike in unison replied, "Yes, Father." I didn't know what was going on — apparently I was the only one left in the dark — and then it all dawned on me … Athena and Mike were also getting married. We all changed places, and a smile as wide as the heavens crossed my wife's face as she watched Athena and Mike sitting and standing before the priest, reciting the wedding vows. For a second time, the priest said, "I pronounce you husband and wife," and looked at Mike and continued, saying, "You may kiss the bride." Mike kissed the girl of his dreams, and Gabrielle and I clapped and then we all kissed.

I turned around for a moment, and saw my father, standing erect at the back of the room. He was dressed in a suit, and was walking directly toward me. We shook hands and he said, "Congratulations, Son!" And then he hugged me for one of the few times in my life and whispered into my ear, "I heard about everything, and I doubt there is a prouder father in the world. I am blessed."

I introduced him to Gabrielle, and he welcomed her to the family and kissed her on the cheek and said, in French, "You are incredibly adorable, my sweet and lovely daughter-in-law."

"Thank you," Gabrielle replied, blushing and beaming at the same time.

My father then walked over to his favorite person in the world and hugged and kissed her, and for the first time in my life I saw tears run down the cheeks of both my sister and my father. He reached out and shook Mike's hand and said, "I don't need to tell you that if you don't treat her right, she will rip you apart and make you wish you were never born."

"I'm fully aware, sir," Mike replied as we all laughed.

With these brisk reunions behind us, we left for a local restaurant to celebrate and eat. We sat around a table like a real family and talked about sports, about the pristine beauty of this small upstate town famous for the Hall of Fame, and then my father stood up and raised his champagne flute and toasted to long, happy, and healthy lives for Gabrielle and me, and Athena and Mike. He finished by saying, "And to the rebirth of our great country." We all raised our flutes and repeated, "To the rebirth of our great country."

My father left after he paid the bill at the restaurant. He promised to visit a lot and to stay in touch, and I believed him. He had a plane to catch, to God only knows where. We newlyweds then went back to cabin and sat around the living room drinking, snacking, and having a good time.

Athena and I had made a promise to each other years ago that we would always live together, whether we got married or not. We were finally ready to make that promise a reality and to start we would make the cabin our primary home for at least a few years. Athena remarked, "If anyone has a problem with that they are free to leave right now." She looked at Mike and Gabrielle who nodded their approval and she continued, "You see, I can be so persuasive." We all laughed as she laid her head on Mike's chest.

Gabrielle and I were going back down to the city for a short honeymoon. I had promised to take her to see the Statue of Liberty, and that was another promise I planned on keeping. I told her that I thought it would be wise if we put off visiting the Lincoln Memorial for a little while and she agreed.

I asked my sister and Mike if they wanted to come and they politely declined. I then asked them if they planned on taking a honeymoon anywhere and Mike replied, "No, I have the best view and the loveliest piece of scenery right here beside me. I've seen enough of the world, and now that I have finally found paradise, I don't plan on letting it out of my sight."

Athena wrapped her hands around her husband's waist and remarked, "He's so full of shit!" We all laughed as Mike reached down and lifted her head off his chest and looked into her beautiful face and said, "I have never been more serious or more honest in my life."

They kissed passionately.

Chapter Forty-Six

The professor's experiments were an overwhelming success, just as he predicted.

The secretary of state stood at the podium addressing the members of a NATO delegation. Sweat poured down his face, even though the room temperature at the convention hall was a comfortable 68 degrees, and his eyes bulged out like those of a rabid pit bull. He was rambling about how he had documentation that clearly showed that Greenland, Switzerland, and the island of Haiti were planning an imminent, deadly invasion of the United States. The members pretended to be listening … after all they had heard similar, bizarre theories leaking out of the secretary's mouth for nearly a year now … and if the government of the United States didn't care what he was saying, why would they even bother to object.

The secretary suddenly put his hands tightly to his head and started screaming at a decibel level so high that many of the members recalled feeling like their eardrums were ready to burst. "The pain! The pain! The pain!" He kept repeating those words, and then his head literally burst … yes, I said burst… and all those dead brain cells, blood, and shards of bone went splatting over the members as they desperately tried to escape. And if that wasn't unusual enough, video footage shows the headless torso of the secretary walking out from behind the podium and doing an awkward little jig before finally falling over dead.

A few days later, the director of the CIA, sitting on the same bench where he sat with Mike and me, overlooking the waterfalls, took out a gun, put it to his head, pulled the trigger, and fell over dead. A few minutes later a group of overweight joggers, completely out of breath but continuing the good fight, accidentally stumbled upon the director's body and became tangled up in it, causing it to roll away and tumble down the cliff and into the waterfalls. The joggers figured that it was simply a dead, large brown bear and continued on their mission without giving it a second thought. After all, there were signposts throughout the park warning of large brown bears.

A few days later, a couple of kids fishing downstream caught hold of what they thought was the biggest fish in the world, and with all the strength they could muster they reeled in their catch but after further inspection they came to realize that it wasn't a fish at all but a dead brown bear … so they cut off pieces of what they thought was a bear and used it as bait and as luck would have it they would catch more fish that day than they had caught in their entire young lives. In wasn't until a park ranger came upon the carcass that he realized that it was a human being and in fact the director of the CIA.

Our fearless leader, sucking on the professor's poisoned pen, started espousing conspiracy theories similar to those that had been heard from the secretary of state before his unfortunate explosion at NATO. As the poison gradually took hold, he threatened nuclear war, fire and fury, against the nefarious countries of Greenland, Iceland, and Haiti. He claimed to have undeniable proof that these three countries were on the verge of an imminent invasion of the United States. When asked to provide the proof, he said the evidence was of such a sensitive nature that it had to remain classified, and he declared "executive privilege" to keep it so.

He started to complain of severe headaches while the entire time refusing to let go of the pen, sucking on the sweet-tasting poison like a piglet at its mother's nipple. He was shipped off to the Walter Reed Army Medical Center in the dead of night, screaming as he pressed his hands tightly against the sides of his head, "The pain! The pain!

The pain!" The doctors, unable to control him or relieve the pain or to remove the pen from his mouth, shot him up with enough barbiturates to trigger a medically induced coma, yet he continued to scream, "The pain! The pain!" and then, just like the secretary of state, his head exploded like that of a late-season pumpkin that had been left out in the sun too long, and he was declared dead.

Researchers from the Infectious Disease Center in Atlanta, Georgia, were flown in and wearing hazmat suits took samples of what remained of the president's shattered brain. After intensive examination of the samples, they recommended that the president's body be cremated as quickly as possible.

A hastily devised funeral was arranged and the very next day the body of the president was placed in an iron cast box and thrown into the back of a hearse, which was driven by a driver in a hazmat suit. The family, a known group of cowards, refused to ride in the hearse with the president, even though they would have also been fitted in hazmat suits. They drove in a limousine that stayed five hundred feet back from the hearse.

A few crowds gathered along the funeral route and at one point a couple of citizens threw cow dung at the hearse and the limo carrying the family, and at another point a young lady, in a dress, stepped in front of the hearse and pulled down her panties and urinated. The secret service agents, not wanting to get flying urine all over themselves, let the lady finish, and as they went to arrest her she kicked one agent in the crotch and took off into the crowd that quickly shielded her from the pursuing agents.

The hearse stopped at an undisclosed location, away from a scattered crowds, and the iron box containing the president's remains was put onto a gurney and rolled through a funeral home and down into the crematory. The president's body, draped in an American flag, was put onto a slab and slid into the oven and like the professor and his entourages' bodies went up in flames ... our fearless leader becoming the first president in American history to be cremated.

Chapter Forty-Seven

By this time the virus had struck, and the world had changed, and Gabrielle and I were in lockdown with Mike and Athena. As odd as it sounds, we were happy to be on our own. Looking back, I still feel guilty that the pandemic became a time of healing for us, while so many others suffered and died. We were forced into a cocoon, and that suited us all perfectly.

Gabrielle's night tremors drastically decreased, and she slept more like a teenager than a woman tormented by her past. She seemed to be settling comfortably into her new life, and part of that involved catching up on years' worth of sleep lost to terrifying nightmares. Athena's influence and patience with her had worked miracles, and if I could allow myself any credit, I thought that my own gentleness might also be helping. Gabrielle might never be a warrior, but then I didn't really want her to be ... I simply wanted her to be happy and confident.

I've said I was happy, but it was more complicated than that. Mike, who had had his own experiences with PTSD, told me that my own anxiety about the events in Paris would pass with time, but it didn't, or not really. My nightmares about Abdul continued with new twists and turns. It wasn't just his floating head coming toward me and our final scene together when we hugged each other near the taxis and whispered "I love you like a brother." Now the dreams switched scenes to one of the bars we used to visit, and as I tried to explain that I never meant him any harm, the music just got louder and louder until he couldn't hear a word I was saying. I might have lost the battle but won the war, and to the victor belonged the spoils, but sadly in this case the rewards included wounds that refused to heal and a betrayal that cost my friend his life.

At a certain point, I just knew that any happiness I experienced with Gabrielle — and there were many moments of happiness — would always be tinged by this loss. The only thing that seemed to work at all was to talk about Abdul with Gabrielle. About a month into our marriage, with all of us still quarantined together and talking constantly, I began to ask Gabrielle to tell me more about Abdul. I even pressed her a little on why they had never been able to get along. She fought me at first, saying she didn't want to talk about it, but I kept at it, gently, until she opened up. After many of these conversations, she broke down in tears and sobbed for her lost brother. She told me that she'd always known he wanted to be close to her, but that she couldn't bring herself to accept his kindness. Any time he offered her anything, the scenes of her brutal attack played over again in her mind, and she confused the boy in front of her with the evil men whose only connection to Abdul was that they worshipped the same God (if, in fact, the men who attacked her could ever be said to worship anything other than violence).

Over time, Gabrielle began to piece together a new Abdul. One closer to the man I knew. A brilliant, funny, flawed person who made a huge mistake, but whose default mode was to be giving and sweet with anyone who needed his help or wanted to be his friend. After weeks of this, I had the strangest sensation — I felt Abdul smiling down on us, with open approval. Maybe I was losing my mind, but I could swear he woke us up with his laughter one day just as we were opening our eyes to another day in quarantine. It might have been the wind, or the cat who adopted us that month, a gray that wandered in from a neighboring property and refused to leave. I guess we'll never know.

www.ingramcontent.com/pod-product-compliance
Lightning Source LLC
Chambersburg PA
CBHW020400030726

47496CB00007B/2226